Snowbound at Christmas

Also by Jennifer Ryan

Montana Men Series

His Cowboy Heart

Her Renegade Rancher

Stone Cold Cowboy

Her Lucky Cowboy

When It's Right

At Wolf Ranch

The McBride Series

Dylan's Redemption

Falling for Owen

The Return of Brody McBride

The Hunted Series

Everything She Wanted

Chasing Morgan

The Right Bride

Lucky Like Us

Saved by the Rancher

Short Stories

Can't Wait

(appears in *All I Want for Christmas Is a Cowboy*)

Waiting for You

(appears in *Confessions of a Secret Admirer*)

Also by Maisey Yates

From HQN Books

Shoulda Been a Cowboy (prequel novella)
Part Time Cowboy
Brokedown Cowboy
Bad News Cowboy
A Copper Ridge Christmas (e-book novella)
The Cowboy Way
Hometown Heartbreaker (e-book novella)
One Night Charmer
Tough Luck Hero
Last Chance Rebel

From Harlequin Desire

Take Me, Cowboy
Hold Me, Cowboy

Look for more Copper Ridge

Seduce Me, Cowboy (Harlequin Desire)
Slow Burn Cowboy (HQN)

Also by Lia Riley

Brightwater Series

Best Worst Mistake

Right Wrong Guy

Last First Kiss

Coming Soon

The Darling Hellions Series

Snowbound at Christmas

JENNIFER RYAN,
MAISEY YATES,
LIA RILEY

EPub Edition NOVEMBER 2016 ISBN: 9780062658784
Print Edition ISBN: 9780062658791

10 9 8 7 6 5 4 3 2 1

Contents

Close to Perfect
by Jennifer Ryan
1

Hot Winter's Night
by Lia Riley
149

Snowed in at Copper Ridge Lodge
by Maisey Yates
255

Close to Perfect

BY JENNIFER RYAN

Prologue

Ten years ago . . .

DEX SAT ON the hard bench outside the sheriff's office knowing he hadn't done anything wrong, but shaking in his Converse just the same after a deputy showed up at the high school batting cage, cuffed him, and brought him down to the station. They charged him with stealing a car, drinking and driving, and in a drunken stupor, ditching the car in Crawford Pond.

The car had been pulled out of the murky water, a case of beer in the backseat—mostly empty cans—along with his baseball cap with the MVP pin the team awarded him last season.

How the hell did it get there?

Laurie walked out of her father's office and turned the butterflies in his stomach into hummingbirds.

Oh God. I'm in deep shit.

He'd thought landing Laurie as his girlfriend made him big shit. Hell, he was seventeen and she had a hot body he wanted to get his hands on, even if she never let him past second base.

Then he met someone . . . different. Interesting. Nice.

Abigail Swain was barely sixteen and in the senior class. She was that smart. Really smart.

Paired with her for a science class project, he'd gotten to know her and wondered why he'd never really noticed her. Small town, small school; still, she kept under the radar. Her parents believed school was more important than friends. Instead of spending her free time playing sports or hanging out at the diner downtown with other girls, she spent every spare minute at church or studying.

Abigail might come off weird and brainy, but really she was shy . . . quiet. And genuinely nice. A perfect target for Laurie, who made it known she didn't like him spending time with Abigail, even for a class project.

Five days into working with Abigail, something inside him shifted while she explained the intricacies of photosynthesis right off the top of her head. The way her eyes lit up. She planted her chin in her palm and looked right at him. Open and filled with kindness, she did something to his insides. He moved without thinking about it, leaned across the coffee table in his living room, and tentatively pressed his lips to hers in a soft kiss. He didn't know why he had to do it until their lips touched and the wonder and softening in her eyes undid him. To his surprise, she kissed him back, and if he hadn't been sitting on the floor already, he'd have hit his knees.

That kiss changed everything and put a lot of things into perspective. Like he'd rather be with someone he liked and enjoyed spending time with. He and Laurie had more fights than good times and it wore thin. Quick. Despite Laurie's many protests, he ended things with her with a promise that he wouldn't back out of taking her to the dance so she wouldn't be humiliated and have to go alone.

From that moment on, he secretly spent more and more time with Abigail, though they kept their relationship hidden. Something about the way her overprotective father hovered nearby when they worked on their project at her house warned him that she'd get into deep trouble if her parents knew about them. Abby never said so, but he got the sense she feared her own dad.

As the mayor of their town, he had a reputation for advocating strict morals. A lot of people outside their church congregation found him judgmental. Including Dex.

He might not be valedictorian material, but he made better than good grades, was the best pitcher and hitter Crystal Creek High ever had, and he planned to take his team to the championships this spring. He had baseball and college to look forward to over the next couple of years, and still Mayor Swain looked at him like he was nothing but a thing.

His dad sat beside him, ready to do battle, and nudged him with an elbow in his side. "Laurie's here. She probably told her father the two of you were at the dance all night, and you couldn't have stolen that car." The hope in his father's voice destroyed Dex.

I am so screwed.

Laurie walked right past him, smiling that sweet smile he and the other guys she'd caught in her web knew hid her devious side. She was out for blood. Since her dad was the sheriff, he had a feeling she was going to get it. Every last drop she thought she deserved because he'd had the audacity to dump *her* and ruined her plan to get back together at the dance.

The sheriff waved them into his office. "Let's go, Dex. You've got some explaining to do."

"Listen, Sheriff, Dex had nothing to do with the theft of that car, or how it ended up in the pond. Dex was at the dance with Laurie last night."

Dex wished he deserved his father's devotion and unwavering confidence. He wasn't guilty of the charges, but he wasn't innocent either.

"Step into my office, Steve. We'll just see what Dex has to say about what really happened last night."

His father turned and gave him one of those dad looks, telling him without words that Dex had better have a good explanation for not telling the whole truth this morning over breakfast about how great the dance was last night.

Dex took a seat in front of the sheriff's desk and refused to say anything. Not until the sheriff gave up whatever he thought he knew. Or rather, what Laurie wanted her father to believe.

Dex stared up at his father, standing with anger flashing in his eyes after the sheriff laid out the evidence against Dex.

"Why didn't you take Laurie home?" his father asked.

"She didn't want to leave with me, said she'd get a friend to take her home, so I left."

"And you can't account for your time after leaving the dance," the sheriff pointed out, an angry I've-got-you gleam in his eyes.

"I drove around *in my truck* for a while to cool down after the fight with Laurie."

The sheriff snorted and rolled his eyes. "I suggest you call a lawyer and come up with a better defense than the bullshit you're feeding your father." The sheriff stood and waved them out of the office.

Dex walked out behind his dad in a daze. Even his father seemed at a loss for words. Dex wanted to explain what really happened, but couldn't give them the whole truth. If Abigail's strict parents found out he was seeing her behind their backs, she'd be in deep shit.

His father pulled out his cell and dialed.

"Who are you calling?"

"A lawyer," he snapped, then moved a few steps away.

The sheriff stepped out of his office ready to process Dex and lock him up.

His dad glared and bit out, "Sheriff, you don't have any proof he was in that car. I could drive a truck through the holes in that story. It's Dex's word against Laurie's."

"His hat was found in the vehicle. He claims he's never been in the vehicle, nor does he know or associate with the owner of the car, Mr. Fowler. Laurie, along with her friend, saw him on their way home." The sheriff turned on Dex. "We'll book you for DUI, grand theft auto, and destruction of property. You're looking at three years minimum."

Abigail stepped through the door and stopped dead in her tracks, her eyes wide with shock as the sheriff's last words sank into Dex's head. He'd spend the next three years in jail. No scholarship. No college education. No life as he'd planned it. This charge would follow him the rest of his life.

He'd lost everything.

Dex yelled in his mind for Abigail to turn around and go home before she got caught up in this mess. He didn't want her here. He didn't want these lies to touch her.

Confessing everything and dragging her into this wasn't worth it. He didn't want to hurt her. He'd never hurt her to save himself.

And yet, a small voice whispered she was his only hope of making this right.

ABIGAIL HAD DASHED out of the store, the groceries her mother asked her to pick up and her father waiting for her in the parking lot forgotten, after she overheard two girls from school talking about Dex.

They picked him up an hour ago and took him to the sheriff's office in handcuffs.

I can't believe Dex stole that car.

They found Dex's ball cap in the backseat and a bunch of empty beer cans. Dex is so busted.

He'll probably go to jail for drinking and driving and stealing that car.

She ran down the street thinking of what she'd say and the consequence. She rushed into the sheriff's office, knowing she was ruining her life to save Dex's.

Her only consolation, she loved Dex, and this was the right thing to do . . . no matter what happened to her.

Abigail hesitated when her gaze locked on Dex's desolate face, his disheveled blond hair, and his green eyes pleading with her. "Go home, Abigail. There's nothing for you to do here."

He'd take whatever came and leave her out of it. Her heart welled with more love than she'd ever felt for anyone.

"Sheriff, Dex didn't steal that car."

The sheriff hooked his thumbs on his gun belt, his chest puffed out. "Young lady, we have a witness who saw Dex in that car."

She didn't need to ask the witness's identity. "Laurie lied." The uncharacteristic boldness in her voice made Dex's eyes widen.

"Young lady—" the sheriff began sternly.

"Let her speak," Mr. Manning cut him off.

Abigail turned to Dex's father. "Mr. Manning, after Dex left the dance, he picked me up."

Someone walked in the door behind her.

An ominous chill went up her spine a split second before her father's booming voice reverberated through her. "Abigail, don't say another word. We're going home." He'd followed her from the store. Her shoulders sank and her head fell. With his presence heavy and foreboding behind her, she refused to shrink, as her mother always did under his oppressive will, and stood tall again.

"Abby, go home," Dex whispered.

He used the nickname he'd whispered in the night after he'd made love to her. *Ah, Abby, you're perfect.*

For the first time in her life, she'd felt perfect lying in his arms. No one was there telling her what was wrong with her, pushing her to be better, smarter, more presentable, like her father did.

Instead, in the quiet dark, she was connected body and soul to Dex, and he'd thought her perfect.

In his arms, she'd discovered that she really was enough.

She looked directly at Mr. Manning, found her courage, and spoke the truth. "I was with Dex last night from about ten-forty until four-thirty this morning."

"Abigail!" Her father's outrage didn't stop her.

"I snuck out my window. We hopped in his truck parked around the corner, drove to a small motel just outside of town, and got a room."

"That's enough. You may like this boy, but lying is a sin," her father scolded.

Abigail refused to keep quiet. "We were in the room for more than an hour when Dex went to take a shower." Heat rose to her cheeks, her heart thrashed in her chest, but she pressed on. "I left the room for a few minutes to get some ice and a couple of sodas from the vending machine. Before I went back to the room, I noticed a commotion in the parking lot near Dex's truck parked outside our room."

Her father said something scathing under his breath at the mention of "our room."

"Laurie walked toward Dex's truck. Well, weaved her

way there is more like it. Drunk and belligerent, she tried to free herself from Frankie Sherman's grasp. He tried to drag her back to his car, a dark blue four-door with a white sticker on the left side of the back bumper. After Frankie got Laurie back into the car and handed her another beer, he went to Dex's truck and stole his baseball hat from the front seat. I don't know why he took it, or if the car they were driving is the one found in the pond. I only know Dex didn't steal a car last night."

"Listen, young lady, because your father is the mayor, I'll overlook the fact you are interfering in an investigation and lying to the police," the sheriff admonished. He would think it was okay to let her get away with lying to a cop, especially when he'd overlooked his own daughter's underage drinking when he or his officers broke up high school parties. Others at those parties didn't get off so lucky.

She thought being the mayor's daughter would make him believe her. Seemed she had no voice at home or here. If she couldn't convince the biased sheriff, she'd focus on convincing Dex's father, who seemed to be the only one interested in what she had to say.

"Abigail, I mean it," her father cautioned. "You will not disgrace yourself or me further. Not. Another. Word."

She didn't heed that warning, knowing all too well the severe punishment she'd receive for going against him.

"After Laurie and Frankie peeled out of the parking lot, I went back into the room. I never told Dex they'd been there." She gave Dex a sad smile. "I didn't want to spoil the rest of our night." Turning back to his father, she went on. "Later, Dex drove me home and I snuck back through my window before my parents knew I was gone."

She left out the part about Dex kissing her good-bye with such intensity, she'd felt her toes tingle. And as she slipped into her bed, she could still taste him on her lips and feel the sweet echo of his body pressed to hers. "Before I fell asleep, I looked at the clock. It was four-thirty-seven."

"You don't have any proof." The sheriff did not like Abigail calling his daughter a liar.

Abigail pulled out a piece of paper she'd stuffed in her purse after Dex left it on the counter and handed it to Mr. Manning. "The receipt from the hotel room. The clerk will tell your lawyer I went in with Dex when he paid for the room and when we checked out." She hadn't hidden in the truck, but proudly stood beside Dex. Not her usual behavior, but last night she'd been bold enough to reach for heaven—and she'd found it.

Mr. Manning took the receipt. "Thank you for coming forward, Abigail. It can't be easy to tell us the truth."

No, it wasn't. Soon, the entire town would know the mayor's daughter had slept with the star baseball player. The publicity and talk this would generate would enrage not only her father but the church council her father belonged to, jeopardizing his coveted position.

Mr. Manning glanced at Dex. "I can't say I'm happy about what you were doing, but I understand your reluctance to pull Abigail into this." He looked at the slip of paper in his hands again. "I have no idea how a seventeen-year-old managed to get a motel room, but at least we have proof you didn't steal that car."

Mr. Manning glanced at the sheriff. "Let Dex go. You have two other people you need to question in this matter. I can't believe your daughter holds such a grudge against my son for breaking up with her that she lied and tried to frame him for this crime. A charge you can add to the others stacked against her."

This time the sheriff couldn't look the other way or sweep what his daughter did under the rug. Red-faced, he exhaled his frustration and did his job. "Abigail, I'll need you to sign a sworn statement to what you've told us here today."

"Of course." Abigail dropped her gaze to the floor, unable to take all of them staring at her, knowing what she'd done with Dex last night.

Her father gripped her arm; the bite of his fingers digging into her skin brought her head up as he gave her a shake and said gruffly near her ear, "You've shamed yourself and our family. We will discuss this when we get home."

The angry look in his eyes told her to expect far worse than a stern lecture and a litany of the many ways she didn't measure up and had disappointed her father over the years. This time, in his eyes, she'd gone too far and marred his good name in public. He wouldn't stand for it, and she would pay dearly.

Someday she'd find a way to break free before she ended up like her mother, a meek woman ruled by her domineering husband, her every thought and deed dictated by his unrelenting demands and the Scripture her father distorted.

As if things weren't bad enough, her father turned and glared at Dex. "You will never see her again."

Dex's green eyes filled with regret and fear. She stared at him for a long moment, memorizing every little detail about his handsome face, praying she'd see him again soon, though none of her other prayers had ever been answered.

Her father not only meant that promise, he'd make it happen. How scared her to death.

Chapter One

Present day . . .

DEX'S STOMACH TIGHTENED and a band squeezed around his chest when he made the turn onto Oak Way and saw the moving truck in front of Abigail's old place. Not for the first time, he wondered how Abigail was, where she was, what happened to her after she'd walked out of the sheriff's office, never to be seen by anyone in town again.

The guilt hit him like a sledgehammer to the chest. It always did when he thought of her. Which was all the time. He never knew when it would strike, but something would spark a memory and he'd fall back in time to her. Always her.

Since she'd never had a cell phone, a Twitter or Facebook account, not even a Snapchat or Instagram, all his attempts to find a trace of her online were unsuccessful. She virtually vanished.

He passed the house slowly, noting the contractors had done a nice job fixing the house after the fire burned down the back portion and took Mr. and Mrs. Swain's lives. Whoever conceived the new plan for the house had certainly done a fine job updating the outside and using the spacious property to add on to the place. Just in the nick of time too, with winter finally taking hold and the first snow of the season on the ground, even if it started late this year. Thank you, global warming.

In his mind's eye, he could still see the house as it was the last time he'd come to try to talk to Abigail. In the dead of night, he'd tapped on her dark window, nailed shut after her parents found out about her sneaking out, and looked inside, only to find her bed as empty as the room. The walls, the tops of the furniture, even the bed had been stripped bare. As if she'd never been there.

He'd asked his father the next day if he knew what happened to Abigail. The look on his father's face told him he wanted to spare Dex. After a long, tense, silence, his father told him the cold, bitter truth. Mayor Swain had made good on his threat and sent Abigail away.

Dex walked right out the door without a word, got in his truck, and drove to the Swains' house. He'd knocked politely on the door, though he'd wanted to pound his fists against the wood and break it down and demand to know where they'd sent Abigail.

Her mother answered with a polite but definitive *"Please leave."*

"Mrs. Swain, please, where is she? Can I at least call her or send her an e-mail or a letter? She didn't do anything wrong. She told the truth."

"You defiled my daughter. She's no longer pure. She

went against God. She went against us. She's a sinner and needs to repent."

The slam of the door rang in his ears even now. His insides ached with the ineptitude to turn back the clock and keep her out of it. To this day, he wondered what happened to her because she'd stood up for him.

Missing her got harder every day.

Judging by the moving truck and SUV parked in the driveway, Abigail's grandmother had found a tenant for the renovated house. To him, it would always be Abigail's. It would officially be hers once her grandmother Mrs. Gilbert signed the papers she'd requested he draw up to put the house in Abigail's name.

He pulled to the curb in front of Mrs. Gilbert's house at the end of the road, grinned at the laughing Santa in her window, and cut the engine. Thinking about Abigail always made him feel sad and guilty and angry. She was unfinished business. He'd promised himself, standing on the porch of her parents' house, that someday he'd make it right. He'd tell her he was sorry for turning her life upside down. He'd give her the thanks she deserved, because after that day, he had vowed to make something of himself and prove her brave act didn't go to waste.

She hadn't saved him from jail for nothing.

He figured he was doing pretty well so far living up to that promise.

Climbing out of his car, he walked up the path, his boots crunching on the thin layer of icy snow. The scent of pine from the wreath on the door hit him on the steps. Since Mrs. Gilbert had taken a shine to him years ago, he gave a hard rap on the door, opened it, and walked in calling out, "Hey, Mrs. Gilbert, it's me, Dex."

"Well, hey yourself, handsome. I'm in the kitchen. Come on back."

Dex walked through the house feeling as comfortable as he did in his own grandmother's place. Mrs. Gilbert sat at the table smiling at him with an odd look in her eyes that sent a shiver running up his spine.

He gave her a friendly peck on the cheek and sat across from her. Her hands trembled a bit before she brought the mug of tea up to her lips for a sip. Lemon and the scent of something else hung in the air, teasing his senses, making him think he should remember that sweet smell.

"I saw a moving truck at the house."

Mrs. Gilbert eyed him intently. "Now that the work is finished, it's time the house had some life in it," she said with a smile. "A family is exactly what that place needs."

"It's certainly big enough for one. I hope your tenant can cover the mortgage you must have needed for such a large addition." The house had been left to Mrs. Gilbert free and clear upon the Swains' deaths.

"The insurance paid for the major damage. Abigail paid the rest."

The mention of her name made his gut ripple. It was his fault Mrs. Gilbert hadn't seen her granddaughter in ten years. And yet, she'd hired him as her lawyer and treated him like family. He didn't deserve her generosity or her friendship, but she offered him both without reservation.

He had a million questions he'd like to ask, but the

day Mrs. Gilbert hired him and he asked about getting in touch with Abigail, she shut him down with an unequivocal "I can't tell you where she is or how to get in touch with her." He'd wanted to push, but something in her sad and wary eyes warned him to let it go even if he didn't want to.

Sticking to business, Dex took the papers out of his briefcase and placed them on the table in front of her. "Sign on the dotted line. The house and property will be Abigail's." Her name stuck in his throat.

She signed the papers and that odd feeling crept over him again. "Do you need my help with a rental agreement for the new tenant?"

"I didn't rent it. She's moving in."

His world rocked off center. "She?" The swell in his heart told him how much he wanted to believe it true.

"Hello, Dex."

Abby.

Her familiar soft, husky voice stopped his heart. Her sweet scent, the one teasing his memory since he'd walked in the door, wrapped around him. It took him back to that motel room and the smell of her in the room, on the sheets . . . on his skin.

He stood slowly and turned to face her. His brain didn't want to believe she was really standing there staring at him. All thoughts fled, except for the simple fact that she was more beautiful today than she'd been ten years ago. Her dark hair disappeared behind her shoulders, hanging down her back in soft waves. Gone was the simple braid she'd always worn. He scanned from her beautiful face down her curved and rounded body to her hips and long legs snug in a pair of tight jeans. No long, drab-colored skirt. Her full breasts rounded in the V of her red blouse. The sleeves ruffled over her shoulders in a soft, sheer material. The pretty blouse suited her far more than those long-sleeved, buttoned-up-to-her-neck shirts she used to wear. Her bright, golden brown eyes glistened in the light, so pretty and intent on him.

The shy girl he used to know stood before him now as a confident, beautiful woman.

He stood stunned by her beauty and the complete unreality of the moment. He'd waited so long to have the opportunity to see her again, to tell her . . . so many things. All of them lodged in his throat at the sight of her.

Something inside him clicked back into place after all these years of being lodged off center.

He closed the distance between them, wrapped his arms around her, and crushed her to his chest. "Abby." Her name came out sounding like a plea, a promise, a wish, a gift.

Abigail's hands slipped from his back around to his chest. Her fingers clutched his shirt a second before she pushed back and stepped out of his arms. He took her hand, his fingers sliding over the puckered scar. He stared at the slash marks on both her hands and one forearm.

Abigail pulled her hand away, tucked both hands behind her back, and with a nervous smile, ignored the questioning look he gave her and said, "Congratulations, Dex. You've really made something of yourself. I always knew you would. You took your scholarship and the promise of a bright future and ran with them. You graduated top of your class in both college and law school, took a job with a small but high-profile law firm and worked your way up, winning more than a few tough cases. Just when they were about to offer you a coveted partnership, you moved back home and opened your own practice."

"Have you been keeping track of me?" Maybe he wasn't the only one who thought of them and what they'd had together.

She didn't answer. "Sit down, Dex. There's something I have to tell you. It's long overdue."

"Where have you been all these years?"

"Closer than you think," she said cryptically. "Listen, I don't have a lot of time. What I have to tell you is very important. Life changing. Please sit."

He remained on his feet, rooted to the floor. He needed to stand face-to-face with her when she said her piece. He owed her that much, and more. So much more.

"Just tell him the best way you know how, honey." Mrs. Gilbert encouraged.

The front door slammed shut and a little girl's voice called out, "Mom!" just as Abigail looked up at the ceiling and said, "Nothing in my life goes as planned."

Dex stared in amazement as two small feet and slim legs in jeans appeared behind Abigail's. He wanted to smile at the tiny pink, and wet from the snow, Converse shoes.

Abigail, a mother. She made a life away from here and it included a family. Trying to be happy for her, he fought the disappointment rising inside him. Some other man held Abigail's heart and shared a child with her. Unrestrained jealousy and regret raced through him.

Abigail turned her back on him and addressed the child. He had an overwhelming need to see Abigail's little girl. Did she look just like her mama?

"I said to wait outside for five minutes."

"I'm a kid, not a clock. Besides, it's really cold out there."

Dex smiled at the sarcastic comeback.

"Did you tell him?" The hesitancy in the girl's voice sent a shaft of worry through Dex's chest.

"If you'd waited the five minutes, I would have. Are you ready?"

"I think so."

Abigail turned back to him. "Dex, I'd like you to meet Kelly."

The little girl walked out from behind her mother. Dex stared in wonder at the little girl with long blond hair and the same green eyes he stared at in the mirror each morning while he shaved.

"Your daughter," Abigail added softly as recognition dawned in his heart and mind.

His knees buckled. Lucky for him, Mrs. Gilbert kicked a chair behind him. He fell into it. Abigail's words hit him square in the heart, gripped it in a fist, and squeezed. His whole world stopped, even as his mind raced with thoughts of the past, questions, what this meant to his future.

He had a daughter.

"I'm sorry to surprise you like this. I promise we'll

talk, but right now, it would be nice if you said something to her."

Abigail brushed her hand through Kelly's thick hair. "She's yours, Dex. She looks more and more like you every day."

"Mom says I have the same birthmark on my shoulder as you," Kelly said, and looked up at her mom for reassurance.

"Why? How? Why? What?" He stumbled to ask . . . everything . . . but didn't have the words to make anything clear when only one thing mattered. He had a child, a daughter.

"I can explain," Abigail said.

Kelly's face remained hopeful, but her eyes held a touch of fear.

The last ten years of his life flashed through his mind. He'd always believed Abigail had given him his life back that day. But she took something too. The sting of betrayal zapped through his heart as all the things he'd missed with his daughter struck him hard. Nine years of her life—gone.

Then he looked at Abigail watching him and realized she had Kelly at sixteen. A child herself. How did she do it? The ever-present *why* flew through his mind.

All that jealousy he'd felt a few minutes ago turned to possessiveness. Kelly was his daughter. And he was tied to Abigail through her. He needed answers, but that could wait; he needed to meet his little girl.

Choked up, he asked, "Can I hug her?" He wanted to touch her and know she was real. This wasn't another dream about Abigail coming back into his life. Though those dreams never included a child.

The relief in Abigail's eyes went a long way to soothing the anger he felt about being denied his daughter all these years.

Abigail squeezed their daughter's hand and touched her fingers to her softly rounded cheek. "You've waited a long time, sweetheart. There's your dad. He wants you."

Dex felt those words all the way to his heart. Combing his fingers through his hair, he tried to choke back the lump in his throat and think through the sludge of thoughts and emotions running through him and reassure her that he wanted her more than anything.

"Kelly." He paused. It felt strange to say her name and know she was his daughter. "I have to admit it's a bit of a shock finding out I'm a father." He rubbed the heel of his hand over his throbbing heart. "Okay, it's a big shock. But turning my back on you never entered my mind." He stood and went to her. Kneeling on one knee in front of Kelly, he was surprised she stood at nearly his eye level. He'd never gotten to see her as a baby, or when she was learning to walk. "I've missed a lot of your life."

"It wasn't Mom's fault. She—"

"Kelly," he interrupted because she didn't need to defend her mother. He took her hands. For a second, he just looked at her small ones joined with his much larger ones. "I'm not mad at your mom. Well, okay, maybe I am. I've missed so much, but I don't plan on missing another day."

"Really?" Kelly's shy smile tugged at his heart.

He cupped her soft cheek in his palm. "Yes. Since you moved back here where I live, I assume your mom wants us to have a relationship."

"Since her mom and dad died, we could come back." Kelly glanced over her shoulder at her mom.

That one statement said a hell of a lot about why Abigail stayed away so long.

Kelly walked right into his chest and wrapped her hands around his neck. "I'm glad you're not too mad."

He wrapped his arms around his daughter for the first time and held her close. She smelled like her mother and the fresh wind and lemon drops. His eyes misted over at the overwhelming sense of love he felt for this girl. His little girl. Everything inside him said, *Mine*. He stood up with his little girl held tightly in his arms against his chest and stared at Abigail, tears shimmering in his eyes.

Tears fell down her cheeks faster than she could wipe them away. She'd also waited a long time for this moment.

"She's beautiful, Abby."

"She's been the light in my life since my parents sent me away." Abigail wiped the tears away while Dex set Kelly back on her feet.

"Why? Why didn't you tell me?"

"It's a long story. I'll tell you the whole truth and nothing but so help me God."

"Then start talking."

Instead of explaining, she glanced down at Kelly. "Enjoy some time with great-grandma. I'll be back in a little while for you after I talk to your father."

"I want to come too."

Abby caressed Kelly's round cheek. "You'll see him again soon."

Abby clasped the side of his shoulder, and a wave of heat shot through him with the tidal wave of memories her touch invoked. "Let's walk over to my place and I'll tell you." She gave his arm a tug before she dropped her hand.

"Come, peanut, let's decorate these sugar cookies," Mrs. Gilbert coaxed Kelly over to the racks of cookies on the counter with a bowl of icing and containers of red and green sprinkles.

Conflicted about what to do, stay with his daughter and figure out what to say to her, or go with Abby and find out what the hell was going on here, he went to Kelly first. He hugged her close again. She held on to him too. Though it felt awkward at first, they both settled into the embrace. He kissed the top of her golden head. Choked up, he barely whispered out, "I'll see you soon." He reluctantly let her go, giving her one last long look before he walked out of the kitchen with Abby, conflicted by his anger and wanting the beautiful woman beside him so damn bad, he wanted to rage at her for keeping him from his daughter and kiss her like he'd dreamed of doing again for far too long.

Chapter Two

ABBY STOMPED HER feet into the brand-new pair of snow boots by the front door. She opened it and walked out into the way too cold outdoors, wishing she could have brought some of the Arizona heat with her to Montana on their move. The wave of heat that washed through her had more to do with Dex's proximity and his intense gaze on her than the thick coat she pulled on.

Rushing and not watching where she stepped, she hit the second tread on the stairs and slipped. Dex caught her under the arms and pulled her up before she landed on her ass on the pathway.

He held her with her back pressed to his chest, then moved his hands to the outside of her shoulders and gave her a squeeze. "Careful, Abby."

She stepped away, needing the space to regain her equilibrium, the loss of which had a hell of a lot more to do with his deep voice rumbling at her ear than the almost tumble she took.

She needed to stop reacting to him like this. As much as she'd like to believe they could have back what they used to share, she expected his emotions would catch up to him soon and the anger would wipe away any good feelings he had at seeing her again.

Walking down the path with Dex beside her, she didn't know how to start explaining, so began with something easy. "Mrs. Cobb is still putting out that deranged-looking gingerbread man." The silly Styrofoam cutout stood at least eight feet tall, with his arms up too high like he was after you. His eyes were uneven and too big. His mouth drawn back in a creepy Joker's sneer.

"It's better than the pig in the Santa suit that lights up."

She laughed, though Dex's voice held absolutely no humor.

They crossed the street, and a truck with the Rambling Range logo on the door drove by as they stepped up onto the opposite sidewalk. The gray-haired man at the wheel tooted the horn twice and Dex gave him a wave.

"Wayne Travers is getting up there," she said to fill the tense silence.

"Yeah. He's one of my biggest clients. He's probably on his way down to the diner for his date with one of the waitresses."

"That's sweet."

Dex raised one eyebrow and gave her a conspiratorial grin. "Luna is younger than Wayne's sons. Rumor has it they're having a steamy affair."

"No," she scoffed.

Dex shook his head. "Wayne thinks of her as a daughter. He looks forward to their 'dates' after his wife passed away several years ago. He says, 'She's good company.'"

"That's sweet." Abby walked up the steps to her front door, opened it, and waved Dex in.

His lips drew back in a lopsided frown. "We never went on a real date. Your father would have killed me if he caught us out together."

"That's what I want to talk to you about." She led him past all the moving boxes and into the kitchen. She'd made a fresh pot of coffee before she went over to her grandmother's house.

"What the hell, Abby? Why did you keep this from me?" All the anger he'd tamped down for Kelly's sake came bubbling up to the surface.

"Sit. We'll start at the beginning."

Dex fell onto the stool at the breakfast bar. "Where the hell did you go after you left the sheriff's office? What happened to you?" His frustration and hurt simmered underneath his words and intent gaze.

She understood both and hoped her explanation helped him to understand if not forgive what she'd done.

She took a deep breath, hoping she could get through this hard part so they could find a way to, if nothing else, co-parent Kelly without animosity or anger between them.

She poured him a cup of coffee and set it in front of him. "I never really talked about my parents with you."

"You avoided it. I got the feeling you didn't like them

much. The few times we worked here on our project, your father talked at you, not to you."

She remembered her father's way of always looking for any little thing she did wrong. Any little misstep called out and admonished with some verbal cut-down and never-ending disapproval.

Dex frowned, thinking back with her. "If you sat too close to me, he snapped at you. If you got excited and spoke too loud, he shushed you. I hate to say this, but it felt stifling to be here. Every little thing we did under the microscope of your parents' scrutiny. Every word and gesture, no matter how innocent, taken as a means of me corrupting you."

"I'm sorry, Dex. They never welcomed you, or gave you a chance."

"At first, I thought they were just protective of their teenage daughter. But the way your father acted, saying you'd disgraced him, your mother telling me I'd defiled you, it went much deeper, didn't it?"

"When did my mother say that to you?"

"I came to see you the night after everything happened. Your room had been cleaned out. I came back the next day, but your mother refused to tell me where they sent you or how to get in touch with you."

"I didn't know you came."

"Too late, it turns out. Help me out here, Abby. Did you hate me that much you kept my child away from me all this time?"

"Hate you? No, Dex. I wanted so badly to stay with you. I never wanted to give you up."

Dex slammed his palm on the counter. "Then why, damn it? Why didn't you call me?" He raked his fingers through his golden hair. "I waited so damn long for you to call me."

She reached out and placed her hand over his. The connection helped her to tell the terrible truth. "They took me to a retreat the church runs for families in crisis. I use the word 'retreat' loosely. In my parents' eyes, I'd sinned and needed to repent."

Dex's hand balled into a fist beneath hers. "I knew I shouldn't have let you go home with him. I tried to tell my dad we needed to go back and get you."

"There's nothing you could have done. I was a minor and under their thumb." She tried to contain the bitterness in her words, but it leaked out with the anger still souring her gut even today. She boldly gave him the truth. "They had me on my knees for days. Hours and hours of fasting and reading Scripture, until I had no energy, terrible bruises on my knees, and no voice left. Still, they made me rasp out the words and pray for my soul. The minister prayed over me, hoping to rid me of the evil I'd let into my heart and life."

Dex sighed and looked her right in the eye. "They never believed you rid yourself of the evil, did they?"

"No. They didn't." The minute they discovered she was pregnant, they'd thought the evil had taken root and was growing inside her. They couldn't see past their deeply held beliefs and love her and the child she carried unconditionally.

"What happened when they found out you were pregnant?" He didn't sound like he really wanted to know after what she'd just told him.

"My parents transferred me to a home for pregnant teens who wanted to give their child up for adoption. It didn't matter how many times I refused; at my parents' direction, the minister and his followers running the place pressured me to go along for my own good. They drilled into me a hundred times a day that what I was doing was best for my child. They promised me that she'd go to a good and loving home that I couldn't provide for her. If I didn't, they swore they'd have me declared mentally unfit. The lawyer who worked for the ministry had the papers for the adoption and my incompetency all drawn up, ready to use against me."

He choked out, "What did you do, Abby?"

"Whatever I had to do to keep her." Abby raked her fingers through her hair, the echo of fear and anger exploding inside her even now as she remembered how close she'd come to losing Kelly. "They took her away not five minutes after I had her. I barely got to see her. I waited until they settled me into my room, then I snuck out, went to the nursery, found my mini-you crying in her bassinet, and I took her while the adoptive parents were signing the papers in the other room."

"Abby." Dex barely got her name out. If not for Abby's desperate actions, he might never have known about his daughter. Ever.

"I'll spare you the details of sneaking out after just giving birth and being scared and hurting and sleeping in a Laundromat with a newborn and not knowing what to do with her or how to take care of her. I had nothing. No diapers. No place to go. No one to help me in those dire hours."

Dex's anger came back full force. "Why the hell didn't you call me then? I would have come and gotten you both."

"I wanted to, but I couldn't."

"Why the hell not?"

"My father swore that I would never be allowed to raise Kelly. The ministry followed his orders. They had a couple there to adopt her already. If he found me, he'd take Kelly away. I couldn't risk it. I had to protect her and you."

"Me?"

"He threatened you to keep me in line. If I tried to contact you and tell you about the baby, he'd ruin you and your family."

Her chest rose and fell with an exasperated sigh. "My father would stop at nothing to prove us unfit parents. He had the resources and clout in this town to affect your father's business and turn people against your parents. How long would it take for them and you to hate me for coming into your lives and destroying them? I had already lost everything. As much as I wanted to tell you about Kelly for your sake and hers, I couldn't do that to you, so I made the hard decision. I walked away knowing you'd hate me when you found out. I cheated you. I cheated Kelly. I knew exactly what I was doing, and I did it anyway. Seeing you happy, with a good job and a good life now, I'd do it again."

Considering her father's position in the community

as mayor and his placement high up in the church organization, and that the ministry had effected changes by pressuring the city council and manipulating local elections and businesses in their favor, Mayor Swain did in fact have the resources to back up those threats. A few changes in policies and restrictions and his father's business would be in jeopardy. The ministry had grown into a powerful force in the community, so Abby's perceived embarrassment to her father had really hit him hard, might have even jeopardized his position in the group, and made him turn on her like that to save face.

Mayor Swain chose the ministry over his own daughter and granddaughter.

Dex wanted to rage at her father for trying to make her give up their baby. For making it so damn impossible for her to come to him for help. For threatening his family.

If the bastard wasn't already dead, Dex would kill him.

Mayor Swain sent the girl Dex loved away and stole the life he might have had with her and his daughter.

Her sad eyes locked on him. "I'm sorry."

People said they were sorry all the time, the words nothing more than a concession, or said without any feeling or atonement behind them. She said the words with all her regret and remorse packed into them. The weight of those simple words hit him with an impact he didn't want to admit made a world of difference and helped ease the anger simmering underneath his questions and roiling emotions.

She meant it.

And because she meant it, he couldn't ignore it.

"I'm sorry too."

Her eyes narrowed. "Sorry? For what? You didn't do anything."

"Exactly." He threw up his hands and let them fall. "I did nothing."

"You didn't know." She defended him.

"I should have guessed, or at least wondered if you were pregnant after our night together." They'd been careful the first two times, but the last, before he'd had to take her home, he'd been desperate to have her. The intensity of what they felt wiped away their good sense.

But what she thought could last forever got crushed by reality in her young heart. "The only thing you were thinking about was college, ball, and whatever girl you were seeing at the time."

"What?"

"Despite my father's threats, I wanted you to know about your daughter. I went to Arizona and found you. I thought it would be so easy to walk right up to you and tell you, 'Look, here she is.' But reality has never been that easy for me. There you were, walking out of your dorm with a pretty brunette hanging on your arm. You must have spent five minutes kissing her good-bye."

Dex tried to put a face to the picture Abby painted. He'd had several girlfriends in college. None lasted long. He used his minor celebrity status as a star athlete to fill his bed and try to find that same thing he felt in Abby's arms. He never did, though; young and dumb, he'd convinced himself he didn't want to be tied down.

That's exactly how it appeared to Abby. His fault.

"What was I supposed to do, Dex? Seeing you so damn happy, playing ball, living in the dorms with all your new friends, proved I couldn't tell you. How was I supposed to walk into that amazing life, tell you about Kelly, then sit back and watch my father destroy it, you, your family, everything to the point you hated me.

"Up until I saw you kissing that girl, I was living in a dream world thinking we could be together and raise Kelly."

"Damn it, Abby, despite how it looked, I hadn't forgotten about you."

Her eyes softened and glassed over.

"I don't know what else to say, Dex. All that mattered was that I got away, and I still had my baby."

Yes, not losing Kelly mattered more than anything. "How did you do it?"

Abigail raked her fingers through her hair. "We bounced around from one shelter for runaway teens to the next to avoid my parents finding me and taking Kelly. I had the motivation and drive to get Kelly out of those places as fast as possible, so I took whatever job I could find. Maid. Dishwasher. Janitor. Construction cleanup. One of the counselors saw that I was smart and a hard worker. She got me a job at a family-owned restaurant as a bookkeeper. Friends she knew well, who offered me a room in their home as part of my pay. They took Kelly and me in like family. They saved us from a very rocky life living one step away from being on the streets."

Dex swore, thinking of the dangers they faced on

their own in shelters surrounded by desperate people in desperate times. His stomach soured with all the gruesome thoughts swirling in his head of what could have happened to them. What might have happened to them without him ever knowing about it? He didn't really want to know the details now, though his mind conjured one nightmare after the next. Reality for Abby had to be much worse.

"My grandmother helped as much as she could, but my father watched her like a hawk trying to find me. There were days, weeks, where . . ." Abby shook her head, a haunted look in her eyes that echoed with the desperation and fear she felt in those dire times. "If not for Selena's family, I don't know what would have happened to us. When I had time and the money, I took online classes and earned my GED and later a degree in business finance. Selena and her husband were immigrants. The business did okay, but I used what I learned in the night classes they helped fund and taught them how to maximize the business and financials. I helped them build the business from one restaurant to four and they made me a partner."

She'd come a long way.

"That's amazing, but I thought you wanted to be a biochemist and researcher."

She gave him a half frown. "I didn't have the luxury of being picky."

"Do you regret it?"

"Not a single day. I made a good life for Kelly and me. Maybe it's not the life I imagined, but it is infinitely better having her in it. I have a good job, a home of my own, and an amazing daughter who is happy and thriving with the possibility of anything she wants in her future. It hasn't been easy, I didn't make all the right decisions, but so long as she's happy and healthy, I'm satisfied."

"What about you, Abby?" he asked gently. "What kind of life have you had raising our daughter alone? Or did you find someone else to be her father?" The thought of some other man raising his daughter sent a fresh wave of pain racing through him.

"No, Dex. I've had some help along the way, but for the most part, I've raised her alone."

The depth of sadness in that "alone" made his heart ache.

He tried to imagine what he would have done had he known.

Would he have married Abby and been a good husband and father at eighteen? How would he have supported them?

Abby had raised their daughter with nothing and no one to help her. She'd given up her college dreams to be a scientist while he took advantage of all the opportunities his academic achievements and baseball accomplishments gave him and became a very successful lawyer.

The life he'd have had with Abby and Kelly would be nothing like the life he had now. Could they have been happy? Yes. Or maybe they'd have come to resent each other for losing the life they would have had if they'd both followed their dreams and not been tied down. He'd never wish away Kelly. He loved her already, and though he had not even imagined life as a father until this afternoon, he was overwhelmed by the things he'd missed, all the time lost. And yet he could see even more clearly the price Abby had paid to keep his little girl safe, to keep him and his family safe. It enraged him that her parents had done this to her. Them. The fact that he lived a life without obligation while Abby carried the burden riddled him with guilt. He'd do and give anything to have been there alongside Abby on every birthday he missed, every skinned knee she kissed, every sleepless night she faced alone.

Abby had put everything on the line to make sure he didn't go to jail and rot in a cell with his life in ruins, then spent the last ten years keeping him, his parents, and their daughter safe from her father's wrath.

Dex slid his hand over the back of his neck and squeezed the tight muscles. His mind swirled with thoughts and emotions he couldn't handle right now. "Truthfully, I don't know what to say or do. I have a daughter I don't even know. She doesn't know me. I don't know what to do with her or for her."

Abigail's lips tugged back in a smile that didn't quite reach her eyes and held a note of sadness. "I had no idea how to take care of her." He didn't think his fear and uncertainty about being a father showed, but Abby read it in him well. "Welcome to that feeling. Don't worry, you'll muddle your way through it."

"Is that what you did?"

"It was a lot of sleepless nights and crying the first few weeks. And that was just me," she teased, though the truth infused her words.

"Listen, Dex, spend some time with her. Let the idea of being a father sink in and settle. When you've had time to digest it, we'll talk again, and you can tell me how awful I am for keeping her from you."

Did she really expect the worst from him? "Why would I do that?"

"Because she's an amazing girl. She's so much like you in so many ways. It'll hit you hard that I cheated you. And because you're you."

"What the hell does that mean?"

"Only that you've chosen a profession in which you fight for people's rights, and I took yours away. When that really hits you, you'll want to take a bite out of me."

He did want to take a bite out of her, but for an entirely different reason than she thought. Everything in him ached to touch her. How many nights had he dreamed of her and the night they spent together? Too many to count.

She was right about one thing, he couldn't wrap his head around what happened. The questions and worry and the inability to settle the storm inside him left him unsettled and unsure.

"You're angry, Dex. I understand. I've been angry a long time. You didn't deserve it. I know that, and I did it anyway. I hope you find a way to, if not forgive me, then at least understand the choices I faced and that I did the best I could under the circumstances."

"I'm angry about all I've lost." He stared at the now cold coffee in front of him. "Nothing can change the fact I've missed nearly ten years of Kelly's life. I'll regret it for the rest of my days." He looked up at her. "But I'm grateful for what you did to keep our girl. I'm amazed by how hard you've worked and all you sacrificed to raise her. I can't tell you how happy I am you finally brought her back to me."

He didn't want things to be difficult between him and Abby and Kelly. He didn't want to get stuck on the past, so he tried to find a way to move forward.

"Tell me about Kelly."

Abby pressed her lips together and nodded that she understood his anger wasn't directed at her. "Kelly got your lawyer gene." That made her and him smile. "The girl can argue a good case. As smart as she is, she's got a soft heart. She's wanted you in her life always and I denied both of you."

"Did she really think I didn't want her?"

"No. Not at all. Never. I explained things to her over the years in a way that she could understand. Now that she's older and we were coming back here, I was able to explain more plainly why I kept you apart and could come back now. She says she understands why I did it, but she's a little girl who wanted her dad every day. I'm worried that now that she has you, she'll let out that anger toward me. I've let her down where you're concerned. I take responsibility for that. I hope we can work together to raise her now."

"I want to be a real part of her life."

"She needs you. She really wants to get to know you. In fact, she's been saving her allowance and wants to take you out on a father-daughter date tomorrow night."

He had to admit that was the best offer he'd had, or made, in months. "She does?"

"It's all she talked about on the road trip here."

He loved that Kelly was excited to spend time with him. He wished Abby had the same enthusiasm. Instead, she kept the counter between them, and her beautiful eyes remained guarded. They might not know each other well now, but they weren't strangers. You'd never know it by her defensive posture or the watchful way she kept an eye on him.

For all she'd told him, she still held something back.

"Your parents died months ago. Why didn't you call me right away?"

"I wanted to, but I didn't want to tell you over the phone, so I planned to come back here."

"Yet the repairs and renovation on the house were done over a month ago."

Something came into her eyes, something sad and haunting. "There is nothing I wanted more than for you to be a part of Kelly's life. That's why I moved us here. I did it as quickly as I could, but I know it isn't soon enough for you. Given time, you'll think long and hard about all you've missed, the milestones big and small in her life that you didn't get to witness, every little detail you don't know, and you'll charge me with every single count."

His heart ached at the sad look in her eyes. Yes, he was angry, angrier still that he couldn't lash out at her parents for stealing so much. "I don't want to prosecute you, Abby. I want to understand. I want to go back and change it. I want to make it right."

"I wish I could make it right, Dex. For you. For Kelly. For all of us. I never wanted to hurt either of you."

It hurt like hell.

"What really brought you home? It's more than just your parents dying and you feeling safe enough to come home, isn't it?" He stared pointedly at her scarred hands.

At first he'd thought the marks came from the punishment meted out by the ministry, but the scars looked newer. Red and bold against her pale skin, they hadn't had time to fade.

She folded her arms across her chest, tucked her hands under her arms, and avoided the question. "Kelly's probably wondering what's taking so long. I should go and get her."

"Stalling won't stop me from digging for the real reason you're here." He worried about how she'd gotten those devastating marks.

Abby's gaze fell away. "Kelly is the reason I'm here."

He let it go for now. "I'll walk you back to your grandmother's. I'd like to say good-bye to Kelly and let her know I can't wait for our date."

As much as he wanted a relationship with Kelly, he wanted one with Abby even more. He didn't like the distance she kept between them. He'd find a way to make her trust him again. She and Kelly were his family. One he didn't know he had, but one he wanted more than anything.

ABIGAIL WALKED INTO her grandmother's kitchen and smiled at the racks of decorated cookies. Santas, reindeers, wreaths, and balls glistened with colored sugar and sprinkles. Their sweet, sugary vanilla scent filled the air. Her grandmother hugged Kelly close to her side as Kelly stacked cookies in a plastic container. The two smiled with their happiness. Dex wasn't the only one who'd missed out on spending time with Kelly. The regret and guilt weighed heavy in her heart.

"You two look like you're having fun. That's a lot of cookies."

Kelly spun around, her sweet smile falling into a frown. "Where's Dad?"

Abigail's heart cracked again. "He had to take a call from a client. He's outside waiting to say good-bye to you."

"Is everything okay?" Hope filled Kelly's voice. She wanted them to be a real family.

Abigail yearned to find a way to be friends with Dex again for Kelly's sake. "Fine, honey. I told him everything."

"Everything?" She narrowed her gaze on Abigail's clasped hands.

"Everything about you and my parents," she clarified.

"But . . ."

"One thing at a time. Go say good-bye to your father. He can't wait to see you for dinner tomorrow night."

Kelly beamed Abigail a smile, took the box of cookies Gran handed her, and ran out to see Dex.

Gran placed her hands over Abigail's. "He's a good man. Let him show you."

"He doesn't have anything to prove to me."

"If he hasn't already, he'll come to understand you had no choice. Keeping Kelly safe and with you was the only way to protect everyone."

"He missed so many years of her life." Memories of Kelly growing up played through her mind along with the one thought she always had when she looked at her daughter: *I wish Dex had been there.*

"There's a reason in that fire taking your parents and bringing you back here now. Unfinished business smolders in a person's soul. Finish this, honey. It's the reason you're here."

Her grandmother's faith sounded too much like her father's devout spewing. "I don't want to hear about reasons and divine plans."

"God is what we make him, honey. Your father, and eventually your mother, took an extreme view. Wrath and punishment and sin twisted together without love and forgiveness and acceptance is not God."

"Don't I know it." She tried to keep the scathing note from her voice, but this topic set her off.

"All I'm saying is that the events that took you from this place and brought you back all stem from one point in your life. What might have been will never be known for sure. You have a chance to right the past and make a new future with Dex. Don't let your fear keep you from trying for something you dreamed of having before it was all taken away."

"That's just it, Gran. Those were a girl's dreams of happy ever after. The reality is, that girl doesn't exist anymore. I'll be satisfied with Dex becoming a true part of Kelly's life. That's all I want."

"Want more," Gran demanded. "You deserve more."

"I don't deserve anything from him. Given time with her, he'll come to realize all I stole from him and can't give back. It's why I fell in love with him, Gran. He's that kind of man. Good. Kind. Decent. He fights for people. What do I say to him when he decides he'd have given everything he has to be a father to her instead?"

"It can't be changed. You watch, this time he'll fight for you."

She wanted to believe that, but after what she'd done, it seemed impossible. A sad smile crept across her lips to match the ache in her chest. "You don't find forever love in high school. I was just one girl he dated. Not the first. Not the last. Not the one he wanted forever."

She gave Gran a kiss on the cheek and walked out to collect Kelly and take her home to finish unpacking. She should have known Gran wouldn't let her get away with the last word.

"You gave him a child," she called out from the kitchen before Abigail opened the front door. "That means something to a man. You're also the one who got away. Nothing a man likes more than a challenge."

Abigail walked down the icy path, her heartwarming just watching Dex oohing and aahing over the cookies Kelly decorated.

Dex's smile didn't waver when she stepped up to them. "She's got a future in baking."

"She loves to cook with me." Abigail swept her hand

down the back of Kelly's hair. "Head up to the house, honey, and put those away. We'll get dinner started soon."

"I'll see you tomorrow, right, Dad?"

Dex's eyes softened the moment Kelly called him Dad. "Yes," he choked out, as caught up as Abigail in the long overdue moment. He hooked his arm around Kelly and pulled her close, kissing her on the head. "I can't wait for our date."

Kelly hugged her dad back, then skipped off with the cookies toward home, looking over her shoulder a couple of times to spy on Abigail and Dex.

"She's amazing." Dex stared after their little girl, all the wonder he put in those words filling his voice.

"Yes, she is."

"We have a lot of unfinished business, Abby. But all I want to focus on is getting to know my daughter. And you again. You owe me for all the sleepless nights you left me wanting you. From this point forward, Abby, it's you, me, and Kelly."

Dex left her with those words and got in his car and drove away.

Abby felt the pull between them pulse.

The flicker of hope she tried to keep smothered flamed to life.

Chapter Three

Evening temps will *drop to the low thirties and upper twenties tonight in some areas of the county, with cloudy skies and snow to the north in higher elevations. Our futurecast shows the storm that left several feet of snow and devastated much of the Western states with gusting winds reaching forty to sixty miles per hour is moving up from California into Nevada and gaining intensity. Stay tuned for updates as we watch the severe weather system headed our way.*

Dex opened his car door, cutting off the rest of the news report. He worried about the storm, but had other pressing matters to attend to right now. Nothing was more important than his dinner date with his little girl. He walked up the path and stairs to the porch and rang the bell, anxious to see Kelly, and especially Abby, again. He didn't know what possessed him to practically admit to her face that he still wanted Abby when he left her yesterday, except that it hit him that they shared a child and he wanted to share a hell of a lot more. He'd missed her so damn long, he didn't want to miss her another day.

That went double for Kelly.

He spent long hours last night analyzing everything Abby told him about what happened to her, how she managed over the years, everything he missed with his daughter; and sorting through the anger to the guilt he felt that Abby had endured her parents' wrath and felt she couldn't come to him. He understood the why. He'd probably have done the same thing. But it didn't stop him from raging at the fact that the girl he fell in love with, who loved him back, didn't tell him about their daughter, and he'd let her go way too easily. His feelings for her scared him at the time. Young. Dumb. Not ready for something so intense and confusing, he'd let the best thing to ever happen to him slip through his fingers.

He wouldn't let that happen again.

Kelly threw open the door. "You're finally here."

He glanced at his watch and noted he was five minutes early. It did his heart good that she was looking forward to this as much as he was.

"Come in. Mom's unpacking boxes in the kitchen."

Abby stepped into the living room. She'd tied her hair up in some messy knot on her head. He wanted to take it down and run his fingers through the dark, silky strands.

As much as he'd thought about what happened to Abby and Kelly, he'd spent even more time remembering Abby with him back when she belonged to him.

She smiled softly, still keeping that cautious distance and look in her eyes. "Hi, Dex."

"Abby. You look great."

She stared down at her simple white T-shirt and snug jeans, then eyed him with even more suspicion in her eyes. "Are you ready to go, Kelly?"

"I can't wait." She practically danced on her tiptoes with anticipation.

Dex smiled down at her. "Where do you want to go?"

"I don't know. We just got here yesterday."

"Okay, I'll pick the place, you buy dinner. We'll get to know each other."

"Awesome!" Kelly ran from the room.

At Dex's confused face, Abby said, "She went to get her backpack. She has something to show you."

"What is it?"

"You'll see. It'll be a way for the two of you to break the ice and get to know each other. Though you'll find she knows an awful lot about you."

Kelly came bouncing back into the room with her coat on, backpack over her shoulder, and a ball cap on her head.

His heart did a little leap in his chest just seeing her again. "Nice cap, honey. I went to school at Arizona State."

"I know. Mom and I went to a few of your games."

His eyes narrowed and a zip of shock shot through him. "You saw me play?"

"Well, I was really little, but yeah. I have pictures in my bag to show you at dinner."

Dex looked at Abby, trying to contain his shock. "You

said you came to see me in Arizona. You never said you stayed."

She scrunched her mouth into a frown. "I needed a place to live. I found it there. I couldn't bring Kelly to you, but I stayed close to make sure my father didn't cause you any trouble. My grandmother kept me posted on your parents here." She bit her lip. "We didn't discuss it yesterday, and I'm not sure you've had a chance to talk to them, but Kelly wants to meet her grandparents."

Dex hadn't had a chance to even think of talking to his parents yet. "They're out of town until tomorrow. I'll tell them as soon as they get back."

"Sooner is better. Once the two of you are seen together, people are going to ask questions and talk," Abby pointed out.

Dex knew all too well how the grapevine worked in this town. "I guess it won't be long before everyone knows she's my daughter. There's no reason to hide it."

Abby pressed her lips together and nodded, but he read her trepidation.

"Is there?"

"No," Abby answered immediately. "It's up to you. This is going to change your life forever. Once people know we had a daughter after what happened, they'll talk. You have a reputation and a business in this town. You need to be prepared for whatever gossip and rumors this creates. If you want to take a couple of days, let people know in your way, Kelly and I will keep a low profile until you're ready—"

He held up his hand to stop her from saying anything

else. "I can handle the blabbermouths. I'm worried about you. You've endured so much, the last thing I want is you hurt by the rumor mill's petty accusations and stories they'll make up, thinking they know what really happened."

The resignation and sadness in her eyes told him she'd already mentally prepared herself for the worst. "I've talked to Kelly about it and tried to prepare her for small-town living where everyone knows everything and has an opinion about it."

"It doesn't matter what they think, Mom. Only what you and Dad think."

God, how he loved hearing her call him that.

Abby brushed her hand over Kelly's head. "It still hurts your feelings when people talk about you behind your back. They don't know you, sweetheart. They know me and your dad and what happened ten years ago. This will dredge all that up again. I just want you and your dad to be prepared."

She acted like she didn't care about what happened to her.

He did. "And what about you, Abby?"

"I brought Kelly back to be with you. That's all that matters to me."

Since the moment he'd seen her, he'd wanted to know if she came back to see him. Yes, she brought Kelly back to him, but he wanted it to be more.

"You two should get going."

Tonight he'd spend alone with Kelly getting to know

her better, but after, they were going to start doing things together. All three of them. Like a real family.

Abby walked them to the door. "Please try to have her back no later than nine."

Dex swung his hand out for Kelly to walk to his car. "Climb in."

"Backseat. Don't forget the seatbelt," Abby warned.

Dex turned back to Abby.

She wrapped her arms around her middle. "She's so excited to have you all to herself."

"Once upon a time you wanted me all to yourself."

Abby took a step back literally and figuratively. "Dex, after all that's happened, I don't even know that girl anymore."

"That's okay, Abby. I never forgot her. The girl I wanted is standing right in front of me. Nothing has changed about the way I feel about you. So stop anticipating that I'm going to rage at you any second."

She flinched. "No, Dex. That's not it at all. It's not you."

"Dad, are you coming?" Kelly called from the open car door.

Dex sighed. "This is a glimpse at what it's like to have a kid, right?"

Abby finally gave him a smile, though like the others it didn't light her eyes. "Welcome to parenthood."

Why did she look so sad and lost? "We'll talk about what isn't me, and you're avoiding telling me, another time."

Dex reluctantly walked away without offering Abby any of the comfort she so obviously needed but wouldn't welcome from him. Not now. Not until they found their footing again and hopefully found their way back to each other.

Kelly smiled at him as he slipped into the front seat and closed the door against the cold. He adjusted his coat and clipped his seatbelt. "Ready, honey?"

"Ready." She shifted over to the seat behind him, so he could see her in the rearview mirror. And he guessed so she could see him.

He started the car and turned onto the road. "Let's hit the diner. You'll love that place. Everyone hangs out there. It's a real local spot and since you'll be living here, you should get to know all the cool spots in town."

"I don't know how long we're staying." She turned her gaze out the side window with those ominous words.

"What do you mean, honey? Your mom is unpacking your stuff right now."

"Most of that is new stuff. Mom had everything from her parents taken out of the house. She didn't want to keep anything that belonged to them. We still have our house in Arizona."

"Is this just a visit, then? You're going back to Arizona?" The thought made his gut twist. "I hope not. I've only just met you."

"Mom enrolled me in school here. It's just that she said if this didn't go well, we could always go home."

"You are home, Kelly. This is where you belong. Here with me and your mother."

Quiet settled over them both at his words. He wanted nothing more than to make his words reality.

"We're here." He pulled into a spot in front of the diner. He loved this place for its simple, small-town charm. Though the years were wearing on the building, you couldn't beat the home-style food. Even the snowflakes and Santa in the cowboy hat painted on the windows took him back to his childhood.

They both got out of the car and he motioned with his arm to the door, "After you, honey."

Her shy giggle, so much like her mother's, settled his nerves. A stiff scotch would smooth out a few more of his rough edges, but he'd have to wait for that. As much as he looked forward to this dinner, it left him off kilter. He didn't know her, had no idea what to ask first, or what to really say. All he knew was he wanted this to go well. He wanted her to like him. More than anything, he wanted her to love him as much as he already loved her.

"Jingle Bells" played cheerfully over the relatively quiet diner. He recognized many of the other patrons. None of them were his close friends or clients. He didn't want to put off his talk with Kelly by getting detoured with introductions and explanations.

"Are those guys real cowboys?"

He followed Kelly's gaze to the booth at the back and the two men sitting together, their cowboy hats on the seats next to them. "Yes, they are. That's Rory and Colt Kendrick. They're brothers. They own a huge ranch."

"That one guy, Rory, is really big. He keeps staring at that waitress."

Dex chuckled under his breath. It did appear Rory had a thing for Sadie. Even his client came down here for dinner dates with another waitress. Luna, who wasn't here right now. What was it about the women in this place that drew the Montana men faster than the smell of fresh apple pie?

Kelly bounced into a booth seat by the painted window with Rudolph and his big red nose and dragged her backpack off her arms, her ball cap off her head, and set them on the seat next to her. He slid in across from her. After they discarded their jackets, he handed her a menu, hoping to buy a minute to settle his mind with nothing more strenuous than deciding what he wanted to eat.

"Did you ever bring Mom here?"

"No."

"Yeah, I guess not."

He glanced up at her. "Things with your mom and I were complicated."

"She told me. You had another girlfriend, who tried to have you arrested. Mom stepped in and gave you an alibi. That's the night I was conceived."

"Alibi. Conceived. Big words. What grade are you in?"

"Eighth. I skipped first, third, and sixth. Mom won't let me skip any more. She says I need to be a kid." Kelly rolled her expressive green eyes.

"Wow. My daughter's a total Brainiac. You amaze me more and more."

"Mom says I'm a lot like her in that way. She skipped first and fourth grade."

"Two years younger than me. I don't think I've ever

met anyone as smart as your mom. Well, maybe until you." That earned him another of her pretty smiles.

Abby had given up a chance to attend a top university to protect Kelly and him. For all he'd lost, he kept getting glimpses of what Abby had to do to care for their daughter and what she'd given up.

He didn't want to interrogate his daughter for more information about Abby, so he stuck to getting to know her. "What are you having, honey?"

"Is the pot roast good?"

"The best. It's one of my favorites," he added.

"I'll have that. Can I have a soda?"

"Does your mom let you drink soda?"

She eyed him over the menu. "Only on special occasions."

He'd never gotten to spoil her, so he gave in to the urge now. "I definitely think this ranks as a special occasion."

"Me too." She beamed.

The waitress arrived. One who served him often. "Hi, Kate."

"Mr. Manning. What'll it be?"

"We'll have two pot roast dinners. Make mine with French fries instead of mashed potatoes."

"Mine too," Kelly chimed in.

He smiled, thinking it cute she wanted to be like him, then she changed his mind when she added, "I thought you'd think I was weird if I got it with fries."

"Not at all, it's my favorite way." He turned back to

Kate. "We'll also have a couple of sodas, make mine . . . . root beer," he and Kelly said in unison.

Kate laughed and wrote their order down. "If I didn't know better, I'd think you two are related."

Kelly stared down at her hands in her lap and didn't say a word. She couldn't even look at him. No way around it, people were going to find out one way or the other.

"Kate, this is my daughter, Kelly. She and her mother, Abigail, just moved to town. Kelly and I are having our first of many father-daughter dates."

A glass fell over, silver clinked, and a plate crashed to the floor at the bar in front of the kitchen, drawing all of their attention.

Dex narrowed his gaze on the woman he avoided like the plague. The last person he wanted to know about Kelly. No telling what kind of drama she'd cause him and Abby this time.

Laurie mopped up her spilled beer, tossed the wet napkins down, eyed him for one long moment, then pulled several bills from her purse, dumped them on the counter, and rushed out of the diner.

Kate shook her head. "Good Lord, she's a one-woman wrecking crew."

Laurie hadn't been out of trouble for any length of time since she set him up in high school. Seeing her around town always reminded him of what she'd almost cost him. He stared across the table at the little girl he'd missed seeing born and watching grow into a beautiful young girl. If not for what Laurie did, Abby might have been able to tell him about the pregnancy before her parents interfered. Things could have been so different. Too many outside forces and people interfered in their lives. Never again. No one would get in the way of him getting to know Abby again and forging a real and true bond with his daughter.

"Anyway, hello, Kelly. It's nice to meet you."

"Nice to meet you too," she responded, her eyes locked on him.

"I'll put your order in." Kate left, and he gave Kelly his full attention.

She narrowed her gaze. "Why did you do that?"

"It's considered polite to introduce two people who don't know each other."

"You didn't have to say I'm your daughter."

"You are." He hoped to ease her mind by making it sound matter-of-fact and as if he'd accepted it. He had, even if he was still getting used to it.

"She'll tell people."

He nodded, knowing the grapevine just lit up. "I'm sure she will."

"They'll talk about you and Mom and what happened."

He nodded again. "They will."

"Aren't you worried about what they'll say?"

He really didn't care. But Kelly did.

"You're worried about your mother and what people might say about her. Whatever happens will happen, but there's no getting around the fact that you two moved back here, you're my daughter, and people are going to find out about it. The stuff between your mother and me is private and personal. Your mother and I will work out how we'll deal with each other in the future concerning you."

She crossed her arms on the table and looked him dead in the eye. "Are you going to file for custody?"

His turn to frown. "No."

"Why not?" Apparently she thought he didn't want her if he didn't file papers saying he wanted to spend time with her.

He set her straight with a simple truth. "I don't need to file for custody because your mother brought you here so we could have a relationship. She doesn't need to keep you from me anymore." He let that realization solidify in his mind and heart. Even though he understood with her parents gone she could finally come home, something else drove her, that something that delayed her return. After all his wishing for her, no matter the why, he only cared that she'd finally come back to him.

"She never wanted to keep me from you, you know? She didn't have a choice."

Kelly's belief in that erased any seeds of doubt that Abby had stayed away because she'd been angry at him for letting her go after she'd saved his ass at the sheriff's office. She was there, his, then she was gone. He still couldn't believe how it all went down. How it all went wrong.

"What's in the backpack?" He eyed the bag, trying to move the conversation back on track and keep it about him and Kelly and not on Abby and their past.

"Pictures. Want to see?"

"Yes." The word burst out of him. A band clutched his heart and squeezed his chest, making it hard to breathe. Pictures of her growing up. A chronicle of everything he'd missed. "I want to see them."

She pulled out a thick dark blue binder with "Kelly" emblazoned on the front in silver script. "Mom said blue is your favorite color. Mine too," she added, and opened the cover to reveal the first page.

Kelly Ann Manning

"She named you after my grandmother and gave you my last name?"

"Isn't it normal to give a child the father's last name?"

"Well, yeah, but I thought . . ." He didn't know what he thought. He'd always wanted a child someday. Someday arrived yesterday with his daughter. Not only did she have his eyes and looks, she had his name. It meant too much to him that Abby gave him that gift too.

"She remembered the stories you told her about spending summers with your grandmother and how much you loved her farm. You liked collecting the eggs from the chicken coop the best."

He smiled, remembering lying in the back of his truck, looking up at the stars with Abby lying down his side, her head resting on his shoulder. Even now, he felt her hand over his heart and the warmth of her body heating his.

Their time together might have been short, but he'd shared so much of his life and dreams with her because she'd been so easy to talk to.

"My grandmother liked to give the chickens crazy names."

Kelly snickered. "Kitty and Nugget were your favorites."

Her laugh brought him back to Abby's in the bed of that truck and a night he'd never forget. That Abby remembered it too, shared it with their daughter, made his heart melt and ache and beat faster with hope that they could settle their past and find a way to be friends like that again. Hopefully more.

"I can't believe Abby remembers."

"She told me all kinds of stories about you."

Kelly turned the page and his whole body went still. Several pictures of Abby filled the two pages. Each one showed her standing in front of the same tree, her belly expanding from one shot to the next. She looked lovely pregnant. Beautiful, but for the sadness in her eyes.

"There aren't many of her pregnant. Gran snuck over to where she was staying and took these."

Even her grandmother had to sneak to see her. Her father tormented Abby and an old woman to get his way and save face for something that was nothing more than an innocent error in judgment because two kids were crazy for each other and wanted to be together. He shook his head at the injustice of it all.

Kelly turned the page, revealing a couple of photos of her in a hospital bassinet. One showed Abby, exhausted from the birth, holding a chubby-faced Kelly with a vibrant smile and tears running down her face. God, she looked so young and vulnerable. A mix of happy and sad, very much the way he felt right now.

"A nurse ran down to the gift shop and bought her a disposable camera. They took this one picture of her. She used the rest to take pictures of me."

"I don't see her parents with you guys."

"They weren't there," she stated simply and turned the page. No, Abby's parents wouldn't show up and face their daughter and granddaughter as they tried to separate a mother from her child and give that child to strangers. The rage roiled in his gut.

"This one is my favorite." Kelly drew his attention back to the picture of Abby bent over with Kelly standing on tiptoe to give her mother a kiss.

"How old are you there?"

"About a year and a half."

"Where are the pictures of you from your birth to these?"

"There aren't any. We moved around a lot and Mom didn't have a camera."

They moved from one shelter to the next on the run from her father, hoping he didn't catch up to them and force Abby to give up Kelly. The rage turned to a fiery ball in his gut.

The next page nearly undid him. They'd been so close and he'd never seen them. He never knew they were there.

"She took me to your games. She tells me stories of how I'd cheer for you in the stands."

Sure enough, Kelly stood all of two feet tall, her hands raised in the air, fists tight as he ran for home in the background. Another showed her cheering as he stood at home plate batting. The tickets with the dates of the games were taped next to the pictures. Kelly turned pages and his life in college baseball played out as Kelly grew up to the age of about three.

"You really look like you love the game," she said because he'd gone too quiet on her.

"I did. I wanted to go pro, but after what happened with your mom and the false charges against me, I changed my direction and went to law school."

"I play softball. Mom thinks I'm as good as you." Her bright smile dimmed. "She might be biased."

He laughed because that kind of dry humor with a not-so-hidden smile reminded him so much of himself and his dad.

"I'd love to see you play."

"Mom promised she'd sign me up for a team in the spring. It'll be a good way to make friends my own age, since my classmates will all be older than me."

"Is that hard for you?"

"It's okay. Mom says it'll be harder when I get to high school. Smart kids are teased for being nerds."

"You're not a nerd, honey."

"I think you might be biased," she teased, and he fell under her spell even more.

Their food arrived and Kelly set the photos aside. They spoke little over the meal, giving each other time to settle and think about the last hour. Kate cleared the dishes with a smile for both of them and left them bent over the photos again. Dex watched in wonder as his daughter grew up on the page. She told him stories and he added stories about his life during those times. The evening passed with ease, reminding him again of being with Abby. Kelly reminded him of her in so many ways, but his mind always reveled in all the similarities they shared.

Kate slipped the bill on the table and Kelly snatched it up and read the total. She dug through her backpack and pulled out a Taylor Swift wallet. She counted out several fives and many dollar bills to cover the total and tip. Since he caught a glimpse of the bill, he mentally calculated that she'd left Kate a twenty percent tip. Generous. Pride welled in his chest.

"You must have saved up for this a long time."

Kelly beamed with pride. "All my allowance and work money."

"You work?"

"Odd jobs for Mom at her work."

Dex nodded his approval. He thought learning about managing money and responsibility was a good thing. "You like working at the restaurant with her?"

"It's fun. I get to spend time with Aunt Selena. I only get to see her at the restaurants because we moved into our own place a few years ago. I got to spend a week with her and Uncle Antonio after Mom—" She clamped her mouth shut on her next words.

"What?"

"Nothing." She drew his attention back to the photo album, but not away from thinking about whatever she didn't want to tell him about Abby and the secret he knew she was keeping from him. "This is the last one. Halloween at my other school."

He laughed when he saw the picture. "Sherlock Holmes?"

"I'd just finished reading the books and was obsessed with him."

"Very cute. Did your mom help you with the costume?"

"Her and Aunt Selena." She closed the book with a snap. "We should go. Mom's probably worried."

"She knows you're with me. Why would she worry?"

Kelly's eyes turned solemn. Her gaze dropped to her lap. "Lately, she doesn't like to be alone." Kelly scrunched a napkin into a ball. "We should go."

"Kelly, is something wrong? Do you want to tell me something, but you can't."

"She'll tell you. Just . . . I don't know. Give her some time," she pleaded, "to tell you what happened to her."

"It happened recently I take it."

"Several weeks ago. We were supposed to spend Thanksgiving with you, but we had to wait."

Right, just like Abby alluded to during their conversation.

"I wish I never missed a day with you, and I am so glad you're here now." He went on instinct and took her hand across the table and squeezed it in his to reassure her, no matter what and from now on, he was there for her.

Chapter Four

ABIGAIL PULLED THE sheet over the corner of the mattress, tucked it underneath, and smoothed the top with both hands. She couldn't wait for Kelly to see the new barn-wood headboard and pretty bedside lamp with the crystals that sparkled on the new blue painted walls she'd finished a half hour ago. With this move, she wanted to give Kelly a big girl room and a fresh start. For both of them.

After what happened in Arizona, Abigail needed one.

A shadow shifted in the window beside the bed. She jumped back and gasped. The lights in the room reflected off the glass; she spun around to see if someone rushed in behind her. Fear shot through her despite being alone in the room. She rushed to the lamp and switched it off, sending the room into darkness and allowing her to see out the window. No one stood outside looking in. No one was coming after her with a knife.

This was a different time, a different place. "Get it together." She tried to breathe, though her thrashing heart and wild imagination made it near impossible.

She raked her fingers through her hair and brought her hands down. The scars on her palms sent another bolt of cold fear through her veins. She shivered with the memories, crossed her arms over her chest, and tucked her hands out of sight in her armpits, and held herself.

He's not here. He can't hurt me again.

She stared out the window, checking every dark corner of the yard beyond but seeing nothing out of the ordinary.

To conquer her fear, she sucked it up and opened the window several inches to help clear the pungent paint smell.

She couldn't keep living like this. What happened to her ended that night. Yes, it was scary, but no one was after her now.

She turned the light back on to ease her mind and chase away her imaginary bogeyman. She picked up the pillow and the case to finish making the bed. Something to do to distract her from her dark thoughts.

Hyperaware of her surroundings after her scare, scrapes against the outside wall and a mysterious thump she wanted to but couldn't pass off as her overactive imagination froze her in a never-ending nightmare.

"Mom."

Startled, Abigail broke out of the spell that had frozen her with fear for God knew how long. She stared down at Kelly, and just like that, the darkness cleared.

Kelly approached with a cautious air that made Abigail sad. She reached out and placed her hand on Abigail's arm. "Everything okay?" Kelly asked.

"Fine," Abigail responded automatically. Her eyes roamed the room and settled on Dex and the concern etched on his face and in his eyes before going back to Kelly's face. "How was dinner?"

"Great. Dad and I like a lot of the same things." Kelly's soft laugh eased the last of the tension in Abigail, and she smiled back.

"You always reminded me so much of him. Now you see it yourself."

"How are you?" The familiar flutter in her belly happened every time she saw him.

"I'm good. Are you okay?" His genuine concern touched her, but the truth was she was far from okay.

She quickly looked at Kelly before responding without answering his question. "I finished painting your room, sweetheart. I got your bed put together and just finished the sheets."

"It's awesome." Kelly's enthusiasm eased her mind even more.

"I think we'll still sleep in the master bedroom until the smell clears."

A cold breeze filtered in through the cracked open window, battling the heat pouring out of the overhead vent. She tried to keep her imagined demons at bay.

Dex's gaze roamed the room that used to be hers. "The house is so different from what I remember. You've added quite a bit more living space, along with the new rooms."

"I couldn't come back to the same house." Anger filled her words. Thinking about what this house used to be like brought on a fresh wave of nightmares.

Abigail stuffed the pillow into the case and tossed it onto the bed. Without further explanation, she walked past him and down the hall.

He followed her back to the kitchen, Kelly on his heels. Abigail grabbed the bottle of pills next to her half-eaten turkey sandwich and hurried to stash the anti-anxiety meds in a cupboard.

Dex opened his mouth to ask about them, but Abigail turned back and gave him a look to keep him quiet. Her gaze shifted to Kelly and back, a silent plea. He nodded, letting her keep her secrets for now, but the first chance he had her alone, he'd demand answers.

She hoped she could find the words to talk about one of the worst days of her life.

"You should have come to dinner with us," he said, nodding toward her measly meal.

"The food was really good," Kelly added.

"The company was better," he shot back.

Kelly smiled shyly, but walked into Abigail's arms and held her close. "We had a really great time, Mom."

Abigail's gaze met his and they shared a moment of remembrance of simpler times. "I told you, he's great."

A flood of memories came back to her. Quiet moments they shared talking in the cab of his truck. The way he held her hand, brushing his thumb over the back of hers. Funny things, like singing along to the radio, Dex getting all the words wrong, but still singing at the top of his lungs just to make her laugh. Passionate kisses they shared that warmed her from the inside out with a love she'd never felt before or since. The closeness she felt to him and the emptiness that followed when her parents sent her away. The longing she felt then and now to get that back.

Abby cupped Kelly's face and stared down at her. "It's late, sweetheart. Go get ready for bed."

"Ah, Mom, can't I stay up a little while longer and talk to Dad?"

"It's been a long day. You're as tired as I am. You'll see your father another time."

"Tomorrow," Dex suggested, eager to see both of them. "Maybe we can do something together."

"Promise?" Kelly asked.

"Tomorrow is Saturday. You said your parents would be home. How about dinner? I'll cook," Abby offered. One more obstacle to overcome. She'd made it through telling Dex; she could explain to his parents and hope they understood too.

Kelly bounced on her feet, her hands clasped together at her chest. "Please, Dad. Mom's an awesome cook." When he didn't answer fast enough, her face fell into an unsure frown. "Unless you think they won't like me."

"They're going to love you." He reached out and ran his hand down her golden head and smiled to reassure her. "I'll bring them for dinner. It'll be fun."

And quite the surprise.

"It's late. I'll see you both tomorrow." Dex opened his arms and Kelly walked into them.

Such a sweet picture. Abigail's heart melted.

"Thank you for dinner, honey. I had a great time. I love you." The words held all the emotion she saw in Dex's eyes. He leaned down and pressed his lips to her hair. His arms drew tight in one last squeeze before he reluctantly let Kelly go. Their eyes locked. Abigail saw the bond they already shared.

"Walk me out, Abby."

"I will," Kelly volunteered.

"Go change for bed and brush your teeth," Abby coaxed. "I'll see your father out."

Kelly huffed, but did as she said. Just outside the kitchen entry, Kelly turned back. "You'll be here tomorrow, right?"

"Absolutely. I never turn down a date with a pretty girl." He gave Kelly a wink, which seemed to ease her mind and put the smile back on her face.

Alone in the quiet kitchen, the only sounds in the house came from Kelly opening and closing drawers down the hall.

"She's amazing."

Abigail stared, seeing her sweet girl in her mind. "There have been many moments over the years when I've looked at her, or thought about her, and wondered how someone so amazing came into my life."

"I've sometimes wondered the same thing about you."

The words hung between them, their meaning expanding to fill the silence with a thousand thoughts and dreams. His gaze locked with hers. She wrapped her arms around her middle, uncomfortable with his undivided attention.

His gaze skimmed over her curves and down her lean legs to her bare feet and pink painted toes. He grinned. "Long ago, you confided how much you wished your parents allowed you makeup and nail polish like the other girls at school used."

"I wanted to be like them."

"You're better."

She didn't know what to say to that sweet statement.

He studied her face, probably frowning because of the dark circles she saw in the morning after each night of restless sleep. She'd carried this weariness a long time. "You should eat more and get some rest. You look tired." He stepped toward her, but stopped when she crowded into the corner of the countertop. He stood his ground in front of her, but stuffed his hands in his pockets to appear more at ease, but she felt his stare. "I don't know what happened to you, Abby, but I promise, I'll never hurt you. I hope you know you can talk to me about anything," he coaxed.

She rubbed her hands up and down her arms, contemplating opening up to him, but in the end she held back because she didn't want to add her drama to what he was already dealing with finding out about Kelly. "Things are different now."

"Tell me about it. We have a kid." A nervous chuckle erupted from his gut.

"Thank you for going along with her tonight. She's

waited a long time for this and you didn't disappoint. I see how much you love her."

Abigail's father hadn't loved her. Not when he'd sent her away, tried to take her child, threatened her, and made her life hell. She appreciated so much the easy way Dex cared so deeply for Kelly.

Dex sighed. "I don't know if I lived up to her expectations, but I'm happy to say everything went well. I promise you, Abby, I will always do right by you both."

She believed that because he was nothing like her father.

From the bathroom, water splashed in the sink. Kelly's electric toothbrush echoed down the hall.

He waited for Abby to open up, but it could wait until they were alone and on steadier ground. She waved a hand toward the front of the house. "I'll walk you out."

"Will you let me in?"

She ignored him and walked through the house, out the front door, and down the icy path leading to the driveway. Reminded of the noises she heard earlier, she searched the yard and up and down the street, but found only the same shadows and her ghosts.

"Abby, we used to be close friends. Talk to me."

"We aren't kids anymore with a bad case of raging hormones."

He gave her a look so filled with need it said, *Speak for yourself.*

She had to admit, ever since the first moment she saw him again she felt the sizzle and pull of attraction. When he got close to her, she burned with it. But ever cautious, she backed away, even though a voice inside her coaxed her to leap.

"We had something."

In the weeks before moving back, she'd tried so hard not to wish for too much. "Whatever we had ended a long time ago."

"We had a hell of a lot more than 'whatever.'" He closed the distance between them and cupped her face in his big hands.

Hers clamped onto his wrists. The unreasonable panic bubbled up even as her heart told her she had nothing to fear from him.

"Dex, let me go." Her breath panted out in wispy clouds in the cold.

"I was forced to do that once and look what happened. I lost you and my daughter."

Deflated of her unwarranted fear, she stood before him, her heart heavy with sadness. "I'm sorry."

"I'm sorry too. For a lot of things. Especially the fact you felt like you couldn't come to me when you needed me. It hurts to think of you pregnant and raising our daughter alone. But you know what kills me? That the girl who used to sneak away with me, who confided her hopes and dreams to me, who listened and laughed and loved with me, can't stand to be within three feet of me."

She barely held back the tears. "It's not you."

"I know. You still like to touch me." His eyes drifted from hers to where her fingertips lightly caressed his arms. His gaze dipped to her lips. She licked them, but didn't lean in. Not a good idea. Especially with so much unresolved and unsaid between them. But the urge grew almost too much to bear.

The tingle of Dex's hands on her face, the warmth of his touch, and the care he infused in the soft caress of his thumbs across her cheeks lingered. She remembered many tender moments like this with him, but this one didn't come from a young boy bent on stealing a kiss. This was Dex, the grown man, asking her to let him into her world again.

She'd hesitated when she wanted to leap the way she did when she was sixteen and overtaken by her need for him. But they had Kelly to think about, and going too fast too soon meant the potential for it all ending in disaster again. She wanted to put her heart on the line, but she couldn't do that with Kelly's. Besides, Abigail was still fighting her demons and trying to find her equilibrium in a world that got knocked upside down by her parents' sudden death, moving back to be with Dex, and what happened to her in Arizona that left her scared and off balance.

Surprised by her actions, she sucked in a breath and released him, clasping her hands together in front of her. He swept his thumbs across her cheeks and slowly released her.

He didn't take a step back, but remained just a step away. She held her ground instead of moving away, as instinct told her to do, but she fought to stay close to him. In an odd way, he both comforted and scared her. She wanted him close, but feared letting him in and losing him again.

He held back a smile at her obvious indecision. "What time do you want me and my parents here tomorrow?"

"Huh?"

"Dinner. Tomorrow. What time?"

"Oh, six?"

"Are you asking me, or telling me?" he teased. It was still way too easy for him to discombobulate her with his touch. And he appeared to enjoy it way too much.

"Six. Bye."

She fled toward the house.

"Running away won't work this time."

Yet she did just that, flying up the steps and rushing into the house before she gave in to the urge to run out, fling herself into his arms, and kiss him. Instead, she stood in the living room and let the house settle around her while she tried to find her footing.

"You can come out now," she called in the general direction of the boxes stacked by the windows.

Kelly stood and rounded the boxes, coming to stand beside her like she hadn't been spying out the window. "What did he say? He's coming back, right?"

With a soft smile, she said, "Tomorrow. Dinner with his parents. Six o'clock." She placed her index finger below her daughter's chin and raised it up, so their eyes met. "The most important thing he said, he loves you. No matter what else happens, that will not change and is forever yours." She brushed her hand down Kelly's hair and settled it on her shoulder. "The next few days will be the hardest, but then we'll settle into this house and town and you'll forge a relationship with your father. Everything will be okay."

"Are you okay? I saw you staring at the coffee table, but it didn't seem like when I got home or the other times you're quiet."

"I'm fine, honey. Really," she tried to reassure Kelly, though it never eased her worry. "My mother bought this coffee table right after she married my father. He wanted a different one, but because he wanted to please his new bride, he gave in and bought the one she wanted."

The only piece of furniture she'd kept because it reminded her of her time with Dex. They'd sat on the floor, opposite each other, their books and papers spread before them. They'd pretended not to notice the air snapping with electricity between them. She'd hid behind the need to get the project done and prattled on about the scientific method and theory just to spend more time with him.

"That was nice of him," Kelly said about Abigail's father.

"No one is all bad."

"Are you very mad they forced you to leave?"

"I wanted out of here, but the way I was made to go hurt." Not being wanted hurt like hell. She hoped Kelly never felt that way. She leaned in and kissed Kelly's brow.

"Your dad didn't want you anymore after you had me." Her too smart daughter sometimes had insights far wiser than her years.

Abigail bent and cupped her daughter's face and looked into her eyes. "You weren't to blame for what he did. Your grandfather was a very rigid man, who had definite ideas about what a young girl should and should not do. He made it very hard to live up to his standards and unachievable expectations, because no matter how hard I tried I'd never make him proud or even happy, because nothing I did would ever be good enough."

"You didn't do anything wrong," Kelly said.

Being with Dex hadn't been wrong, but keeping Kelly from Dex was, and she'd spend the rest of her days trying to make it up to both of them.

Abigail put her hand to Kelly's back and led her down the hall to the master bedroom. "Bedtime. I'm exhausted."

"You look it."

"Hey. Not nice. Especially, after I spent most of the evening finishing your room."

"I love it."

"I'm so glad, honey. I want this to be a home for the two of us."

"What about Dad?" Kelly climbed into the big bed. Abigail covered her and tucked her in, turning off the light on her way around to the other side. Moonlight streamed through the sheer curtains, making it just bright enough to see Kelly's face.

"I'm pretty sure he has a home," she teased, though she found it very easy to picture him in the bed instead of Kelly.

"That's not what I mean," Kelly pushed.

Thinking of the strange noise she heard earlier, Abigail closed the drapes and stripped off her paint-splattered clothes. Too tired for a shower, she pulled on a clean nightgown and crawled into bed beside Kelly. They lay facing each other, and Kelly's earnest eyes pleaded for more information.

"Your father and I haven't seen or spoken to each other in ten years. We have completely separate lives. That hasn't changed." She didn't want to get her hopes up, or Kelly's, despite the sexy way Dex looked at her.

"You let him touch you."

Abigail brushed her fingers through Kelly's long hair. "He knows I'm keeping something from him and wants to know what it is."

Kelly placed her hand over Abigail's scarred ones. "You'll tell him, right? You said you would."

"It's been one day. One piece of shocking news is enough for the man to deal with right now."

"You'll tell him tomorrow."

She eyed her pushy daughter. "With his parents here?"

"I guess that might be kinda strange."

"Kinda," she mimicked. "Not everything has to happen all at once. You spent the evening with your father. How awesome is that?"

Kelly smiled her father's smile. "I really like him. Does he look like he did when you knew him?"

Better, but she didn't say so. "He's taller, I think. Filled out. His hair is shorter."

Kelly giggled. "You think he's handsome."

"Kelly, don't," she warned.

"What did you like most about him?"

"His eyes. I love the color and the way he looked at me, like he saw something in me no one else could see.

His hands. So big. When he held my hand, his were warm and rough, they engulfed mine."

Kelly held up her hand and Abigail matched hers and clamped her fingers over Kelly's.

And when he held her, she felt safe.

"Did you love him?"

This was the first time she'd ever asked. Abigail often wondered if she ever would. "I don't know," she answered honestly. "When you're sixteen, all you want is the boy you like to like you back. My parents were strict and not affectionate. I can probably count on one hand the number of times my father hugged me. My mother tried, but my father would always scold her to stop coddling me."

"So, when Dad paid attention to you, you liked it."

"I craved it," she admitted. Just like she did now. "The things he made me feel: safe, protected, wanted, loved. Those are powerful things to a young girl." They were powerful even now when he held her face and looked down at her with such tenderness her heart longed for more.

"Do you still love him?"

"A part of me will always love him because he gave me you."

"That's not really an answer," Kelly complained.

"I don't know him anymore, sweetheart." *But I want to.* Because some dreams are too good to give up. And even unanswered prayers might finally be heard.

"He watches you."

"No, he doesn't." The thrill that zipped through her,

hearing that he watched her, shouldn't please and terrify her at the same time.

Abigail reached out and placed her hand on Kelly's soft cheek.

Kelly's hand came up to cover hers and hold it in place. "I love you, Mom."

"I love you too."

"I can't wait until tomorrow." Excitement that she'd get to see Dex again filled Kelly's soft and sleepy voice.

Abigail felt the same way. Facing Dex had been difficult. His parents and the town were another matter altogether.

She wished telling him was the end of it.

But this was just the beginning.

Chapter Five

DEX SAT IN the chair facing his parents sitting on the sofa in the living room. He'd asked for this meeting before they went over to Abby's for dinner, but had trouble finding the words to tell them about Kelly and what happened to Abby. The longer he'd had to think about what her father put her through, the years he'd missed with Kelly, and Abby, the angrier he got and the more he wanted to have right now what he should have had all along with them.

"What is it, Dex?" His mother coaxed him to talk, because he usually didn't have this much trouble spilling his guts to them.

"I told you on the phone that Abby moved back into her parents' house, but I didn't tell you why."

"I still can't believe her parents sent her away. She didn't deserve that." The sadness in his mother's eyes warmed his heart. He hoped she still sympathized with

Abby after he told her the truth of why Abby finally came home.

"Her parents did a hell of a lot more than send her away."

Dex spent the next ten minutes giving them all the sordid details about the "church retreat," her parents trying to force her to give up their baby, Abby on the run from one shelter to the next, her father constantly harassing her, and after her parents' death Abby finally being able to come home. He ended with the threats her father made against him and his parents.

They shared a lingering glance filled with a dawning understanding that made them both sad.

"What is it?" He really didn't want more bad news, but with Mayor Swain involved, expected it.

"After what happened at the sheriff's office, business dipped about twenty-five percent. About a year after that, we wanted to expand the business but couldn't get a loan anywhere in town."

Dex swore. "He used his position as mayor and with the ministry to influence your business."

"We had our suspicions," his mother said.

"Great. I'm sure Abby's grandmother told her, and that made her believe even more that she had to stay away." Dex raked his fingers through his hair. "I'm sorry, Dad."

"Not your fault. We rode out the hard times. I wish things had been easier for you."

"What do you mean?"

"You tried to buy out that law practice downtown and partner with a few other law firms."

His father didn't have to say anything more. He'd wondered why, in such a small town with few lawyers and most approaching retirement, none of them wanted to work with him, so he'd opened his own practice. He'd had to earn every client, but his work eventually gained him a good reputation. Now he understood why he'd had to work so hard at it.

"Sonofabitch. If you knew what was going on, why didn't you say something to me?"

His father looked him right in the eye. "Because any time her name came up it made you sad. We knew how much you cared about her. We wanted to spare you."

"This is such a damn mess."

"What about the baby?" his mother asked.

"She's not a baby anymore."

His mother glanced at his father. "We have a granddaughter." He hadn't seen his mother smile that big in a long time.

"She's nine and beautiful. She's super smart and starts school in the eighth grade here on Monday."

"She takes after Abigail," his father said, pride lighting his eyes.

"And looks just like me."

"Really?" His mother's eyes glassed over.

"Whenever you're ready, we can head over there. She can't wait to meet you."

"We have to stop at the store on the way over."

Dex cocked up one eyebrow. "Why?"

"I'm not meeting my granddaughter for the first time without a gift."

Dex hung his head and rubbed the heels of his hands over his eyes and forehead before he looked up at them again, relieved their enthusiasm to meet Kelly overrode any animosity they had toward Abby for keeping her a secret all this time.

"Things are kind of tenuous right now. Abby feels guilty about what happened, so I'd appreciate it if you didn't grill her about her past."

"Work on building a relationship with . . . What's her name?" his father asked, realizing Dex never told them.

"Kelly."

His father smiled. "Everything else will fall into place between you and Abigail." His dad gave him a look that said, *I know you want her.*

Yes, he did. Both of them. One big happy family. The way it should be.

He wished he knew how to make that happen.

FORECAST MODELS PREDICT *the slow-moving storm will dump anywhere from ten to thirty-five inches of snow in areas over two to three days. Again, the storm is expected to reach southern Montana on Thursday. State and local agencies recommend stocking food and supplies. Expect major road closures and power outages.*

Dex pulled into Abby's driveway and parked behind her SUV, cutting off the engine and the radio news bulletin.

"It's going to be a big one." His father glanced out the

window, looking for any sign of the dark and dangerous storm clouds headed their way.

He slid from the car and noticed both broken taillights on Abby's SUV. With no other damage, he wondered how it happened.

He rounded the car and met his parents on the shoveled walkway to the porch. No less than three of the neighbors around Abby's house had come out of their warm homes to stand in the cold and stare, or simply appear to be adjusting Christmas lights and decorations while they tried not to be openly interested in them.

Nothing like living under the nosy-body microscope.

His mother stared up at the renovated house. "The house is lovelier than I remember."

"Abby added on to it after the fire."

"She must be doing well for herself if she can afford to do this. What does she do?" his father asked.

"She runs four restaurants back in Arizona. The family she started working for made her a partner."

The front door opened and Abby stepped out onto the porch to greet them. God, she took his breath away. She was dressed in gray slacks and a navy blue sweater that flowed over her body in a soft material that hugged her curves and hinted at the swell of her breasts at the neckline. She gave him a soft smile, but her eyes and the way she clasped her hands in front of her didn't hide her nervousness. His gut went tight and he fisted his hands at his sides to keep from reaching out and pulling Abby back into his arms.

Before everything happened, they'd only begun to explore the force pulling them together. The years apart hadn't dimmed the charge that shot through him. This time, he wanted to know exactly what it was about her that made him want things he'd never wanted with anyone but her.

His parents stepped up to the porch first. Abby's smile faltered a bit, but she recovered and said, "Mr. and Mrs. Manning, I'm so pleased you came tonight."

She took a step back, and fear filled her eyes when his father came forward and embraced her in a light hug. Taken off guard, she stood with her hands at her sides and seemed to endure the awkward embrace.

His father stepped back and held her at arm's length. "It's so good to see you again, Abigail. You've grown into such a lovely woman. In fact, I hardly recognized you."

Understatement of the century. Lovely. Abby had transformed into a beautiful goddess.

"I just want to get this out before dinner. Thank you," his father began, his voice catching a bit with emotion. "What you did for Dex, coming forward with the truth and standing up for him. I can't thank you enough. Who knows how long it might have taken to clear his name. By then, it would have been tarnished and no one would have cared that he didn't do it. He might have lost his scholarship and spent God knows how many days or weeks in jail. So thank you. I can't express how grateful I am for what you did."

His mother moved forward and gave her another awkward hug. He hated it that Abby shied away from everyone.

"That goes double for me," his mother added. "I wanted to speak to you right after it happened, but your parents asked that the matter be dropped."

"You spoke to my parents?" Abby asked, confused.

He had no idea his mother had tried to talk to her either.

"Steve and I came after Dex got arrested. Didn't they convey our gratitude to you?"

"No. They never mentioned it." The words came out clipped and tinged with anger and resentment.

He could just imagine how alone she felt, locked away in this house, her parents feeling as if she'd irreparably shamed them.

"Well, I'm sorry," his mother went on. "I wish I'd known. You were very brave."

"I wish I'd found a way around my father and the ministry and been able to share Kelly with you all this time. I'm so sorry. I never meant—"

"We know, Abigail." His father stopped her from saying more. "You're here now." That simple statement allowed them all to accept and move past it.

Kelly walked out behind her mother. She looked up at his parents, and both of them sucked in a startled breath in utter shock when they saw her face. He stepped close to Kelly and Abby. The three of them faced his parents like the family unit he wanted them to be. "Mom, Dad, this is Kelly."

His father, overcome by seeing his granddaughter for the first time, choked out, "Kelly is a very pretty name. My mother was a Kelly too."

"Mom named me after her. She's Dad's favorite."

His mother turned a disgruntled frown on him and smacked him in the arm for choosing his father's mother over any of his mother's relatives.

"What? You know how much I liked spending summer's on Grandma Kelly's farm."

"Apparently, Abigail knew that too," his father said.

"I did talk to her, you know." Dex smiled when his mother glared at him for implying he did a lot more than just sleep with her.

"Let's move this inside," Abby suggested, shivering from the cold and noticing the nosy neighbors milling around outside their homes.

"Is that for me?" Kelly asked about the bright purple bag with the sparkly white tissue paper sticking out, which his mother carried inside.

"It's a bit early for Christmas, but we wanted to welcome you to the family." His mother handed the gift to Kelly, who plopped to the floor and tore into it immediately.

Kelly squealed and pulled out the tablet and headphones his parents got her.

Dex leaned into Abby's shoulder and whispered. "Look how happy she is."

"This is what I wanted, Dex. I hope you know that."

He did. And seeing his parents with Kelly, all of them coming together for a family dinner, made him think of how much they had to look forward to from now on.

He took Abby's hand and held it, rubbing his finger over one of the long scars on her palm. He didn't ask about them. He didn't acknowledge the tremble in her hand. He just stood there watching his daughter explaining some zombie game she loved.

Since Kelly and his parents were occupied on the couch across the room, he asked Abby, "What happened to your taillights?"

"I had some business at the diner in town. Someone broke them in the parking lot."

While he wondered about the business, the vandalism took precedence. "Any idea who or why?"

"I'm not sure. Even though my father is gone, maybe someone in the ministry is holding a grudge that I live here now and my grandmother went against his wishes and gave me the house."

Maybe. "Seems kind of juvenile and petty." Still, he thought there might be something more.

"Tell me about it. I've got an appointment to get it fixed. They said it's going to be over five hundred dollars."

"What business did you have in town?"

"Oh, just a job."

"What about the restaurants back in Arizona?"

"We hired a new manager. I'll have to go back a few times a year. Maybe a few days once a quarter, but I don't want to keep dragging Kelly back and forth."

"You don't have to. That's what I'm here for. Plus, my parents would love to have her. She's their only grandchild. I'm pretty sure they thought I'd never give them one, so they'll spoil her rotten."

"Don't you want to settle down and have a family?"

He squeezed her hand. "I already do." He brought her

hand up to his mouth and kissed the back of it. "You and Kelly are my family. As for settling down, all I do is work these days. Now I'm holding the most beautiful woman's hand, watching my daughter charm her grandparents, and you and I have nothing but time to get to know each other again.

"You're the only woman who ever stayed stuck in my heart and head. You're the only woman I want."

"Dex."

"There you go, saying my name the way you do. All I want to do is kiss you."

Her gaze met his. He leaned in to kiss the shocked look right off her face. A breath away, he hesitated when a bell dinged several times in the kitchen and she started out of her daze.

She tugged her hand free and walked away. "Excuse me. I need to get dinner out of the oven."

"Saved by the bell," he teased. He'd get his kiss. Soon. Because wanting her for the past ten years had nothing on the way he needed her right now.

His father came over to join him. "Kelly is amazing." The smile and pride in his dad's eyes couldn't be matched by any other grandfather. "How is Abby?"

"Still settling in." He'd give her a little more time, but he wasn't inclined to wait too long to have her back in his arms.

"I hope you're able to work things out."

"Nothing to work out but the details of how we blend our lives. I don't want to be a weekend dad. I want them. All the time. Every day. Forever."

"What did she say about the taillights?"

So his father noticed them too. "Vandalism. Maybe someone from the ministry who holds a grudge because she's living in her father's house again."

"She's made it her own."

"It's a great place." He could certainly be happy here with them. The empty room off the living room, which overlooked the front yard, would make a great home office. His couches and chairs would fit in the empty living space off the back of the house next to the dining room. He liked Abby's simple, elegant taste. It complemented his comfortable and rustic furnishings. The blend would make for a warm and inviting home. Especially once Abby finished unpacking and he moved in. Soon. He told himself to be patient, but ten years of waiting had worn thin and he wanted everything right now.

"She's been through a lot. Don't push too hard, too fast, son. I know you want to, but you both need time to come to terms with what happened and the new future you both face."

"As long as we do it together, that's all I want."

Abby carried a platter out of the kitchen to the dining room table, scenting the air with mouthwatering garlic, rosemary, and chicken.

His mother and Kelly jumped up. "Abby, let us help you with that."

He and his father stood back as they came out with more food. Mashed potatoes, gravy, biscuits, and green beans with bacon and onions. The table looked great with the simple white dishes, gleaming crystal glasses, a bottle of wine in an ice bucket, and silverware placed on navy blue napkins.

"The flowers are so pretty," his mother commented on the white roses mixed with holly leaves.

"Thank you. I wanted everything to be perfect." Abby brushed her hands down the apron she'd tied around her trim waist.

"It's lovely. And smells so good." His mother took a seat next to Kelly at the table. "Dex mentioned you run a few restaurants. I'd love to hear all about it," his mother coaxed Abby into conversation as they all took their seats at the table, his father across from his mother, Abby at the head and next to Kelly as well, and him right beside her and across from his daughter. "Maybe we can exchange some recipes. Oh, and come up with our menu for Christmas. Shall we do it here? Your first Christmas home. I bet your grandmother is just overjoyed to have you here again."

And just like that his mother drew Abby out. Abby put her hand over his and squeezed, looking at his parents, Kelly, and the rooms around them. "This is what was always missing in this house. Warmth. Love. Family. Thank you for coming," she choked out past the lump in her throat.

Dex felt it too. A start. A new beginning. One that he would do anything to ensure ended with their happiness.

Chapter Six

DEX PARKED AT the curb in front of Abby's house and stared out the windshield at the light snow piling atop the six inches that came down last night. The forecast called for light snow on and off over the next couple of days as the huge storm, which everyone was stocking up for and talking about, lumbered up and across the western states toward Montana, dumping record levels of snow, blowing catastrophic winds, and leaving a path of destruction in its wake. They hadn't seen anything like it in years.

He didn't look forward to the storm, but he didn't object to a few days snowed in with Abby. They'd generate enough heat to melt the expected ice.

He stepped out of his Jeep and carefully made his way up the icy walk. A snowball splattered against his back, stopping him in his tracks. A soft giggle sounded behind him. He schooled his face, hiding his own smile, and turned slowly. He didn't see Kelly, but suspected she hid behind one of the bushes to the left.

"You're playing a dangerous game." He leaned down and scooped up a ball of snow in his hand, slowly making his way toward the garden, following the trail of tiny fresh footprints in the snow.

Another snowball hit him in the back of his shoulder. The giggle that followed tightened his gut and reminded him of the girl he used to know.

"So, it's the both of you ambushing me." He reached down to fill his other hand with snow. He ran over to the bush, threw the snowball over it, hitting Kelly right on top of her head. She shrieked and made a run for it. He grabbed her around the waist and hauled her up against his chest and ran toward the Tahoe parked in the driveway. Abby stood and threw two snowballs at him, hitting Kelly as he used her as a shield. She laughed so hard, her little body vibrated against him. Abby made a break for it, but he hit her square in the chest with the snowball, sending ice into her coat and down her sweater.

She pulled the garments away from her body and shook them to get the ice off her bare skin. "Oh my God, that's cold." The bright smile on her face belied the hint of censure in her voice.

"You started it."

"Kelly started it," she accused.

He tickled Kelly's ribs, then set her on her feet. She immediately picked up another snowball and lobbed it at his chest.

He grabbed a handful and tossed it back at her, hitting her shoulder and cheek as the snowball exploded.

"Mom, save me." Kelly ran behind Abby, using her as a shield.

Abby sidestepped so he could hit Kelly again.

"Mom, you're supposed to be on my side."

Abby laughed. "You had to know when you pulled him into the game he'd play to win."

Dex stood spellbound, seeing Abby so open and carefree, her hair softly blowing in the breeze, quickly turning white with the snow falling on her dark hair. Her cheeks were pink from the cold, her breath a wispy cloud on the breeze, her pretty golden brown eyes bright and filled with happiness.

"God, you're beautiful." He stared because he couldn't take his eyes off her.

"Mom, you're supposed to say thank you when someone gives you a compliment."

Abby lost her smile, shook herself out of her stunned silence, and softly said, "Thank you," as ordered. "Um, Kelly, go get your backpack before we're late for school."

"Is he going to kiss you?"

"No." Abby's gaze bounced from him to Kelly and back. "Go."

Kelly shrugged, eyed him one last time, then did as her mother said and went to get her bag.

"Yes."

"Excuse me," Abby said, eyeing him.

"I am going to kiss you again." He didn't take a single step toward her.

Apprehension and anticipation warred in her eyes.

"When you want me to kiss you, I will."

"Dex."

"I missed taking her to the first day of school. She's probably too big to need both her parents to take her today, but thanks for including me."

"She talked nonstop about you yesterday."

"You should have called me. I'd have come over, taken her off your hands for a while so you could unpack."

"I'm used to having her with me."

"I can't wait until I can say the same."

All the light went out of her. "Dex . . ."

"I miss the way you say my name. Just that and seeing your face is all I need to know everything you're thinking. The anger comes and goes, but one thought always sticks. You saved her, Abby. You kept her close and protected her. If she couldn't be with me, at least I know she had you to love her. I see it in her. All the love you poured into her for you and for me. I don't know how you did it, but my daughter knows me the way you used to know me because you made sure she knew I loved her even though I didn't know about her. She wants so badly to be close to me. I want the same thing."

"You can have all the time you want with her."

"I plan to take it. I don't know what your plans are for living here, but I'd like to take her to school every day on my way to work. Afternoons are kind of tough for me, but I can pick her up once in a while if you need me to."

"No. I can do that. She'd love to see you every morning."

"Good. If you're agreeable, I'd like to have dinner

during the week with you too. We'll keep her on a schedule, but I can help her with homework, put her to bed, hang out with her." *And with you.* This was just the beginning of his plan to get to know his daughter. And Abby again.

"I never got to be a full-time dad. I don't want to be an every-other-weekend dad."

"I don't want to get her hopes up that . . ."

"What? Her mother and father actually like each other. That even though we aren't a conventional family we can still sit down to a meal together each night so she has both of us with her."

"I don't want her to hope that we will be that conventional family."

"You know she's already hoping for that. I am too." No time to fool around; he gave her the honest truth.

"You are?" The amazement and hope in her voice and eyes encouraged him.

He tried to reassure her. "This is what I want. To spend time with my daughter before she's a teenager and can't stand to be around me. I've got a lot of making up to do with her, and you, Abby. I have been such a huge part of your life, every day you see me in her, tell her about me, and share our memories with her. I carried those same memories. I pulled them out all the time, hoping for just a moment to feel the way I felt whenever I was with you."

Her gaze softened. "You're the ghost that's haunted my life since the day I left. You're there, but it's not enough. Her missing you, wanting you, asking for you broke my heart over and over again."

"I broke your heart over and over again, Abby, because I wasn't there and you wanted me to be."

Tears slipped past her lashes and cascaded over her cheeks. She nodded, telling him without words how much she wanted him in her life.

"I'm here now, Abby. I'm not going anywhere. You don't have to do this on your own anymore." He took her in his arms and held her crushed to his chest as she sobbed out all her grief, anger, frustration, loneliness, and sorrow for all she'd been through, all the wishing for him to be there and make it all right. In her grief, he found that he could let go of the anger, knowing they both wanted the same thing: a chance to rewrite the past.

Kelly wrapped her arms around him and Abby, holding on tight to both of them. "Don't cry, Mom. It's going to be okay now."

Abby's hands clutched at his jacket, but she didn't push him away. She held him closer. "I know, sweetheart."

"We're going to be late on my first day."

Dex ran his hand over Kelly's snow-covered head. "You need a cap. Go get in the car. We'll be there in a second."

Kelly shook the snow from her hair, pulled a knit cap out of her coat pocket, and pulled it on. She picked up her backpack and ran off to his car.

Dex turned his attention back to the woman still in his arms, setting off waves of heat through his system. She smelled like wind and honeysuckle and spearmint. He wondered if she still tasted like plums and her skin still felt like satin.

He hugged her close and leaned down to her ear. "You are not alone anymore, Abby. Lean on me. I will be there any time you need me. I know you don't yet, but I hope you'll trust me again."

She leaned back in his arms, her hands on his shoulders. "I do trust you."

"With Kelly, yes. But not with you. I let you down in so many ways. Give me a chance to make it right."

Her gaze fell to his chest. "We have to go."

"I won't give up on us this time, Abby. You can count on that too."

Chapter Seven

DEX STOOD NEXT to Abby by the car. Close. And still too far away. She came home to fulfill her promise to Kelly. In her wildest dreams she imagined what it would be like to be with Dex again. She anticipated his anger, but never let herself believe he'd be interested in her again. She got a glimpse of the kind and caring boy she used to know this morning when he held her and promised her the world. Or so it seemed.

"First day of school, sweetheart. Give me a smile." Dex held his phone out and snapped several photos of Kelly in front of the school sign.

"Dad, seriously, it's not that big a deal."

"It is, honey. Your dad missed preschool and kindergarten and watching you excel and skip grades. Remember what we talked about; for him, this is all new. He's excited for you. He can't wait to see you do well and enjoy this experience."

"It's school," Kelly reminded her. Not exactly amusement park fun. "I'll be on Christmas break soon. But I get it. Sorry, Dad."

Dex took it in stride. "It's fine. Are you nervous?"

"A little. They're all bigger than me." Kelly eyed the other kids walking into the building.

Abby touched Kelly's shoulder. "Remember what we talked about, anyone gives you trouble, tell a teacher or the principal."

"It'll be fine."

Abby didn't know if Kelly tried to reassure her, or herself.

"Do you want us to walk you to class?" Dex asked.

"No!" Kelly bit her lip. "I know you want to do the whole thing, but I'm already the outcast, please don't make me look like a baby who can't get to class on her own in front of all the other kids."

Dex nodded. "Got it. Can I kiss you good-bye or at least get a hug?"

Kelly ran into Dex's arms and hugged him close. Dex gave her a sweet peck on the head. Abby's stomach tightened and her heart melted seeing the utter joy in Kelly's eyes.

Kelly gave her a quick hug, sighed, sucked in a breath, and marched off to her first class.

"I'm worried," Dex confessed.

"You're not the only one. She's so smart, but I worry she's not ready to be with a bunch of kids she doesn't know. She's a sweet girl. She makes friends fast, but she's nine and they're twelve and thirteen. The more grades she skips, the harder it is for her to connect with the older kids."

"You gave her everything she needs to fit in. Her own phone. Confidence that being young and smart isn't a social death sentence. Cute clothes. She looks just like all the other girls I saw walking into school."

Abby smiled. "I came to meet with the principal and her teachers a couple of weeks ago. I purposely stayed for lunch and scoped out the other kids. To help her cope with the move and missing her friends back home, I got her some new clothes. Not just for the weather." She shivered.

Dex chuckled. "Not used to the temps anymore?"

"It's not Arizona, that's for sure."

"Just wait until that big storm hits."

"I'm not looking forward to it. Storms scare me."

"I can help you get ready for the storm far better than I did getting Kelly ready for school. I wouldn't have thought to make her look like she fits in, so the kids would instinctively think she does."

"They'll still think she's different, but the less ammunition they have against her, the less she'll be teased until someone accepts her, and hopefully the rest of the kids will fall in line. Just one good friend can make all the difference in the world. You showed me that."

Dex glanced down at her. "I should have been a better friend."

Abby didn't get a chance to respond.

A familiar voice from the past broke into their private

conversation and sent a warning chill up her spine colder than the early morning Montana temps. "I can't believe you'd show your face in this town again."

Abby turned to face the person who'd tried to destroy Dex's future and succeeded in changing Abby's life forever.

What was she doing here?

Laurie stood with a smug smirk and menace in her eyes, but she didn't have the same bright, pretty looks she did as a girl. A little heavier, lines around her eyes and bracketing her mouth—not from smiling, but the frown she wore now that seemed a permanent fixture to go with the unhappiness underlying the spite in her eyes.

"The whole town will never forget what I did to the golden boy, but it pales in comparison to what you did to him. Man, you stole his kid. I may have been petty, trying to get back at him, but you're a royal, vengeful bitch. You kept his kid from him. Now that's low."

The words stung, but Abby expected them and a lot worse. But she didn't have to take it, especially from Laurie.

"At least I own up to the things I've done. Is Daddy still bailing you out of trouble?" Abby seethed that Laurie got away with nothing more than a slap on the wrist and two months community service despite trying to frame Dex for her crimes. The boy who helped her had spent six months in juvenile detention.

Dex stepped close, standing right next to Abby. "Three DUIs and she's still got her license and her son, despite the fact he was in the car the last time she got arrested. All outside your father's jurisdiction. Wonder how many times your father's guys looked the other way?"

"Not all of us lead a charmed life." Laurie seethed. "But you got yours. It must burn you up inside, nine years old and you missed everything in that girl's life." Laurie turned her narrowed gaze back to Abby. "I hope he hates you 'til the day you die. You deserve it after what you did."

Dex wrapped his arm around Abby's shoulders and pulled her close. "Are you done?" Dex asked Laurie. "What is it? Are you pissed that even now I choose her over you? Are you so insecure and jealous that you have to tear her down to make yourself feel better? Seriously, do you think I would ever look at you when I've got someone as beautiful and kind as Abby?"

He exaggerated that last bit, but Abby couldn't squelch the hope that rose in her heart that he truly meant those words.

"She'd never put our daughter in harm's way the way you do with your kid. She's got a warm heart. I'm not even sure you have one at all. Stay away from her, or you'll answer to me."

"She ruined everything." Laurie meant breaking them up and the downhill spiral her life descended into after everyone found out what she did to Dex. "You're going to let her get away with what she did?"

"You have absolutely no clue about her life and what she's been through. If you had a heart, you might find some compassion and understanding instead of lashing out at someone who did nothing but save my ass and tell the truth about what *you* did."

Laurie's frustration came out in a cloudy huff. "This isn't over." Laurie stormed off with her hands fisted at her sides.

"It's been over since high school," Dex called after her. "Get over it already."

Laurie didn't get over things, she got even.

Chilled to the bone by more than the weather, Abby walked to the car and got in, waiting for Dex to climb in behind the wheel. Dex sitting so close next to her seemed to overheat her inside and out. He took up the space in the car like he'd filled the emptiness in her heart all those years ago and never left. "Everyone is going to feel exactly the way she does. I'm sorry to put you through this."

Dex turned in his seat and leaned back against the door. "We need to stop doing this."

"What?"

"You and I taking one step forward and two back. Enough already. I'm so damn frustrated with the whole thing. Let's just be honest. I'm pissed your father forced you into keeping Kelly from me. You came back to make it right. I'm so damn happy to have you both back in my life. I want Kelly to have the best of everything, including you and me."

"Dex, we can't just pick up where we left off like nothing happened."

"Why not? I felt it the second I saw you and when you were in my arms. You can't deny that, Abby. We gave it up once, I won't do it again. Aren't you tired?" He didn't give her a chance to answer. "I'm tired of missing you." He hooked his hand behind her neck and drew her in for a kiss.

The moment his lips pressed to hers she fell back into the past. The touch of his fingers on her skin, the taste of him on her lips, the passion and need he put into the kiss reminded her of how things used to be when she couldn't wait to be with him. It reminded her how much she'd loved him. That love pulsed strong and bright and so warm in her chest. She'd given up and lost so much, but memories of Dex were the one thing she'd held on to all these years. Here he was. Real. And hers if she wanted him. All she had to do was put her heart on the line and hope he didn't break it again.

Dex broke the kiss, but held her close, their faces inches apart as he stared into her eyes. "You missed me too, Abby. I can feel it. We have a daughter. A chance for a real future together. You didn't leave me because you didn't want me. I let you go, but it's not because I didn't want you. I want you so damn bad. If we don't at least try to make this work, we'll spend the rest of our lives wondering. I've spent the last ten years wondering and wishing for you to come back.

"I've had a pretty damn good life, Abby. Now, if you'll let me, I'll make sure you never want for anything ever again."

She couldn't resist him or those simply put sentiments filled with all the truth and warmth she saw in his green eyes.

She set aside all her reservations and warnings to take things slow, reached up, took his face in her hands, and drew him in for another kiss, telling him without words that she wanted to try.

She wanted a little piece of the heaven she'd found in his arms all those years ago.

Chapter Eight

ABBY STARED AT her reflection in the dark window over the kitchen sink as she washed the dinner dishes, thinking about the last three days that started out with them making out in the school parking lot and progressed to them falling into a routine of him taking Kelly to school each morning, dropping by for dinner each night, putting Kelly to bed, and kissing Abby good-bye under the mistletoe he'd hung on the porch, like he didn't want to leave at all.

Not that they needed the mistletoe or the soft glow of the white Christmas lights he'd strung along the front of the house to fall into each other's arms. She found it harder and harder to let him go each night.

He fit in with her and Kelly like he'd always been there. Kelly adored him. And secretly wished for him to stay too.

Kelly noticed the closeness building between them.

The way Dex shared his day with Abby, touched her hand, brushed his fingers through her hair, the sexy way he smiled at her from across the dinner table. Every morning and night when Dex arrived, their gazes connected for just a bit too long, and he looked at her like Abby was his everything.

Men had looked at her over the years. She'd dated off and on, but no man had made her feel the way Dex did with one look that said so much. It packed a punch that left her burning and winded sometimes.

Lost in thought, she jumped when Dex leaned down and kissed her neck, his big body heating her back. She shivered and shook herself out of her head.

"Where'd you go, honey?"

Abby set the empty bowl Dex handed her in the sink and filled it with water to soak away the remnants of their spaghetti dinner. "Sorry. I zoned out."

Dex leaned back against the counter beside her and stared down at her. "You do that a lot."

She understood exactly what he meant. "You haven't asked about what really brought me back since our first conversation."

"I admit, I'm not normally this patient, but it's more important that you want to tell me."

She gripped the edge of the sink and leaned forward, her head bowed between her shoulders. She couldn't put this off forever.

"I can tell him if you don't want to," Kelly volunteered, walking into the kitchen.

Abby glanced over her shoulder. "I can do it, sweetheart." She needed to be strong for Kelly and show her that despite what happened, she was getting better. "Why don't you go get your boots and jacket on? We'll leave in a few minutes for the Christmas tree lot."

Kelly beamed them a smile and left to give Abby the space she needed to tell her story without worrying about the details and scaring Kelly all over again.

Dex took her hand and turned it over, looking at the scars on her palm. She squelched the urge to pull her hand free and hide it.

"Who hurt you, Abby?" His thumb rubbed over a particularly thick scar.

"I worked until closing at one of the restaurants to cover for Selena's daughter. I didn't normally do that, but she had a date and Kelly had a sleepover at a friend's house, so what was I going to do, stay home and watch yet another rerun or reorganize Kelly's closet one more time?"

"So not that many date nights for you?" Dex teased, but underlying that joking tone he wanted to know the truth.

Her gaze dropped to their joined hands and she couldn't deny the pulse of electricity tingling up her arm or the glowing heat that settled low in her belly. "Not many," she confessed, but didn't feel guilty for those few times she'd tried to have a normal life and a little fun.

Dex held her hand in one of his and ran the other up her arm and back down, setting off a wave of heat through her body.

"Everyone left for the night and I went into the office to finish the paperwork. The alarm went off. I thought

Monica or Santos forgot something and came back to get it. I stepped out of the office thinking they'd enter the code and pick up whatever they forgot. The second I saw the guy I knew by the brightness in his eyes that he was high on something. Then I saw the knife. He ordered me to get him the cash. I turned to do just that, but hit the panic button on the alarm panel, and ran for the office instead. I thought I could reach the office and lock myself in, but he tackled me."

Dex swore. His hand gripped hers tighter.

"I never made it out of the kitchen. He rolled me over. I tried to fight him off, but he was too heavy and strong. I screamed and the alarm's incessant blast seemed to agitate the guy even more. He tried to stab me, but I grabbed the knife." She looked down at their joined hands and turned hers in Dex's. He stared at the deep scar, knowing exactly how she got it now.

She held up her other hand, showing him the crisscross of scars over her palm and forearm. "He wouldn't stop." Her voice trembled with the echo of fear she'd felt that night. "I fought so hard, and all I could think about was that I couldn't leave Kelly all alone. I thought of you and that if that was it, I'd never have a chance to tell you how sorry I am for what happened. She needs you, Dex. I need to know that if something happens to me, she will always have you."

Dex pulled her into his chest and wrapped his arms around her. "She has both of us, Abby." He kissed the top of her head, his grip around her back tight. "How did you get away?"

"An off-duty officer driving by heard the alarm. He shot the man before he stabbed me in the chest." Abby leaned back in Dex's arms, pulled down the front of her sweater, and showed him the inch-long scar where the knife tip sank in and nearly killed her if not for that off-duty officer saving her life.

"God, Abby, I almost lost you." He hugged her close, his cheek pressed to the top of her head. "I'm sorry it took that terrible attack to bring you back."

"I thought to come back so many times, but my parents were unrelenting in their fury and threats. I can't describe the way they taunted me over the years. I couldn't put Kelly through their religious spite, thinking that she's some evil creature and not their beautiful, perfect granddaughter. I hope you understand, I just couldn't come back here and face you and them and the whole town dumping their hate on me for what I did."

"Stop, Abby. It's over now. No one will keep us apart anymore."

"But if we screw this up again, it's not just you and me who get hurt. Kelly will be devastated."

"Exactly. We have more at stake. More to hold on to. More reason to get it right. And when we don't, an even better reason to not just toss it all away without trying to fix it. I see so many people give up too soon. This is me, Abby, holding on and wanting to have what we both want. I want my friend, my lover, the mother of my child, the partner I know we can be to each other for the rest of our lives."

"Dex, I want that so much, but I'm a mess right now."

He cupped her face. "You're strong and beautiful."

She sighed and held on to his wrists and gazed up at him. "So much has happened. Every time I think I can catch my breath something else happens."

"Are you guys coming?" Kelly called from the living room.

Abby rolled her eyes. They'd put off getting the tree too long, and with a major storm on the way, this was the last chance to get it before they got snowed in for days. "We're on our way." She stepped back, but Dex held her still.

"Let's both take a breath and agree to enjoy the time we have together."

She nodded, hoping tonight would be another great memory for Kelly, picking out a Christmas tree and decorating it with her dad.

Chapter Nine

NIGHTMARISH IMAGES HAD flooded Dex's mind since he'd seen the scars on Abby, but once he knew the details of what happened to her, they burned into his brain. He wanted to wipe them away, never think about the pain, trauma, and fear she'd suffered. He wished he could erase that night from her life, but it made her stronger and brought her back to him. He hated the distance she'd put between them from the moment she came back into his life. Over the last few days, she had drawn closer to him. Dinner had been a genius idea to get to know his daughter, be a part of the family, and ease Abby back into his life.

He wanted to rush. She needed him to be patient. Holding her in his arms, the steamy kisses they shared, the soft touches that grew warmer and more familiar weren't enough. He wanted more. The stolen glances she thought he didn't see told him she still wanted him too.

Like the way she stood close. Right at his side. He looped his arm around her shoulder and leaned down and kissed her. She kissed him back. Simple. Easy. The way it used to be but so much better.

"That fat tree over there is perfect." Kelly took off into the rows of trees.

Dex smiled at Abby. "I'll chase down our girl."

She turned in his arms and stared up at him. "I love it that you call her 'our girl.'"

"You're both my girls. Remember, we're moving forward, not looking back, because if we do, we'll crash and burn, and I have no intention of letting that happen." He kissed her on the forehead and went after his devilish daughter, who always seemed to find a way to give him and Abby time alone. It made him smile that she wanted them together so badly.

Not even two rows away, he stopped short when he overheard a woman's angry voice.

"You've got some nerve coming back here, thinking Dex would want anything to do with you. Everyone knows he's just being nice for his daughter's sake. How long until she sees you for the bitch you are and decides to live with her dad?"

Dex took a step to put a stop to this, but halted when Kelly's small hand clamped onto his.

"You walk into the diner like you own the place, giving the Carters your unsolicited advice about redecorating and changing a diner that's been an institution in this town long before you slept with a guy who is way out of your league."

"Obviously, for all you think you know, you really know nothing at all. I walked into the diner like I own it because I do."

A jolt of shock shot through Dex. He looked down at Kelly for confirmation, but she shrugged, knowing nothing about it either.

"That's right. You may manage the diner, Ellen, but I'm your boss. At least for now," Abby warned.

Ellen and Laurie were friends, which explained the woman's feral assault.

"You don't know anything about Dex, our daughter, or the circumstances that kept me from telling him about her. But you're right. Dex is an exceptionally good man. A man who cares deeply about family. A man generous enough to forgive and want to make a happy life with us."

The worry in Kelly's eyes changed to hope at her mother's words.

God, Abby blew his mind. For all his talk about them being together and Abby's caution to move too fast, she did believe in him and wanted to be with him. He needed to step up and tell her exactly how he felt and what he wanted.

"I don't need or want your approval, or anyone else's in this town. You don't know me. You don't know what I've been through and overcome. I don't need your *unsolicited* comments and scorn. Dex is certainly capable of speaking for himself."

Dex hauled Kelly up onto his shoulders and stepped out from behind an eight-foot Douglas fir tree, feeling none of the holiday cheer he'd felt when they started this adventure to find a tree as "Santa Claus Is Coming to Town" played over the loudspeaker.

"The only thing anyone needs to know is that I love you and Kelly. No one in this town is going to tell me how to feel about you or what happened. I'm not blameless, and I don't hold a grudge," he added for all those who'd stopped to witness this scene. "Anyone else wants to go after you for what happened, they'll find me in their way." He pinned Ellen in his gaze. She'd flirted with him often at the diner. He'd never paid her much mind. She obviously thought she had some claim on him, or at least a shot at something. Not a chance.

"You're the second person to defend me and insinuate that the blame lies squarely on her shoulders. Where's the blame for me? She didn't get pregnant by herself. I let her go and never once thought I might have a child. Everyone is so damn concerned about her hiding it from me, but no one seems to be happy that we found our way back to each other and have a real shot at giving Kelly the family and love she deserves. It's Christmas, find some holiday cheer, some charity, and just be happy. We are." Dex walked right up to Abby, leaned down, and kissed her right there in front of the twenty-plus people who'd gathered at the downtown lot.

Someone started clapping as he lost himself in kissing Abby. Her sweet lips tempting him to take the kiss deeper, despite the fact he still held Kelly up on his shoulders.

The applause grew louder. Abby laughed against his lips and he leaned back and smiled down at her.

"You're crazy."

"About you, yes," he admitted. "Let the whole damn town talk about that for a while."

Abby stared up at him, wonder and hope in her pretty golden brown eyes. "Did you mean it?"

"I meant it ten years ago. I mean it now. I'll mean it even more in fifty years. I love you."

"I fell in love with you ten years ago. I love you still. I'll love you forever."

Dex plucked Kelly off his shoulders and set her on her feet in the snow beside him, pulled Abby into his arms, and kissed her again. Lost in her words, the taste of her on his lips and tongue, and the feel of her body pressed to his, he wished they were alone, but settled for branding her with his lips and every ounce of love he poured into the kiss.

Kelly wrapped her arms around them and hugged them close. Dex managed to tear himself away from Abby before he gave everyone even more to talk about.

"Did you really buy the diner?" Kelly asked.

Abby's heated gaze left his and found Kelly. "I didn't mean for you to find out that way, but yes."

"Because we're staying here with Dad and you need a job."

Abby brushed her hand over Kelly's long hair. "You're so smart."

"Then let's get our tree and go home." Dex stared into the distance at the thick clouds rolling in and blotting out the starlit sky. They had one hell of a storm headed their way, but it wouldn't dampen his enthusiasm or excitement for the coming holiday. He pulled Abby along with him, smiling like a kid on Christmas morning who got everything he wanted, because that's exactly how he felt.

With Abby and Kelly beside him, he had everything.

Chapter Ten

ABBY STOOD IN Kelly's bedroom doorway, staring at Dex sitting next to their sleeping daughter. His rich, deep voice faded as he read the last page of the chapter in Kelly's new favorite book obsession—*The Hunger Games*. Dex loved the movies and bought Kelly the books. They'd been reading a chapter a night. Dex enjoyed it just as much as Kelly, despite her halfhearted protests that she was too big to have her dad reading to her at night. Still, Dex found a way to spend time with her, connect, and live some of the things he'd missed out on when Kelly was growing up.

He stood, turned, and leaned over and kissed Kelly on the head. Such a sweet moment. Abby wanted to hold on to it and the warmth in her heart forever. Her father never read to her at night, let alone kissed her with such love and reverence. He never looked at her the way Dex looked at Kelly, with so much love and hope and amazement. Even after the last few days, his wonder of having her in his life hadn't dimmed. If anything, it had grown.

Dex drew off those damn sexy tortoiseshell glasses that made his green eyes brighter and ramped up his sexiness to the point she needed to squeeze her thighs together to ease the ache. His heated gaze roamed over her body as he walked toward her. The need in his eyes matched the yearning in her heart to be with him again.

God, how she missed him. She wanted him even more than when she was a hormonal teenager eager to explore all those hard muscles and feel his rough hands on her body.

"I don't want to go," Dex whispered as she backed into the hallway. He closed Kelly's door and followed her backward retreat toward her bedroom at the end of the hall.

"I want you to stay, but Kelly can't know. It's too soon—"

"It's long overdue," he cut her off, reaching out to hook his hand behind her neck and draw her in for a kiss.

She walked right into his arms, went up on tiptoes, wrapped her arms around his neck, and lost herself in temptation. His big hands slid down her back, over her hips, and landed on her ass, pulling her close. His hard length pressed urgent and tempting against her belly. She'd dreamed of being in Dex's arms again. Those dreams and memories of the last time he held her, loved her, didn't do justice to the reality and overwhelming heat, need, and love she felt for this man. Right or wrong. Too quick or long overdue. For right now or forever, she didn't care. She just wanted more of him.

Eager to feel the heat of his body pressed to hers, she slipped her hands beneath his shirt and dragged it up his hard body, revealing sculpted muscles that had become even more well-defined over the years. His broad chest and shoulders were wider than she remembered. Everywhere she looked, he was the same but different.

"I love the way you look in a suit, but nothing beats you in a T-shirt and jeans," she whispered, leaning in and pressing a kiss to his chest. She rubbed her hands over his six-pack abs and around his waist, and over his hard ass, pulling him close.

A low hum sounded deep in his throat as his bare skin pressed against her breasts. "I promise I'll go slow next time." With that warning, he pulled her sweater over her head, unhooked her bra with a flick of his fingers, hooked his hands at the backs of her thighs, picked her up with her legs wrapped around his waist, and laid her down on the bed.

His strength startled and excited her.

His mouth took hers in a searing kiss, but that distraction didn't stop him from undoing her jeans and deftly sliding them and her panties down her legs. Thank God they'd both left their snow boots by the door when they came in tonight. She didn't want to slow down. She wanted to go faster, finally feel him move against her, inside her.

Dex tried to rein in his need for her, but her hands slid over his heated body, sparking waves of fire and electricity through his veins. He'd wanted her for so long and especially these last days she'd been home and he'd forced himself to say good night to her each night and sleep alone. No more. He loved her. She loved him. He wanted everything, starting with making her his again.

Forever this time.

With every barrier out of his way, he kissed his way up her belly to her round breast. Bigger than he remembered. She'd filled out in such lovely, seductive ways. He took her peaked pink nipple into his mouth and sucked hard. She arched off the bed. He barely contained the urge to sink his rigid cock deep in her heat. He tried to slow down, but he wanted her too much and caressed his hand down her side, over her soft skin, and down to her slick center. With soft strokes, he teased her sensitive flesh, then sank his finger deep, stroking her up to the very edge until she panted out his name.

He flicked his tongue over her nipple as her hips rocked into his hand.

"Dex, please."

He stripped the last of his clothes away, remembered the condom in his pocket, rolled it on, and settled between her welcoming thighs. He held himself above her, his dick nudged tight against her center. He stared down at the beautiful woman who'd come back into his life, saw the girl he'd loved, the mother of his child, and the woman he couldn't live without anymore.

With a soft kiss, his eyes still locked with hers, he sank into her until his body and hers were one. She sighed out her pleasure and relief. He saw the same wonder and welcome and depth of love he'd seen in her eyes all those years ago.

"You belong with me." He proved it to her with his body, pouring everything he was into making love to her, but she showed him with every caress, kiss, and press of her body to his that he was exactly where he was meant to be. Home. In her arms.

He thrust into her harder, faster. Her hands gripped his sides, pulling him in. Her love pulled him under. Lost in her, he gave himself over to the overwhelming urge to ride this thing into oblivion as her body tightened around his. He thrust into her again, spilling himself inside her before he collapsed on top of her, his breath sawing in and out at her ear.

Her fingers traced up and down his spine, then spread wide as she hugged him close.

He rolled off her, landed on his back, and pulled her close to his side, her head tucked on his shoulder and under his chin. He traced his fingers down her arm and back up. Her hand lay over his thundering heart. So filled with love and her, he whispered, "I love you, Abby. I've missed you so much and dreamed about us being like this again."

"Me too. I can't tell you how many nights I wished for you to be with me. The only time I ever felt whole was when I was with you."

"Until you came back, I felt like something was always missing. Whenever I was wishing for something I couldn't even name, you always popped into my mind. I'd think about how easy it was to talk to you. How bad I wanted you and what we shared back."

Abby leaned up on her elbow and stared at him in the dim light. "Are you sure about this, Dex? After all that's hap—"

He kissed her to shut her up. "I'm sure I want to be with you. Not because of Kelly, because I love you."

"I'm afraid to go too fast. I don't want to disappoint her if this doesn't work."

She didn't want to be disappointed, or have one more thing go wrong in her life.

"We work, Abby. You feel it. I feel it. Kelly can see it." He rolled on top of her and proved just how well they worked together. As promised, he took his time, loving her slow long into the night, leaving no doubt in her mind that what they had was special, worth fighting for and holding on to forever.

He held her in his arms for a long time, savoring the feel of her pressed down his side and the love pulsing in his heart. Regretting he couldn't spend the night and let Kelly find him here in the morning no matter how much he knew she'd love that, he slipped free of Abby's hold and smiled when she grumbled her displeasure in her sleep. He couldn't believe for all the times she snuck out of this house to meet him, he was the one sneaking out this time when the last thing he wanted to do was leave her.

He thought about their future. Not inclined to take things slow and lose more time with them, not when they wanted the same thing, he planned to make Abby his forever. He had her heart, this time he wanted her promise.

Chapter Eleven

WARNING BEEPS BLARED out of the TV in the other room as the seven o'clock news came on. *This is a severe weather watch. Several counties are expecting record snowfall over the next forty-eight hours. The storm is expected to sweep from the southwestern counties north and east beginning in the next twelve hours. Ten to twenty feet of snow per day is expected in some areas and higher elevations, with winds gusting to sixty miles an hour. Residents are advised to stay off the roads starting at four o'clock. Expect road closures beginning tonight as early as six o'clock and into tomorrow and the next day in some areas.*

To prove the point and power of the storm headed their way, a gust howled outside and bent several branches to brush against the house, making Abby jump.

"Dex, you can't drive into Bozeman today." The worry in Abby's voice touched him. "The snow is already coming down. By tonight it's supposed to be a blizzard.

The news is reporting record snowfall over the next few days and possibly all the way to Christmas. Most of the Western states have already been devastated by the storm sweeping across the country. They canceled school for the rest of the week."

Which was why Kelly was in the other room watching TV instead of ready for him to take her to school. He stopped by because after last night he needed to see Abby and make sure what they shared in the night remained strong and intact in the light of day. He didn't see a single reservation or regret in her eyes, making him even more eager to set his plans in motion.

"Abby, I have to go. After months working on this case, the judge agreed to hear arguments for moving forward this morning. I can't say no. If we don't do it today, he'll have to wait until the New Year. My client's waited too long for this." He hooked his hand around her waist and pulled her close. "I want to stay here with you."

"Then stay," she pleaded. "It's too dangerous to go."

"Abby, honey, I've driven in worse than this many times. You heard the weather forecast, the worst of the storm won't hit until later tonight. I don't like it, but I'll stay in Bozeman until the storm passes."

"It could be days before the roads are safe again. You can't miss Christmas."

"I won't, I promise. What's really wrong?" The desperation in her eyes made his heart clench.

"I know it's stupid, but I feel like I need you here."

Whether this had to do with the man who attacked her during the robbery, the imminent storm, or just her desperation to hold on to him so nothing happened to tear them apart again, even though that would never happen, he didn't know for sure, but he hated making her feel this way.

He cupped her face, leaned down, and kissed her softly. "I love you, Abby. It's going to be okay. Nothing will stop me from coming back to you. I promise."

ABBY NEEDED TO get out of here. The last customer had left the diner ten minutes ago to beat the worst of the storm home. Snowplows drove up and down the street clearing the way for those daring enough to go out in this weather. Abby didn't like it, but she had a responsibility to make sure the restaurant closed and her employees got home safely.

Ellen, her manager, left in a hurry with the last customer. Though things had been tense between them since she accosted Abby in the Christmas tree lot, her hasty departure tonight and the way she couldn't meet Abby's eyes seemed odd. Maybe she'd found another job and just hadn't told Abby yet. Or maybe she didn't like driving in this weather either.

Kate put the last of the dishes away at the counter where Kelly sat playing a game on her tablet.

"I've got the deposit ready to go." Abby would take the money bag to the bank when the weather cleared. "I'll go out and shovel a path for you and me to get our cars out."

"I can do that," Kate offered.

"I got it. We're parked next to each other. Kelly, I'll come back to get you as soon as we're ready to leave."

"K." Kelly kept her head bent over the tablet, her concentration on planting plants in front of her house to keep the zombies from invading.

Abby picked up the snow shovel by the back door and walked out into the parking lot, snow softly falling. She stopped and looked up at the beauty of all that white fluttering down from the dark sky and wished to be home in her warm bed with Dex wrapped around her.

Pain exploded in the back of her head before the thought could spread a smile across her face, and everything went black.

DEX KEPT BOTH hands on the wheel, his speed steady and well below the posted legal limit, his gaze straight ahead on the icy road. This day couldn't have gone better. His client got the case against him dropped for lack of evidence, which Dex had proven months ago, but it had taken this long to get an actual ruling. He found the perfect ring to ask Abby to marry him and something special for Kelly. He couldn't wait to make this the best Christmas for all of them.

Since everything went his way, he'd been able to leave early enough to beat the storm home, barely, and surprise Abby and put her at ease after she'd been so upset this morning.

His phone rang. He hit the hands-free button to accept the call.

"Hello."

"Daddy." Kelly's tear-choked voice stopped his heart.

"Kelly, baby, what's wrong?"

"You have to come home. Please, you have to come right now."

"I'm on my way," he assured her. "What's happened?"

"S-someone h-hurt, M-Mom," she stuttered, crying harder.

No. This couldn't be happening.

His heart clenched so tight a piercing pain stabbed his chest. He couldn't breathe. "Kelly, is she all right?"

"No."

His throat clogged. He fought to keep his head, get the facts, stay on the icy road, and not let his mind conjure one nightmare after the next.

The phone jostled and a familiar voice came on the line. "Dex, it's Kate from the restaurant. Abby went out to shovel a path for our cars. Someone attacked her and hit her in the back of the head." His stomach soured and pitched. "When she didn't come in right away, I went out to see if she needed help. I found her lying face down in the snow. The back of her head was covered in a lot of blood," Kate whispered, trying to keep Kelly from overhearing and getting more upset. "The ambulance is here. They're taking her to the hospital. I can take Kelly over there, but the roads are getting bad."

Dex tried to think fast. "You live on the south side of town, right?"

"Yes."

"Can you take Kelly to my parents' place?" He rattled off their address. "I'll call them and tell them you're coming. They'll take care of Kelly. I'll go to the hospital. I should be there in about thirty minutes." It felt like a lifetime. In the meantime, he'd call the hospital and get an update on Abby's condition.

"Daddy." Kelly's sweet voice made his heart bleed. Scared, she needed him to be strong for her.

"I'm almost there, baby. Kate will take you to Grandma and Grandpa's house. You stay with them. I'll go to the hospital and call you as soon as I know how your mom is doing. Okay?"

"K."

"I love you, sweetheart."

"I love you too. She has to be okay. We're supposed to be a family."

That's all he wanted too. "She's going to be fine." He didn't know if he was trying to convince her or himself.

He hung up with Kelly, his heart heavy that he wasn't there to comfort and take care of her. He took the turn-off for the two-lane road leading back to Crystal Creek. Thankfully the plows had been down this way already and the roads were relatively clear, though the snow fell faster by the minute and the wind made him work to stay in his lane.

If he'd gotten stuck in Bozeman . . . left any later and couldn't get to Abby when she needed him . . . He didn't want to think about it. He should have stayed home like Abby asked him to this morning.

About to call his parents and give them a heads-up about Kelly staying with them and Abby going to the hospital, he stilled his hand and concentrated on the headlights coming straight at him and the red and blue lights swirling against the falling snow, a siren blasting. The person ahead of the cop car was going way too fast for the icy conditions. Whether by accident, the gusty winds, or on purpose, a split second before the lead car passed him, the driver swerved and plowed right into him.

The seatbelt locked against his shoulder and chest as his body flew forward, carried by the halt of the car's momentum. Pain seared across his shoulder and ribs and all the air pushed out of his lungs. The airbag smashed into his face, breaking his glasses and slicing a cut across his cheek. The blast of pain shocked him. Metal crunched and bent in a sickening screech as his car slid and spun. His head swung and thumped against the side window. The car came to a jarring stop, rocking side to side a couple of times before it settled.

Red and blue lights swirled in front of his blurry vision. An officer wrenched open his door, letting in a blast of freezing air and snow. "Are you okay, sir?"

Disoriented, Dex took quick stock of the many aches and pains his brain masked pulsing below the numbness. Soon, the adrenaline would wear off and he'd feel every bump and bruise. "I'm okay." The automatic response didn't convince the officer.

His eyes narrowed with concern. "Stay put. We have the other driver in custody."

The sheriff pulled a struggling and unsteady blonde out of the front seat of the other car. Her hair quickly collected snowflakes and hung over her face as she slurred, "Daddy, let me go."

"After what you did, you're lucky I don't leave you to freeze in this storm."

Dex stared at the sheriff and Laurie, the shock making everything in him still.

Laurie raised her head and their eyes locked. Surprise and fear filled hers.

The other officer tossed a blue bank bag on top of the car hood along with a bloody tire iron, and Dex's shock turned to rage.

Dex extricated himself from his seatbelt and his totaled car and marched over to Laurie.

She tried to back away, but her father held firm, his mouth set in a grim and resolute line. Her father held both her arms to keep her on her feet in the ice and snow; she had no escape. Dex would make sure she got exactly what she deserved this time.

"Dex, I didn't . . . It's not what it looks like . . . I needed the money . . ."

He pointed his finger right in her face. "Shut up." Right now, he didn't care about her financial struggles as a single mother. He cared about the people she hurt and the lives she put at risk. He'd do everything in his power to ensure she never hurt Abby again.

He pinned her indulgent and reckless father in his gaze. "I want her blood alcohol level checked immediately. I don't care that she's your daughter. She will be arrested and booked for drunk driving, attempted murder, and robbery. That bank bag is from Abby's restaurant.

The blood on the tire iron is Abby's," he choked out, wondering if Abby was okay. She had to be okay. "But I'm guessing you already know that since you were chasing her down yet again."

"Dex," Laurie pleaded as one of the officers opened the back door of her car and pulled out her crying three-year-old son.

He shook his head in disgust at Laurie. "How could you?" He tried to feel sorry for her, but couldn't muster an ounce of sympathy. "You could have killed Abby. Me. Your son. What the hell is wrong with you?"

"She ruined everything." Laurie had been on the road to ruin before Abby came into their lives.

"You did that all on your own."

The other officer climbed out of his car after he radioed headquarters. "The ambulance is on its way, but the roads are getting worse and it's going to be a while."

Dex raised his face to the darkening sky and the snow falling thicker and faster by the second, freezing his exposed face and hands. The chill that ran through him had more to do with thinking of Abby hurt and alone at the hospital than the rapidly dropping temps. "I don't need an ambulance; I have to get to Abby at the hospital." He glanced at his wrecked car and swore.

The officer handed him a wad of bandages and pointed to Dex's bleeding face.

Dex hissed with pain the second he touched the deep gash on his cheek.

"How was Abigail Swain?" the sheriff asked, a nervous look in his eye.

"She's suffered a major head trauma, but she's stable."

"See, she's fine," Laurie whined.

"Shut up," her father ordered.

Dex pointed a finger at the sheriff. "If you don't follow the letter of the law, arrest and charge her, I'll sue every last one of you and the department. Get her behind bars before she hurts someone else."

The sheriff let out a wary sigh. "You have my word, we'll do this by the book."

"Daddy," Laurie wailed.

The sheriff ignored her and addressed Dex again. "Her mother and I will take custody of our grandson while Laurie gets a handle on her life. Hop in my patrol car. I'll take you to Abigail." The sheriff handcuffed his own daughter and handed Laurie off to the other officer, who read her her rights, despite Laurie's continued pleas of "Don't do this" and "You can't do this to me" that turned to nothing but an incoherent string of swear-words around her sobs.

Dex grabbed his phone and briefcase from his car, strode over to the sheriff's car, and fell into the backseat next to Laurie's son. He leaned against the seat and closed his eyes, staving off the dizziness and trying to control the rage roiling inside him.

Laurie's son reached over and brushed the snow from his shoulder. More covered his hair. Maybe the cold would help the goose-egg lump swelling on the side of his head.

"You okay, buddy?"

The boy nodded, his lip wobbling as he held back tears.

"You're going to be okay," he promised. Dex would make sure his mother got what she deserved and the sheriff took care of the boy and kept him safe from now on.

The sheriff took his seat behind the wheel but turned to Dex before starting the car. "For what it's worth, I'm glad you and Abigail found your way back to each other. What her father did, it wasn't right. Abigail deserved better. I know it doesn't look like it sometimes, but I try my best to protect Laurie. Even from herself." The weariness in the sheriff's eyes spoke of his sincerity. "It won't be easy, but I'll get you to Abigail."

Dex acknowledged the sheriff's unspoken but obvious apology with a nod. He called his parents, though his cell signal barely registered and the connection cut in and out, but he managed to tell them everything that happened, made sure Kelly was safe and okay at their place, promised her he was okay and on his way to check on Abby, and he'd call her later.

With more white than light outside, the car slid around a corner toward the darkening landscape. Dex's shoulder pressed to the door before the sheriff gained control again.

"I appreciate the rush, but slow the hell down."

By the time they narrowly escaped several more nail-biting slides, one spinout, and Dex having to dig them out of a deep snowbank, the desperation eating away at him to get to the woman he loved nearly undid him.

She needed him.

He'd get to her even if he had to trudge his way through every snowbank to do it.

ABBY WOKE FROM yet another dream about Dex, desperate for him, and stared straight into Dex's gorgeous green eyes, so filled with love, worry, and elation despite the cut and bruises on his handsome face.

"You're awake." Relief filled his voice and eyes.

Snow fell in a torrent outside the window. Complete whiteout. "How did you get here?" Fear rose up and choked her, thinking of him driving in that dangerous mess.

"You needed me. Nothing could stop me from getting to you." The sincerity and devotion in those words melted her heart.

"Are you okay?" She tried to clear the fog in her mind about why she was in the hospital, but he looked like he needed to be in the bed more than she did.

He stood from the chair, leaned over, and kissed her softly. She pressed her lips to his even as he pulled away, breaking the soft kiss. "I'll tell you everything, but right now, just know I love you so much." The words stumbled out of his clogged throat.

Sudden tears filled her eyes. The pain in her head became an incessant throb that echoed the explosive pain she'd felt when someone hit her. "Where's Kelly?" Panic seized her racing heart as what happened came back to her in sharp clarity.

"She's okay. She's at my parents' place." Dex cupped her face and pressed his forehead to hers. "I almost lost you again."

She touched her hand to his swollen and bruised cheek, avoiding the stitched cut. "Looks like I almost lost you." The words barely made it past her choked throat. "Talk to me, Dex."

"I can't lose you, Abby. I'm moving in with you and Kelly. I don't want to be apart from you anymore. I can't." The desperation pouring out of him undid her.

She wrapped him in her arms and held him, thinking about how close she'd come to dying again. How close she'd come to losing everything she wanted with Dex. "Let's go home."

The relief in his eyes made her heart well with love. No more holding off, waiting for the right time, and making sure, when they both knew exactly what they wanted—each other.

Chapter Twelve

DEX GROANED WHEN Kelly jumped on the bed behind him, leaned over his side, and kissed his cheek. His bruised ribs still ached, but his heart felt full waking up with the woman he loved in his arms and his daughter kissing him good morning.

"It's Christmas! Get up."

Abby burrowed closer to him and hid her face in his chest. "What time is it?" she grumbled.

The storm howled for three days after he brought Abby home from the hospital. They barely slept, too worried about the snow piling up, trees dropping broken limbs or falling around the house, and the power going on and off for long hours. They cuddled by the fireplace, played games, and thanked God they made it through with no major damage and all of them safe.

The storm finally subsided, giving them the last several days of quiet calm before the holiday. A week for them to spend together.

Kelly's excitement for her first white Christmas filled the quiet again. "As promised, I waited until seven."

"No doubt you've been up a lot longer." Dex hooked his arm around Kelly and dragged her over his side and between him and a barely awake Abby. He tickled Kelly's ribs, making her giggle.

Kelly bounded up and bounced to the end of the bed on her butt. "Come on. Presents!" She ran out of the room.

"She's like a windup toy that never unwinds." Abby burrowed back under the covers and into him. They hadn't slept apart since he brought her home from the hospital.

Kelly had adjusted to him moving in with an enthusiastic squeal and an offer to help him pack his place. They'd get to it after the holidays. Right now, he needed to secure a promise long overdue.

He rolled on top of Abby, kissed her good morning like it was the beginning of the very good night they shared before falling asleep in each other's arms. He shifted, sliding out of bed and breaking the kiss and her hold on him as she tried to pull him back into bed and her arms. Tempted by the inferno of heat kissing her ignited, he kissed her one last time and stepped back to pull on his sweatpants.

"Hey, I was trying to unwrap my Christmas gift." She eyed his bare chest and dropped her gaze down to his waist.

He chuckled and held out his hand. She took it and he pulled her up and out of bed. Wearing nothing but his T-shirt, she fell into his chest and hugged him close.

"Our girl is waiting for us."

"I need coffee."

He pulled the T-shirt up and over her head and pulled it on over his. He tried to drag it down his chest, but she held it at his shoulders and kissed his chest right over the bruises and his heart before she pulled it down herself and smiled up at him. He loved how much she loved to flirt and touch him. Everything had changed after Ellen set Abby up for Laurie's attack and then Laurie crashed into him. Ellen lost her job and took a deal to testify against Laurie and keep her own ass out of jail. Laurie would be spending the next several Christmases behind bars. He'd be spending every day with the woman who couldn't stop touching him to make sure he was real.

Abby dressed in a cute pajama set with white and red floral pants, a deep red tank top, and the charcoal gray zip-up hoodie she wore around the house. She stuffed her hands in the pockets and he hooked his arm around her shoulders and they walked out of their room and down the hall. Abby broke off to the kitchen, and he found Kelly sitting next to the lighted Christmas tree by the fireplace with a stack of gifts in front of her.

"You know we have to wait to open some of that until your grandparents get here." Dex eyed Kelly, though she only smiled at his stern look.

Abby walked in from the kitchen sipping her mug of coffee and holding his out to him.

"Dad, where are the gifts from you?"

He wondered how long she'd take to ask him why none of the presents under the tree were from him. He marked the ones he got her from Santa, except one very special gift.

Dex went to the Santa cottage he brought over to add to the decorations, so it would be a mix of theirs and his that was now theirs. He picked up the one-foot-square house and set it in front of Kelly.

"Open the roof."

Kelly lifted one side of the top and peeked inside. She gasped and pulled out the red velvet jewelry box and glanced at her mom, who smiled encouragingly even though he hadn't told her about this very special gift.

Kelly opened the lid and stared inside, tears gathering in her eyes. "It's so pretty." She turned the gold heart-shaped pendant toward her mother to see it.

"Dex, that's beautiful."

"So she never forgets that she doesn't only have my heart, she is my heart."

Kelly and Abby both let the tears in their eyes slip down their cheeks.

Kelly brought the necklace to him. He took it from the box and with her back to him, he reached over her and put it around her neck and clasped it. She turned back to him, her smile so bright it lit up his heart. "I love it, Dad. Thank you." She threw herself into his arms and hugged her close. Well worth the wait to see his little girl open her present and light up over a Christmas gift.

Kelly leaned back and stared up at him. "Where's Mom's gift?"

"Wait here with your mom. I need to go get something. No peeking." He pointed his finger at both of them to make sure they stayed put.

"WHAT IS TAKING him so long?" Kelly asked for the third time in two minutes.

Abby didn't know, but whatever surprise he had in store couldn't be better than waking up with him on Christmas morning, knowing he'd finally get to spend the day with Kelly and watch her in all her young glory opening gifts.

"Abby, Kelly, come out back," Dex called from the breakfast room.

Abby exchanged a look with Kelly and they both glanced out the front window at the snow-covered yard. The storm had passed, leaving the landscape changed, the same as Dex and Abby's relationship after all they'd been through.

With an excited gasp, they both jumped up to see what Dex had in store for them.

Kelly beat her to the kitchen and was stomping her feet into the boots Dex left by the door. Abby left her mug on the counter, pushed her feet into her boots, and went to the door Kelly had already exited through.

Dex stood in the doorway and held his hand out to her. "Close your eyes, sweetheart."

"What is this?"

"Trust me."

Without hesitation, she put her hand in his, closed her eyes, and walked forward as he led her out the door and along the covered back porch. The breeze chilled her face and the cold seeped through her thin pants.

Dex positioned her, then cupped her face in his hands. "Open your eyes."

He stood so close, the only thing she could see was his handsome face. "I love you."

"I love you too."

"I want to spend the rest of my life with you and Kelly. I want us to be a real family."

Her eyes glassed over at the sincerity in his voice. "Dex."

"I promise I will spend the rest of my life making you happy. You will make me the happiest man ever if you agree to be my wife." Dex sank down on one knee and held a ring up in front of him. Behind him he'd spelled out "Marry Me," in red rose petals in the snow.

Kelly stood off to the side, holding up Dex's cell phone, recording them. "Say yes, Mom."

Abby stared down into Dex's love-filled gaze. For the second time in her life, for this man, she threw caution to the wind and reached for heaven, knowing she'd receive another amazing gift—a lifetime of love.

"Yes."

Hot Winter's Night

BY LIA RILEY

To my Brightwater readers, thank you for loving the Kane men (and Grandma). Happy holidays.

The Legend of the Ice Queen's Daughter

(An excerpt from
Brightwater: Little Town, Big Dreams)

IN A FINE house on January Lake, at the foot of Mount Oh-Be-Joyful, there once dwelled the Ice Queen, a woman nicknamed by townsfolk for her cold demeanor. Life had not gone her way and dissatisfaction turned her resentful, particularly against her sunny, optimistic daughter. The poor child learned from a young age that it was better to bury any private dreams before her mother plucked them out by the roots.

One Christmas Eve, a peddler knocked on the door seeking shelter from the coming snowstorm. The Ice Queen sneered at the poor man's shabby appearance and ordered him driven off the property. But before he disappeared into the gloom, the daughter offered him a basket of fresh-baked rolls, smothered in home-churned butter. In gratitude, the peddler pulled two gifts from his sack. For the mother, a delicate hand mirror set in silver, and for the daughter, a leather pouch full of plain brown seeds.

The Ice Queen boxed her daughter's ears for allowing the old man any crumb from their table. But her complaints faded once she realized that the mirror revealed possible futures, ones in which all of her delusions of grandeur came to pass. But the girl knew the mirror was more curse than blessing. Her mother grew consumed by the images, ceasing to eat, sleep, or even dress. She grew weaker and weaker and eventually died during the spring thaw.

After burying her mother, the girl cast the seeds from her pouch in the meadow behind her home. Would an enchanted beanstalk grow and provide a path from this lonely place?

Nothing happened, and she went to bed with a stone-heavy heart. However, the next day she discovered the meadow awash in a rainbow of wildflowers.

As she picked a bouquet, an unfamiliar peacefulness took hold. Lifting her face to the rising sun, her cheeks dampened with happy tears. At last she understood what the old peddler had intended with his gift. Her dreams weren't buried after all, only planted. And at long last, they were ready to bloom.

Chapter One

MARIGOLD FLINT HUMMED along to "Santa Baby" while retying the candy cane–striped ribbon on a holiday centerpiece. "There." She beamed at the exploding red roses, white lilies, mini carnations, and button poms. "Perfectio— wait." She frowned at an off-center pinecone, adjusting it a smidge to the left. "*Now* you're perfect."

A nails-on-a-chalkboard screech tore through the radio speakers, cutting Eartha Kitt off mid-croon. "This is an announcement from the U.S National Weather Service," a robotic voice intoned. "A blizzard warning is now in effect across California's Eastern Sierras until Friday morning. Reduced visibility with whiteout conditions will make for dangerous roads. Record snowfalls are expected, up to forty inches during the next forty-eight hours. Storm force winds gusting up to sixty miles an hour—"

"Son of a motherless goat!" Panicked, she glanced

at the bullet journal open beside the cash register. The week's color-coded to-do list ran over both pages. "This. Can. Not. Be. Happening." She squeezed her eyes shut hard enough to see stars. The storm had been forecasted to pass due north, above Lake Tahoe. What was it doing down here?

Go on, tears, try to make an appearance. She'd squash those suckers from existence one by one.

Thistle Do Flower Shop couldn't afford to shutter ten days before Christmas. The holiday boost needed to keep her financially afloat until Valentine's Day. She ran a hand over her sleek blonde bun before stalking to the bay window. White holiday fairy lights glittered around the plate glass, illuminating her tense reflection. At least her hair was on point, a bonus that helped balance her laundry list of faults: the sharp chin and prominent forehead, the aquiline nose and hooded eyes. An interesting face, worth a second look, but not cute. If anything, she was a reincarnated Viking shield maiden, and squared her shoulders accordingly.

Weather gods didn't scare her.

This storm could go *elf* itself.

But a flicker of doubt remained. What was the failure rate of small businesses that the bank loan officer had shared before her grand opening?

Her temples throbbed. *Never mind. Didn't matter.*

"Because I'm not a statistic." She shook her finger at the poinsettia display. "I'll get through this," she proclaimed to the calla lilies in a vase on the shabby chic table.

The flowers didn't argue back.

Reason #403 why being a florist was a million times better than her previous job burning coffee and flapjacks for disgruntled customers. Last year she'd accepted that running her dead mother's café was scrambling her brain right alongside the eggs. So she sold up and used some of the proceeds to run away to Paris, an once-in-a-lifetime opportunity; the perfect chance to find her passion. She'd ticked the Eiffel Tower and the Louvre off her bucket list. (Eloping with a hot Frenchman for a life of gourmet cuisine, champagne, and high fashion was also on the list, but as Mother had been fond of saying, "You get what you get and you don't throw a fit.")

Everywhere, from the Latin Quarter to the Champs-Élysées, her eyes were drawn to the bouquets at the markets or spilling from shops tucked down crooked side streets. Turned out passion-finding was less of an "aha" moment and more of a long "ahhhhh, of course." Flowers made people happy. Getting them. Giving them. Looking at them. What better way to make a living than spreading joy in a world that too often felt hard and sad? On the return flight, an idea blossomed. She'd open her own flower shop.

Fast forward a few months and such budding hope seemed naïve. Her posture wilted as snow whirled over Main Street in thick flakes. Not a whiteout, but the intensifying gusts hinted that the party was just getting started. Worse, no other local business lights were on. The darkness was unsettling, like being alone on the moon.

Her uneven breath fogged the glass. Losing control of a situation made her want to rock in a corner. Nothing was scarier, except maybe clowns.

She balled her sleeve around her fist and cleaned away the condensation in a brisk back-and-forth swipe. Never again would she allow herself to be at the mercy of anything, or anyone. Her ancestors had rolled into the valley as part of the original Brightwater wagon train. They had grit and gumption, and by God, so did she. One measly bout of bad weather wouldn't lick her. Besides, there'd been another dire storm warning before Thanksgiving and nothing had happened. It petered out over the Sierras and left the valley with only a quarter-inch dusting.

But just in case, she marched to the cupboard by the sink and opened the doors.

Jackpot! A veritable treasure trove of stashed snacks: chocolate pudding cups, granola bars, pretzels, and an eclair from Haute Coffee and Bakery.

Like a squirrel's hoard of precious acorns, these treats would allow her to hang tight, finish every order, clean out the supply closet, redo the display shelves, and tweak next year's business plan. Once that was all done and dusted she could reward herself with planner decorating, break out the Nordic washi tape and ugly sweater Christmas stickers.

Let the storm try its worst, she'd put the P in productive.

The windowpane shook as if the wind took affront, roaring like a wounded animal. Brightwater had been founded in the boom period following the 49er gold rush, and the downtown retained a classic Old West charm. Thistle Do was in a stand-alone building that had once served as a miner supply post. The sides were log-clad instead of sturdy brick, and had the tendency to get drafty. Case in point, the poinsettias rustled as the glass-beaded chandelier swayed.

So did her legs.

A shudder went through her. Capital P productivity was all well and good, but facts were stubborn things. Pondering whether a blizzard would provide a chance to get more work done might be a sign she'd migrated from Type A to a whole other alphabet.

And where would she sleep? She wasn't a camp-on-the-floorboards kind of gal. Plucking the phone from her tote bag, she scrolled to the E's and hit call.

"Hey you!" Edie Banks-Kane, owner of Haute Coffee, answered on the fourth ring. "Hang on, just finagling one last cookie sheet into the oven." Metal squeaked, followed by a grating sound. "There, now we're in business! What's up?"

"You're working late too?" Goldie huffed a sigh of relief. "The storm advisory gave me a scare, but sounds like another tempest in a teacup."

"Working? No, I'm at Hidden Rock. Wait. Hang on. Goldie . . . you're still at the shop?" She was too polite to tack a *Are you few nuts short of a fruitcake?* to the question, but the sentiment was clear, make no mistake.

"Orders are picking up and I wanted to stay ahead of

the game." Goldie reached for her teacup and winced. *Ew.* Cold English Breakfast. She set it back down, dabbing the side of her mouth. "This morning The Weather Channel reported that the storm was going to miss us."

"Now the valley's in the bull's-eye. Snowmageddon. We're talking The Snowtorious BIG."

"Watch out before you bury us in snowperbole."

Edie ignored the sarcasm. "At least tell me you drove today."

"With all the peppermint bark you keep shoveling in my face? I had to get in my ten thousand steps." Her fake laugh didn't win any acting awards. "Seriously though. I can't afford a storm of the century, not if I'm going to pay the quarterly lease. The last thing I want in my stocking is an eviction notice."

"Good Lord, woman, quit thinking about the Thistle Do ledger for two seconds and put yourself first."

Goldie surveyed her small but stylish surroundings—the pressed tin ceiling, robin's egg blue walls, and white-washed wooden floor. "That's what I was trying to do," she whispered. She loved this place. The idea of losing it was unacceptable.

"Okay, okay. Let me brainstorm how to get you out in one piece." Edie spoke fast, her New Yorker roots sneaking in. "Do not, and I repeat, do not think about walking home. You'd be the Bride of Frosty before passing Bab's Boutique."

"Don't worry, I've read all the Laura Ingalls Wilder books, and *The Long Winter* scared me straight. I have no desire to freeze in a snowdrift three steps off Main Street."

"Good," Edie said. "Find a chair and paste your butt." The line went dead.

"Good-bye to you too?" Goldie tucked her phone back in her bag and settled over her journal. A blizzard preparedness checklist would go a long way to settling her frazzled nerves. She was on the fourteenth dot point when the brass bell over the store's front door jingled.

A gust of frigid wind blew in a tall, broad man dressed for an Antarctic solo crossing. Before she could grab the shears from the counter to ward off an ice-pick attack, he flung back his hood, revealing a knit cap with yellow embroidered lettering reading "Brightwater Sheriff's Dept."

"Kitridge Kane?" Her stomach hollowed even as her heartbeat went "pa-rump-pa-pum-pum" in time to "The Little Drummer Boy" on the radio. She raked her gaze down his strapping six-foot-four frame. It wasn't until she reached his black tactical boots—dripping muddy snow all over her pristine floor—that reality set in. At eighteen, she'd sworn to hate this man for eternity, and the past decade hadn't dented that resolve. If anything, the feeling had become a permanent part of her physical makeup, a hard, durable, *weather-resistant* coating. "And just what do you think you're doing here?"

"What's it look like?" He stuffed his hands in his bomber jacket and rocked on his heels. "I'm on a rescue mission. That is, unless you have a better suggestion." His lazy green-eyed gaze locked on the mistletoe display while his mouth slanted in his trademark—painfully hot—smirk.

She blanched even as her back stiffened. He'd lost the right to flirt when he'd split town ten years ago. Hard to believe it had been so long since those strong, sensuous lips covered hers, or since he'd done that tongue trick that had always jingled her bells. Good Lord, her inner thighs zinged at the memory.

She swallowed—hard—knees clamping, vision narrowing. She'd once mistaken him for a stallion, but had ended up in a donkey corral. During a time when she needed him most, the jackwagon had run off without a word, only to return two years ago as a decorated war vet who barely held her gaze.

And now he barged in here, into *her* space, and postured beneath the mistletoe like the past didn't exist, like their shared sad history wasn't graffitied on the walls around her heart. Like she hadn't eaten every tender word she'd ever whispered to him until her stomach filled with sour sludge.

She wasn't aware she'd closed the distance until her trembling index finger poked the center of his chest. "You've got until the count of ten to get lost or you'll find the pointy end of a rose shoved in an uncomfortable place."

His eyes widened. "Come on, Cookie. Cut it out."

Cookie—as in "Tough Cookie."

"Don't call me that." She hissed at the use of his old pet nickname. "And you're already at three. Four. Five. Six—"

"Storm's kicking in." His mouth reset into a straight

line. All trace of humor vanished behind a stony mask. "Edie called and said you'd gotten yourself in a fix. Needed a hero."

The bottom fell out of her jaw. Her friend must have gone and cooked a pan of magic brownies. "A hero?" She made a show of looking around the shop while crossing both fingers. "Well, goody, who's coming? Superman, the Henry Cavill version? Maybe Christian Bale Batman? Wait, no. I've got it! We're a ways from the ocean, but what about Aquaman? A girl can dream, right?"

No one on God's great earth flipped her bitch switch faster than this man.

A muscle twitched in his broad jaw, beneath the chestnut scruff. For a moment it looked as if he'd take the bait. Back in the day, their needling banter drew them together, but now she wanted to prick, to stab, to *hurt*. Give him a taste of how she felt those days. *The days*. That's what she called—if she ever was in the mood for a masochistic stroll down memory lane—the worst forty-eight hours of her life. No word in the English language captured the particular horror of losing everything that mattered, of learning it was possible to sob until past the point of vomiting. When Kit first vanished, it was as if some terrible magic trick had gone horribly wrong.

As the first night closed in, she'd grown convinced he was dead in a ditch, or had fallen down one of the mining shafts riddling the ranges. It was the only plausible explanation for his absence until Kit's cousin Archer called two mornings later.

"We found him," he'd muttered. "In San Diego, at the MCRD."

"A hospital?" She'd gripped the phone with a wordless prayer. "I'll borrow my mother's van and go right now. What's the address?"

"MCRD is the Marine Corps Recruitment Depot. He's enlisted, Goldie. A recruit." He'd cleared his throat. "He's not coming home."

She'd sunk to her knees. Turned out hitting rock bottom had an unexpected bonus . . . not a lot scared her afterward. These days she wasn't soft, but she was strong.

Kit hooked a hand around the back of his neck, heaving a desultory sigh. "Look, like it or not, you need my help. Now we can make this easy or hard."

"The record's damn clear. If either of us ever made anything hard, it was you." She slammed her hands to her hips. The lights flickered. "This town thinks you're a hotshot war hero, but I know the truth."

His eyes darkened to an impenetrable forest green.

These words had logjammed in her throat ever since he'd moved back. She reached to swipe her eyes and froze halfway. No smearing mascara over this loser. Not ever again. She balled her hands into fists, her heart aching like an old war wound.

His Adam's apple bobbed. "You think I'm some kind of coward?"

Their gazes clashed. "I don't think, I've got first hand experience." Between them stretched a wasteland. Once they'd tried to grow something beautiful. But he'd ruined the dream, and the squander of it made it hard not to scream. "Cowards run. You bolted, left me alone in the dark."

Fate must be a jerk with a wicked sense of humor because the lights sputtered a final time before the power went out, plunging the room into blackness.

Chapter Two

THE LAST THING Kit Kane saw before the flower shop lights went out was his first love scowling like he was gum stuck to her boot.

Well, shit. Fifteen minutes ago, he'd been minding his own damn business, clocking out of the Brightwater sheriff's office, when Edie, the wife of his cousin and best friend, called frantic because Little Miss Workaholic here had decided the biggest storm in Brightwater's recorded history didn't mesh with her damn schedule.

For the brief time it had taken to walk from his patrol car to Thistle Do, he'd even entertained a fucking stupid fantasy where he'd open the door and she'd fling herself into his arms purring, "Oh, Kit. My savior. You've come at last."

And even though the dream had lasted only a few seconds, he'd come up with no less than half a dozen dirty ways she could demonstrate her undying gratitude. Especially if she still owned those days-of-the-week underpants.

He swallowed. Hard. Yep, this furious gray-eyed woman had been it for him, ever since the third grade when he'd squirted glue in her blonde platinum pigtails and she'd socked him in the nose. They'd both been sent to the principal's office, and upon entering, she'd informed the school secretary in her no-nonsense tone, "Get the nurse. I punched Kit Kane, and he needs ice."

Classic Goldie—causing pain and making it better, all at the same time.

"You can't stay here—" he said right as she fired off—

"I'm fine," through clenched teeth.

They stood, arms akimbo, locked in a stare-off, backlit by the exit sign's pale red light. Finally he called uncle, unclipping the flashlight from his gun belt and beaming it in her stubborn face.

"Fine, eh? When it comes to women that word's the tip of the iceberg, and I'm not in the mood to be the *Titanic*."

She inched her hand toward the pruning shears on the counter. "Remind me of the difference between murder and manslaughter, Deputy."

"You kiss Santa with that mouth?" Jesus, he missed getting under her skin. He hoped a sardonic smile masked the painful twinge in his chest, like plucking a familiar chord on an old guitar.

After he'd enlisted, he'd get his hopes up on visitor days. Archer had warned him not to. Said Goldie hadn't taken the news of his enlistment well, in fact had frozen everyone out, even more than usual. Back in high school, people had called her the Ice Queen, but in his arms she'd always melted. Eventually he thought she'd understand the reasons he'd given for leaving. Their brush with teen pregnancy had smacked him upside the head with a rusty hammer. He'd come from shit, the spawn of Wally Kane, town loser. He didn't want to grow up and be shit, not for her or any future children.

But her frosty silence never thawed. And finally he got mad. If she couldn't accept that he'd gone = to gain skills and experience to be a real provider, what the fuck?

When his CO plucked him from the infantry, offering a chance to be one of the rare marines to grow a beard, ditch the high-and-tight, and go undercover to work in covert ops alongside the nation's most clandestine agencies, it seemed like the perfect chance for Operation: Get Over Goldie.

But things didn't go to plan.

He and Goldie had more in common than she knew. He too despised the face that stared back every morning from the bathroom mirror. "You don't like me?" he growled. "I'll look for a tissue. Still doesn't change the fact that—"

"Don't like you? Huh." She pretended to mull his words. "Is that what the cool kids call pure, unadulterated hatred these days?"

God, that sassy mouth needed taming.

But not by him.

He didn't get to stand around thinking with his dick when good men had died on his intel. Guys who'd never again smell cinnamon buns on Christmas morning, or sled the backyard hill, or play cards in front of a roaring fireplace. Since he'd been discharged, it seemed like hell had emptied out and all the devils set up shop in his head. A shrink from the VA hospital had said he suffered from survivor's guilt, a symptom of PTSD. Whatever the hell was wrong, it sucked gorilla balls.

His grip on his temper frayed. "You can be pissed, maybe that's even your prerogative, but this storm isn't fucking around, so let's review the facts as they are, not as you want to pretend." He held up three fingers. "One, the power's out. Two, that means you can kiss the building's heat good-bye. Three, the amount of seconds you've got to hightail your sweet ass into my squad car."

Her eyes glinted like sharpened daggers. "Go on, keep talking. I always yawn when I'm interested."

That was their shtick. They'd always bickered like an old married couple. In fact, they'd once teased that when they *were* an old married couple, they'd sit on a porch eating soup in silence.

But one thing was sure as shit, she wouldn't freeze to death out of spite.

Not on his watch.

"Marigold."

She jerked at the use of her proper name.

He made the scout's salute. "I give my solemn word not to speak another word, or so much as look at you sideways, if you leave with me now."

"And if I don't?" Uncertainty crept into her tone.

"Then I've got no choice but to bust out Plan B." He

crossed his arms over his chest. "Ninety-nine bottles of beer on the wall, ninety-nine bottles of beer, take one down—"

Her exasperated sigh greeted him like an old friend. "You're the worst, you know that?"

"Can't argue with the truth."

Her eyes opened a fraction wider as if registering the raw undertone hidden beneath the casual comeback. "It's going to take a minute to clean the mess you tracked in here."

After two, he removed the mop handle from her hand. "Time to go."

She tried to swipe it back. "I just need to—"

"Someday I hope you'll thank me for this." He picked her up and threw her over his shoulder.

Chapter Three

"Is this necessary?" Goldie grabbed the steel mesh separating her from the front of the patrol car, shifting on the hard plastic seat.

"Wanting to get you home safely doesn't mean that I'm careless with my own well-being," Kit drawled. "Ask nicely and I'll turn on the sirens."

"Don't you dare!" She hunched her shoulders as if someone would peer out from a house and see her inside.

In the last two years, since Kit came back from war, she'd never gotten used to seeing him in the role of Brightwater deputy sheriff. He'd grown up buck wild, son of the town drunk, Wally Kane, who'd moved to Reno before his son's return. Used to be if there was a prank, Kitridge Kane was the immediate suspect. He'd masterminded everything from installing a Slip 'N Slide in the hallway on the last day of senior year to hiding alarm clocks around the school and setting them to go off at three-minute intervals.

Now he was the enforcer of local law and order.

Guess there was one constant in life . . . change.

She ignored his lazy grin in the rearview mirror the same way she ignored how her skin tingled in the places where his hands had grabbed her, carrying her to the car. Her body responsive to his touch even through a cashmere turtleneck sweater and a puffy down jacket.

But back when those big hands used to roam her bare skin . . .

Her throat shrank like cheap cotton in the dryer. *Not going there*. Sheer force of will had gotten her this far in life. It could get her through this ride.

The heater fogged the window and she drew a snowflake in the condensation. Damn this snow, and damn this man for breaking her heart into a million and one pieces, and damn him double for the fact that she'd never managed to glue it back together.

Even now she felt seconds from shattering.

He rolled to a stop in her driveway and she grappled for the door. How many steps to the front door—twenty? She could lock the door, run a hot bath, and forget the last half hour ever happened.

"This your first time in a police car?" He propped his elbow on the seat back and turned. "Can't get out from the inside. You're at my mercy."

If looks could kill, she'd be sentenced for life without the possibility of parole.

"Settle down, I'm coming." He climbed out and released her.

Her nose stung as she stepped into the storm, each breath a lung-biting pain. "I'd have been in trouble if you hadn't come." A grudging display of gratitude.

"Nah, don't believe that for a second. You'd have made it." His gaze was intent on her face. "That's what you do. You're a survivor."

She gave a small nod. She'd endured a lot; much of it he knew. Her daddy's fists. Mother's criticism. The baby and the miscarriage. Some he didn't, like the sleazy agent Mother had found after Kit left, determined her only daughter's good looks could take her far. Instead they only got her on the Internet, where the agent posted pictures of her teenage body in a skimpy bra and panties and acted like he'd done her a favor getting exposure.

The only good thing to come from that horrible experience was meeting her friend Edie, who'd been in a similar situation with her ex-fiancé right before moving to Brightwater.

She'd been through so much, scared and alone, and in desperate need of saving.

Instead, she saved herself.

"I can walk myself inside," she shouted over the gale.

"Of course you can." he yelled back, hot on her heels. "But what if I were to drive away, and you slipped in those silly shoes and weren't found until the spring melt?"

"These shoes are not silly. They're damn good Chanel

knockoffs." The heel of her ankle boots skidded on black ice.

He cocked his head. "I could say told you so, but why bother, seeing as you're nice enough to make the point for me?"

"You want to stand out here, freezing and talking nonsense? Fine. You're a big boy. Enjoy the frostbite. Me, I'm going in."

The sight of his unexpected smile shot a wild arrow through her heart. When he came back to Brightwater, the first thing she noticed was how his smile no longer reached his eyes. The one he gave her now was different.

His features were still handsome, but altered, harder-edged, with rugged creases in the corner of his eyes. A man's face, not a boy's, and a closed book. No point trying to read between the lines. Their story had been written and was on Fate's shelf, collecting dust. Spoiler: The ending wasn't a happily-ever-after.

Didn't matter. It was all ancient history.

She fished out the key from her tote. The only good thing about the frigid temperature was that it masked the heat flushing her cheeks. Hopefully they'd look wind-chapped instead.

"Thanks for seeing me home, "she mumbled at last.

"Hot damn, a kind word. One might almost think you wanted to play nice."

"It's French for 'I acknowledge you brought me home in one piece, but don't entertain any ambitions about coming inside.'"

He didn't budge. "Guess I should've paid better attention back in Madame Francoise's class. Wait." He snapped his fingers. "Weren't you were my tutor?"

"I don't remember," she snapped. "That was all a long time ago."

"I seem to remember you more interested in helping me with French kissing than conjugating."

"That's it. *Au revoir.*" She opened the door, fully intending to step inside and give the door a satisfying slam

The first part of the plan went off without a hitch, but before she got through the foyer, a slosh of water pooled around her feet.

His low whistle cut through the wind. "Looks like a burst water pipe."

She closed her eyes, overcome by the urge to hide from the awful sight. He stood behind her, so close that she could lean back and learn whether his arms felt as good wrapped around her body now as they did at eighteen.

But when she opened them again, she was single, twenty-eight, and her home rivaled a child's wading pool. "Burst pipe?"

"Yeah." He sidled past and knocked on the plaster. "It's common for these old places not to have adequate insulation. Temperature drops, they freeze and rupture."

"But everything was fine at breakfast."

He gave a sympathetic smile, his arm flexing as if he wanted to touch her, give some measure of comfort. "Where's your main?"

She threw up her hands. "Around the side, by the cellar door."

He was gone five minutes, enough time for her to dig

out a stack of towels and spread them over the floor. She'd wanted an older home and had fallen in love with the snug miner's cottage character at first glance. It was hers and hers alone, a small space in a big world, one she was determined to fill with happy memories.

Instead, it was ruined.

Tears misted her vision as she trudged over her favorite wool rug, the one covered in golden poppies. Her boot heels made audible squelches. "No!" The kick-pleat skirt to her sky blue love seat had a dark water stain spreading along the edge

"Not this too." She picked up the copy of *Pride and Prejudice* from beneath the coffee table, a birthday gift from Quinn Kane, who'd stopped by the Thistle Do last month on a day Goldie had expected no one to recognize—with that and chocolate cupcakes. She was only halfway through the book, her first time ever reading it, and now the last pages were stuck together. A noise bubbled in the back of her throat, somewhere on the spectrum between a laugh and a sob.

She couldn't even get a fictional happy ending.

"Damn it to hell!" she yelled.

She'd thought she was queen of her own little kingdom, that maybe she couldn't control much in the world, but she could control her life.

Guess not.

And the surprising part was that she was even surprised.

Chapter Four

Kit gripped the steering wheel so tight it was a miracle the fucking thing didn't pop off in his hands. Tonight's agenda had been to ride out the storm in his apartment doing the usual: heating a microwave meal, popping a can of cold beer, and kicking back with ESPN. Fat chance he'd take Goldie there to pass judgment on his bare white walls and rows of unpacked cardboard boxes.

His cousin Archer claimed the apartment was "fucking depressing" with his usual tact, but the smartass had a point. Kit had lived there for almost two years and never made it a home. It wasn't like he'd learned interior decorating tips from his old man. Anyway, that's why God invented bar stools, so men didn't have to sit alone, trapped with their feelings. Instead, they could hang out, talk shit about whatever game was on, and compare hunting stories.

The wheels fishtailed, but he kept it under control, even if inside he felt the opposite. Goldie would have to wait until the blizzard let up before a plumber would be willing to come out, so here he was, on his second rescue of the day. Technically she might even feel like she owed him one.

He flicked on the radio. Classic rock poured into the car. *Better.* Silence made his thoughts sound like they'd been given a megaphone.

"Where are we going?" she asked dully.

"Edie and Archer's place." Archer Kane ran Hidden Rock Ranch on behalf of his cranky eighty-year-old grandma. His older brother Sawyer, town sheriff and Kit's boss, lived on the property too in his handmade log cabin. A third brother, and the only one off-site, was Wilder, a gruff but good-hearted inspector for the regional fire department who lived on the Brightwater outskirts near Castle Falls with his wife, Quinn, and their new baby daughter, Austen.

"Is that a good idea?" She stiffened. "The last thing I want is to turn up and be an imposition."

Why didn't she have a boyfriend, worse, a husband? But it wasn't his place to ask. In fact, never once since he'd been discharged had he ever heard Goldie's name linked to other men, a fact that didn't make sense, not that he complained. Yeah, it was selfish and shitty to be relieved by her single status, but he'd never pretended to be a prince.

"I don't think they'll mind. Way I hear it, you've been getting nicer, maybe not in the running for Brightwater's

Miss Congeniality yet, but with a few more years of hard work, you never know."

She narrowed her gaze, two small lines bracketing her mashed lips. "What do you hear about me?"

"Honestly?" He rubbed his thumbs on the wheel's leather. "That you seem happier ever since selling the Baker's Dozen." Her mom had run the gray, drab café with a bad attitude and worse food. He'd been secretly proud when Goldie had finally sold the place. She needed out of those bad memories.

She heaved a small sigh. "Probably because I am."

"That was always her place, not yours." Goldie's mother worked hard but never seemed to find joy in it.

He felt rather than saw her questioning gaze and refused to sneak so much as a peek. "We'll make it to the ranch fine," he muttered, steering the conversation back to safe small talk. They fishtailed again passing the Brightwater city limits signs, crossing the median, but he slowed and corrected, his whole body stilled. Primed. Focused.

The woman next to him might be a pain in the ass, but she was precious cargo.

"I've never seen the roads so bad." She spoke up after ten minutes, arms locked in place across her chest. "You're putting yourself at risk."

"I'd do anything for you." He ground his molars together. It was either that or groan out loud. Stony silence greeted the admission. Time for damage control before he destroyed whatever fragile truce they'd made in the last few minutes. "Cookie, I—"

"No—I said not to use that name." She blew out a breath, recalibrating. "Look. There's no need for a big deep and meaningful. Concentrate on driving and I'll text Edie and let her know that I'm coming." She fished out her phone. "I hate turning up unannounced."

"And I'm saying they won't care. The old house is plenty big. Besides, we're here." He turned under a wood ranch gate that read "Hidden Rock Ranch" and slowed, the conditions worsening by the second.

Goldie dropped the phone. "There's no signal."

"Yeah, the driveway is a dead zone. But stop worrying. This ain't an inn in Bethlehem. You won't be turned away. In fact—"

The car skidded on black ice, the front end whirling like a sock in a spin cycle. The faster they turned, the slower his mind went, as if his brain moved under six feet of water. A scream blasted his eardrums. A shot of adrenaline. Boom, he was back in the desert. Blistering sun beating his brow and gritty sand crunching between his teeth. The convoy rolled along the shit road, given the go-ahead based on the counterintelligence he'd helped secure, not realizing the information had been fucking compromised. They'd headed into enemy fire like ducks in a row. Dan had been driving and took a headshot. The Humvee careened into a ditch as the enemy unloaded on all sides.

Kit racked up a few medals that day, for saving lives and getting the men in his unit to safety despite a gut shot. He'd been given the hero treatment like he hadn't screwed the pooch in the first place, as if men hadn't died because of him.

Pain exploded across the side of his cheek. He swung out, struggling, shaking the body covering him. The sharp sting came again and he blinked, slamming back into his body. Goldie had half crawled into his lap and was slapping him over and over.

"There. Thank God. You're back." She paused, hand frozen in mid-air. "It was like you blacked out, went haywire." Her voice was unfamiliar. Quiet. Timid. "I didn't want to hurt you, but I . . . I got scared."

Shit. Look at her. Wasn't it enough to lose control of the car, nope, he had to fucking freak out too. "You good. Hurt?"

She shook her head. "We slid off the road. It happened fast, but we didn't hit anything. You didn't even bump your head." She ran her hands over his shoulders. Down his arms. A crease appeared between her brows. "But what got into you? I swear it's like you weren't here."

God help him. She was right. He wasn't. But he was now.

Her gaze met his and a lock of her blond hair fell over one of her ears and he pushed it back, the strands silken against his callused fingers.

"Jesus, Marigold." No Cookie. No Goldie. *Marigold.* The word tasted sweet. "How do you smell the same?" Her floral scent was like being in a secret garden.

She inhaled, sharp, sudden, as if she'd forgotten how to breathe and just now remembered. The apex of her thighs rocked his groin and he couldn't see straight. He was a man, not a monk, and it had been ten years.

Ten fucking celibate years.

No room for thought or restraint. The darkness pressed on all four sides as the wind howled. They were a man and a woman, all alone.

He sat back in his seat, giving her a small grind.

"What's going on?" she asked, leaning back, a gesture subtle enough it could be an accident, except that look on her face came straight from the devil.

"I was about to ask you the same question." He tightened his grip on her hair and pulled, not to hurt, but a teasing tug of war. If she wanted to get any closer, she'd have to work for it, she'd have to admit she wanted this—whatever the fuck this was—too.

Instead, she braced her hands on his chest, a halt gesture that turned him to stone. "Wait. Hear that?"

"No." He strained his ears. Beneath the wind came a whoop.

"I was right, those are taillights. Over here, boys!" Archer yelled.

"Where?" Sawyer.

"There. Drainage ditch," Wilder shouted in a deep, coarse voice.

Heavy boots crunched over the snow as Goldie scrambled off him, a tornado of legs and arms. His erection was going to be a big problem unless he got it under control. These three were almost like his brothers, which meant they didn't hold back when it came to dishing shit.

"Hey, cuz." Archer peered through the windshield with an ear-to-ear grin. "How's it hanging?"

"Hard and high, asshole." Kit shot him the bird, refusing to look at Goldie.

Archer slammed the roof with a fist and crowed over his shoulder. "Told you chuckleheads that I heard a crash. It's like I've got twenty/twenty vision, but in my ears."

"Yeah, yeah, yeah. You're a regular fucking Lassie." One swing of Wilder's huge arm sent his rangy youngest brother flying into the snowbank.

"Are either of you hurt?" Sawyer opened the door and dropped to a no-nonsense crouch.

Goldie cleared her throat. "We're—"

"Fine." Kit undid his shoulder belt and climbed out, wincing at the ache of his thick cock against his boxer briefs. "Spun out on black ice. Got a winch?"

Sawyer gave the stunted tree nearby a doubtful look. "I don't think we can pull you out before the storm gets worse. Wilder, could you run and grab your truck?"

Wilder gave his prosthetic leg a good-natured knock. It had been amputated after a smoke jumping accident in Montana. "Yeah, no prob."

"Enough with the twenty questions," Kit said, taking charge. "We'll lock the doors and leave it. Goldie has to get warm."

She was half out of the car, revealing her impractical high-heeled boots. Christ. No way would she manage the quarter mile up to the big house.

He heaved an inward sigh. "Come on, Cookie."

"I need a minute." She appeared to be gathering up the willpower to get frostbite.

"No." He turned around, presenting his back. "I mean, come on." That's how he used to carry her around the high school halls, piggyback style. He'd meet her in front of a class, say, "Come on, Cookie," and she'd jump on with a giggle, hitching her sweet thighs around his hips.

"I don't know." She frowned. "I'm a few pounds heavier these days."

He wasn't going to say the obvious, that the only thing that had changed about her was that her boobs looked a size bigger. No complaints there. "Think I'll manage."

"Oh, all right, before you three get your faces frozen that way," she snapped. Girl had a point. Archer, Sawyer, and Wilder gawked with undisclosed curiosity. It wasn't every day two archenemies appeared at the start of a blizzard to piggyback to their ranch.

She hopped up and his hands moved automatically, grabbing under her knees. It was like riding a bike, an instinct that hadn't ever gone away.

Ahead, up the rise, the front porch light flicked on and off in a concentrated pattern.

"Annie." Sawyer's stoic voice softened with love and amusement. "She's sending Morse code, telling us to hurry back." He shrugged at everyone's stares. "It's how we used to communicate as kids and . . . later."

Interesting. Sawyer never offered details about his surprising romance with his former next-door neighbor Annie Carson. She'd grown up on the ramshackle Five Diamonds Farm as part of a family that had maintained a long-standing land feud with the Kanes. She'd blown back into Brightwater divorced and with a five-year-old son, Atticus, in tow, to sell the property and use the proceeds to move to San Francisco. Instead, she had a change of heart. These days she and her boy lived in Sawyer's log cabin on the eastern rim of Hidden Rock Ranch.

Goldie shifted her weight, her breath hot against his ear. "Thanks for the lift," she whispered as he sank mid-calf in the snow. The simple words stoked a heat inside him, a fire long extinguished by time and disappointment.

"Anytime."

Goldie's arms tightened on his neck. Did a special sort of hell exist where you were trapped with the woman you loved, taunted by everything you lost?

It must, because he was there now.

He glanced up in time to see the last of the night stars eclipsed by the clouds. His jaw flexed.

The devil was a real asshole.

Chapter Five

GOLDIE TIPPED BACK in the rocking chair situated beside the river rock fireplace. The living room was chaos. Passive observation wasn't her thing, but somewhere between groping Kit in the car and wrapping her legs around his hips in the driveway, she'd lost her ever-loving mind.

Quinn, in a "Books Make Me Happy, You Not So Much" hoodie had draped her shoulders with one of Annie's crocheted blankets while Edie broke an Olympic speed time trial procuring a mug of buttered rum from the kitchen. Kit stood in front of the ten-foot-high Christmas tree, filling everyone in on the events that had reduced her from the organized and efficient proprietress of Thistle Do—to this trembling wreck risking second-degree tongue burns to chugg her drink.

One person wasn't shaking her head like the three Kane brothers, or clucking in sympathy like their three women, or even engaged in what appeared to be a tyrannosaurus ambush beneath the coffee table between Annie's son, Atticus, and a young woman who looked vaguely familiar. The old woman in the opposite rocking chair regarded her with a tight-lipped stare through the bifocals perched on the edge of her hooked nose.

"Happy holidays, Grandma Kane." She lifted her mug in greeting. Everyone in town called the matriarch of Hidden Rock Ranch Grandma.

"What's so happy about it?" Grandma snapped. "From where I sit, it's a noisy, overcrowded mess. Know what day it is?"

Goldie fixed her gaze on the cloves and cinnamon floating in her honey-covered beverage. Could she glug it discretely? Because if so, for once her lightweight reaction to alcohol would be a help instead of a hindrance.

"It's *The Bachelor* quarter finals." Grandma continued. "Guess who's going home tonight?"

"I don't know."

"Me neither. And why might that be?"

"Um . . . because it's not on yet?" Goldie hadn't used this meek tone since she was eight years old and had run through the home goods tent at the Brightwater County Fair, tripping over her own feet and careening headfirst into a table of canned vegetables, breaking Grandma's heirloom tomatoes entry. The old bat still carried a grudge.

Grandma made a "wrong answer" buzzer sound. "Because two fools drove off my driveway and now we've got more uninvited guests joining the big storm slumber party."

"More?" Atticus ducked his head out from under the table. "What do you mean?"

"It means that *you've* got a perfectly good cabin up yonder hill, and the question I have is why you aren't there, tucked in bed like a good boy because you know Santa is watching and—"

"Quit it, Grandma." Sawyer's tone was kind but firm. "I know you're riled up about missing your favorite show, but family first. We decided, and you agreed, that we should face the blizzard together, and the big house has the most space."

"We have a feast in the kitchen." Edie dusted off her red apron that was a near match for her flaming hair. "I've been cooking all day. We could be snowed in for a week and still be eating chocolate chip cookies."

"Maybe not a week." Quinn smoothed her blunt-cut bangs while glancing at the tiny baby swaddled to her chest in a sling. "I thought I was hungry when I was pregnant. But it turns out breastfeeding makes me eat like a teenage boy. But I did bring a stack of romance novels for a wintry read-in."

Grandma perked. "We talkin' man chest?"

"Why settle for a six-pack when you can have eight?" Quinn winked while Archer clutched his throat, making gagging sounds.

"And my contribution is crafts." Annie ruffled her pixie haircut. "We're going to string popcorn garlands and build gingerbread houses." She glanced over at Goldie. "Sawyer, Atticus, and I are taking Margot back to Denver for Christmas and then skiing in Winter Park."

"Margot?" Goldie asked.

"Down here!" The young woman beneath the coffee table popped out her head, tugging down her distressed red and white T-shirt emblazoned with the horn-and-hockey-stick "Denver Hellions" logo and saluted. "Hey, remember me from last year? I worked at Haute Coffee for the summer? Annie's daughter from another mother?"

Ah, right.

Margot Hathaway. Annie's stepdaughter.

Edie had filled her in about Annie's first husband, a philosophy professor who appeared to have slept with half the yoga instructors in Portland. He might be a jerk, but his twenty-something daughter seemed friendly enough, with wide-set hazel eyes, coffee-brown curls, and the tiniest gap between her front teeth.

"Margot, the game!" Atticus ordered.

"Right, sorry." She saluted. "Back to Jurassic Park."

"Wait a second." Atticus scratched his head. "Isn't it stupid that they called it Jurassic Park even though most of the dinosaurs were from the Cretaceous Period?"

It took Goldie a second to realize that the question was directed at her.

She'd kept her distance from children; it was easier than thinking how old her own would have been, marking time, marking a life that never got a chance to be. But Atticus's fine-featured face held such earnestness that she couldn't help herself.

"Hey, what do you call a scared dinosaur?" She used to collect jokes as a kid until Mother said if she heard one more she'd drive her to the White Mountains and leave her for the mountain lions.

"A scared dinosaur, hmmm." Atticus mulled, glancing to Margot for support. His half-sister shrugged.

"A nervous Rex," Goldie said wryly.

Margot laughed as Atticus offered a half smile. "That's pretty good."

"Coming from him that's high praise." Annie winked.

The tenor in the room shifted in a subtle way. Goldie had grown up attuned to checking emotional thermometers in others. After Dad took off, her mother's emotions tended to drop from frosty to downright bitter. Right now, there was a tiny warming, as if she'd broken through some invisible but lukewarm company role and became accepted. Postures got more natural. No one forced polite conversation.

Kit stuck his head out of the kitchen. "Hey Grandma! Get in here, I need you. The mulled wine isn't going to drink itself."

"What you need is Jesus, boy," she muttered, but she shuffled off with a fond chuckle.

The night rolled along merrily. Sawyer challenged Kit to a log-chopping contest outside. Edie set out a plate of sugar cookies on the table, and Margot convinced Atticus to ditch the dinos in favor of frosting sugar cookies with Annie. Quinn's baby girl began to fuss, and Wilder fished a thick, leather-bound book from a diaper bag.

"*The Complete Works of Shakespeare*?" Margot asked.

"He reads her to sleep each night." Quinn gave her serious husband heart eyes.

"That's adorable," Margot cooed.

Wilder made a noncommittal snort, but his ears turned red.

"We're going to turn in. She's fussy, must be cutting a tooth." Quinn waved. "Good night all. We'll make the coffee in the morning seeing as we're up by four."

Goldie watched the happy trio walk up the stairs, a tight ache in her chest. She loved sleep, but there were times when her independence felt lonely. What would have happened if . . . if . . . if things had been different?

"You involved with anyone these days, Marigold?" Where had Grandma Kane come from? Her cheeks were a decided red. The mulled wine she had shared with Kit earlier must have loosened her up.

"Nah, too busy." She strove for her most casual tone.

"Says you. No one's too busy to get busy. In point of fact, I always thought you and Kit would end up together."

"End up?" Goldie tried laughing it off. "You mean in side-by-side jail cells? Or the cemetery after we murdered each other?"

"Pshaw." Grandma adjusted her glasses. "Don't get uppity with me, Missy. I've been around the block a time or two. You should have heard me and Bridger back in the day. Hoo-wee. Fighting is the best kind of foreplay."

Goldie raised the mug to her lips. Oops, all gone.

Loud boots clomped up the outside stairs as Kit and Sawyer returned, their brawny arms filled with split wood, snow dusting their shaggy chestnut hair.

"Time to heat things up." Archer clapped his hands as they heaved the logs in the woodbin. Goldie refused to acknowledge the smirk he sent her way.

Kit gestured to a homemade stocking hanging from the hearth, the word "Archer" sewed onto the side in green felt letters. "You should've stuck yours next to the coal bin and saved Santa a trip, cuz."

"Uncle Archer's getting coal?" Atticus asked with a worried expression.

"Know what, it's past your bedtime." Annie leaped to her feet.

"But I'm not tired."

"Is that . . . Hang on a second, why yeah, it is . . ." Sawyer pointed out the window. "I just spied Rudolph's nose. He must be flying around checking to make sure the good little boys and girls are tucked in their beds."

Atticus beat it up the stairs before Sawyer had finished his sentence. Annie blew her fiancé a kiss and followed behind him.

"Where am I sleeping?" Goldie asked.

"Don't look this way." Grandma wagged a finger. "No way, no how will I share my bed."

"No, of course not!" Goldie clarified in a hurry. "I'll be fine right here on the couch."

"No dice. That's where Margot's set up." Archer rubbed his chin. "My vote's the attic."

"Honey." Edie's nose wrinkled. "We can't put her all the way up there to sleep alone."

"Who said anything about alone? There's our old

bunk bed. We'll stick Kit in too." He mimicked slamming a ball into a net. "Slam dunk."

Goldie whirled. "Enough with the comedy routine."

"I'm serious. All the other rooms are full. Besides, you two are consenting adults." Archer gave a mischievous wink. "Reckon you two can have fun working out who'll be on top and who'll be on the bottom."

Chapter Six

Kit feigned concentration on his game of Texas hold 'em but his real focus was on Goldie and the mugs of buttered rum she consumed in quick succession. If her tolerance was anything like when she was eighteen, she'd wake up tomorrow with one hell of a headache. When she finally made a move to leave with Edie, he tossed down his cards, ignoring the raised eyebrows from Sawyer and Archer.

"I'm going to call it a night, fellas." He pushed back his chair without further ado and strode to the kitchen to fetch water to bring up. And a good thing too. She stood, swaying, on the third floor stairs, the narrow ones leading to the attic.

"Why's it so warm?" she murmured, turning and almost smacking him in the nose with her flashlight. "It's like the Sahara. Or the Amazon. Or, I dunno . . .

somewhere hot. Sultry. Yeah, sultry. That's a good word. Sul-try."

Yep. She was still a lightweight. "We built one hell of a fire downstairs. Heat rises." He passed her the pint glass. "Drink up."

She took a dazed sip. "Everyone's off to bed?"

"Not for a while." He winced as she directed her flashlight at his eyes, frying his retinas. Archer, Wilder, and Sawyer had lost their parents long ago to a deadly house fire. No way in hell would they go to sleep while embers glowed in the hearth.

She gestured to her knee-length bathrobe. "Edie just loaned me pajamas and a toothbrush."

"I scored a toothbrush from Archer," Kit answered. "But no PJs." He planned to crash in his black boxer briefs. Hopefully that didn't offend her delicate sensibilities.

They hit the top of the stairs at the same moment, both reaching for the doorknob. His fingers grazed hers. Electricity danced between their skin.

"You choose the sleeping arrangements." He bent, placing his lips next to the shell of her ear. "Way I seem to remember, you preferred the top."

Her flashlight clattered to the floor.

She grabbed his chin and squeezed. "Let's get one thing straight, Casanova. Nothing is happening here. Nothing. As in 'no things.' Not a thing. Whatever there is between you and me is . . ." She paused, catching herself.

He rested his hand over hers, not for long, but enough for her to register that it wasn't an accident. "There's something here still. I'm not crazy. You feel it."

"I'm feeling tired." She bent and grabbed the flashlight, lurching a trifle unsteadily. "This has been a heck of a day and not only is my house an ice rink, but there is no way, and I mean no way, that I'm getting my holiday orders finished on time. So that means refunds. And that means surviving on snow cones and a prayer for the foreseeable future. So excuse me if I don't feel like playing hanky-panky with the guy who once nuked my heart without a word of explanation."

"You said that before. In the shop." He snapped out of his casual, lanky posture, his muscles locking in place. "Care to elaborate on what you mean by 'no word'?"

"It wasn't like I needed a personalized sonnet or a big fancy speech. I'd have settled for an 'I'm not that into you.' Or an old-fashioned 'Hey, sorry about enlisting in the marines a week after you miscarried our child.'"

"Are you—"

She held up a hand, silencing him. "Unless you want to tell me that you were abducted by aliens, I'm not in the mood." She turned and slammed the door to the attic.

Ten minutes later he still stood in the dark, staring at the shut door, reeling at the implication of her accusations. Finally, with a muttered "Fuck it," he pushed inside. His questions needed answers.

The attic was steep-pitched with exposed tresses of thick, knotted Douglas fir. The furious wind had little chance against the stoutly built roof and resorted to rattling the three dormer windows. The air smelled like old paper, musty clothes, and camphor, and steamer trunks lined the walls, interspersed with cardboard boxes scrawled with things like "Christmas Decorations," "China," "Power Cords," and "Personal Papers." A headless dressmaker's dummy held court in the far corner next to a broken rocking horse. Muffled sniffles emitted from the bottom of a metal, military-style bunk.

"I needed you. I needed you like I've never needed anyone and you were gone without a word." Goldie's voice was woozy, the buttered rum letting her guard down.

"What about my letter?" he said tightly. "I left you words. Two pages to be exact, double-sided in my shitty-ass handwriting." Such a fucking old-fashioned gesture, but at the time it had seemed permanent. A promise she could hold on to, one not easily deleted. Of course it hurt like hell leaving, but them were the apples and he'd sucked it up, tried to be a man, a man of all but eighteen, who didn't know his ass from his elbow.

"I had nothing to give you," he went on. "No money. No job prospects except weekend wrangling or pumping gas at the Kum & Go." Shadows made talking easier. "You'd lost the baby, but if I stuck around there'd have been another one. Way we couldn't keep our hands off each other . . . Shit. It was only a matter of time. And how was I going to look after a family? All Wally Kane taught me was how to fix him a Jack and Coke and place bets on losing horses. Remember how many times he and I moved during senior year alone? The trailer. The rat-infested room behind the Last Chance Saloon out on Highway 395? Oh, and don't forget the converted toolshed we scored after he'd blown his paycheck at the track down in Santa Anita. My belongings could be shoved into two IGA shopping bags." He ripped off his hat, shoved it in his pocket. "You knew this. It's why I snuck in your room night after night. To escape. To be somewhere that felt clean and good and fucking perfect for a few hours."

"You mean it?" She jerked as if he'd struck her and rose to a half sit on the saggy mattress. "You wrote me?"

"Yeah?" Confusion roiled through him. "I laid it all out. For a kid with nothing, the service is a way to be something. You are the one who didn't answer me!"

She swung her legs off the side of the bed and buried her face in her hands. "I don't know if you're telling the truth or feeding me a convenient lie, or what. So I'm going with the facts that I do know." She raised her head and peered through a veil of tears. "I didn't get a letter. I got nothing. End of story."

He didn't want to speak ill of the dead, but Barb Flint downgraded in his memory from a nasty piece of work to a fucking bitch. "Interesting. Because I left it with your mother."

"Um . . . My mother who kept you in a special place in her heart reserved for voodoo dolls and curses?" She huffed a sharp breath. "My God. You trusting her to convey a letter would have given her the equivalent joy of an all-expense paid trip to *The Price Is Right*. The only thing that would have made that miserable woman feel a drop of enjoyment would have been to watch me hurt. You waltzed right into the spider's web."

"A letter seemed like the easiest way to explain, get everything out without seeing you cry—you know how much I hate tears on your face. So I waited until you were at school and stopped by the café. Funny thing was, your mom was actually nice for once, said she'd take care of it." He leaned against the bunk and raked a hand through his hair. Guilt and self-loathing made it hard to remain upright.

"After we found out you'd enlisted, all Mother ever said was that I was better off without you, that she'd sacrificed too much on my behalf for me to end up with a no-account. I swallowed her poison pill without question. If you were an idiot, so was I."

They sat together in stunned silence until at last she stirred. "What did it say anyway—the letter?"

"Ah, shit. What the hell does it matter?" He felt a thousand years old, depleted and hollow. Everything had been for nothing. He'd doomed their chance for a future before he'd ever even driven out of Brightwater. She hadn't been mad at him for joining the service, she'd been hurt as hell because she didn't know that what he'd done was for her, for them, for a better life.

"So much time has passed and whatever my intentions had been, I messed it up. Same way I always do." He rose and heaved himself up into the top bunk, the springs protesting under his weight as he punched down the thin pillow. Much as he didn't want to end up like his old man, the apple hadn't fallen far from the tree. Except in his case, he didn't have to be a gambling drunk to let people down. He did a good enough job of that sober.

Chapter Seven

AT FIRST IT sounded like the low, haunting keening of the night wind. Goldie blinked in the darkness, her brow sweaty, head aching and the baby hairs on her neck rising in sharp attention. From every corner came squeaks and creaks, the occasional sharp pop as a frozen nail thawed in the wood frame.

Kit cried out again, a low, harsh shout that cut from the fabric of his soul. No wonder her heart was in her mouth. She must have woken to that dreadful sound.

"What's the matter?" she called, her mouth a dry cave.

No answer.

She couldn't take the hoarse, raspy breaths another second, and rose from the bunk to stand on tiptoe.

Kit was fast asleep; his mouth parted the same as those nights when he'd sneak into her window and hold her tight after another fight with Mother. After she'd heard the story for the three hundredth time about how Mother had once been a popular waitress at the Last Chance Saloon and a Hollywood executive had stopped in and left his card alongside a fat tip. Said she had a face like Natalie Wood and that it belonged on the silver screen.

Trouble was that later that same day Goldie's future father had sauntered in, a big-talking traveler from Texas, out exploring the West by motorbike. One thing led to another until Mother got pregnant. Eventually, he returned to the open road, but not before leaving them both bloody and battered.

And none of it would have happen if Goldie hadn't been born. Mother had forsaken her big shot at fame and fortune to become a teen mom to a colicky baby and the abused common-law wife of an itinerant biker in a Podunk ranch town.

But Brightwater never felt Podunk to Goldie. It was crisp, pine-scented air and craggy mountain peaks that lifted her spirits every time she paused to soak in the view.

Kit had been like those peaks. Always there. Something she could lean on, count on, and, fine, hurl herself against when she needed to fight something or someone when the pain inside became too great to bear.

No matter how much they ever fought, he was there, rock steady, until she'd gotten pregnant.

After the miscarriage and Kit left, the bleeding returned. The doctors said the hemorrhage damaged her uterus and gave her odds of having another baby somewhere in the single digits. At the time it didn't matter because why would she ever want to be with anyone else?

But life had grown lonely. So damn lonely. And some days that single digit felt like a tiny flicker of hope. Other days a bonfire of despair.

Kit moaned again.

What happened to him? The boy she knew all those years ago never had nightmares. But this was a man, a former soldier. He'd faced battles and bloodshed. She'd never heard him mention a word about his eight years in the service.

She reached out to touch his face, but froze halfway. What if he woke up? Wanted physical comfort? She'd been in his thrall before. He'd taught her about love, but also loss. She survived, thrived even, but had never been quite the same.

He thrashed harder and her pulse accelerated. He punched the empty air and jerked as if running. "Move," he mumbled. "Get back. No, shit! Go, go, go!"

She bit the inside of her lip. He suffered, and this wasn't a spectator sport. She wouldn't stand idle like some gutless tragedy voyeur. Instead, she leaned up and rested a hand on his sweaty head. "Sergeant Kane, stand down. You are in Brightwater, in the Hidden Rock big house, and—"

He thrashed in her direction and the unexpected lurch sent her tripping backward, getting caught up in her own feet and hitting the floorboard butt first with a thunk that vibrated through the attic.

"Jesus, are you okay?" Kit leaned over the rail, his bare, sweat-sheened shoulders illuminated by the diffuse night light streaming through the portico window. "Were you coming to kiss or kill me?" That bulletproof smile didn't fool her for one second. The air was thick with the sharp, salty tang of secret terror.

One of his biceps was inked with a globe, anchor, and eagle, and the letters USMC. Over his heart was inscribed the words "Semper Fidelis."

Always faithful.

She rose wordlessly, hugging her chest. Edie's loaner pajamas were modest, covered all her fun bits and more, but the silky thin material still left her with a sense of being exposed, as if every goose bump pebbling her skin rose in sharp relief.

"How long have you had these nightmares?"

Kit's face turned to stone. "What'd you hear?"

"I'm asking the questions."

He ran a distracted hand through his thick hair. "It's nothing. Stupid shit. Go back to bed or you're going to catch a cold."

Her breath was visible, soft wispy puffs that rose to him like a secret she couldn't bring herself to share.

"You're cagey." Despite his calm expression, his body remained flexed. Muscles rigid.

She didn't want to need him, or anyone. It had taken years of hard work and courage to stand alone on her own two feet. To separate her hopes and dreams from Mother's. But that didn't mean he didn't need her.

Semper Fidelis.

Her tattoo wasn't over her heart. It was *on* her heart.

She took a long, shuddering breath. Yes, she was mad,

hurt, and confused. But no, she wouldn't go back to bed and let this soldier face his long watch alone.

"Scooch," she ordered, moving to the bunk ladder. "I'm coming up."

"But I . . ." He was sitting straight up in bed now, his hair a little mussed, his shadowed face registering shock. "You don't need to bother with me."

"Do you remember a time when I asked for your opinion? Me neither. Now move, or I'm going to sit on top of you, and after three buttered rums and six, okay, fine, seven of Edie's cookies, that puts you at risk of being flattened like a pancake."

He moved to one side and she crawled into the empty space, her body curving against his like a half moon.

"Anyone ever tell you you're bossy?"

"This one jerk I used to know." Bravado was a weak defense. All he'd have to do was reach out, settle his big hand on her hip, and she'd turn into a puddle of ooey-gooey need.

The silence stretched, pulling her insides tight, before he spoke again. "It's been a while since I've had a nightmare," he said carefully. "When I first got back they happened all the time. But these days, I can't sleep well so I guess that's a silver lining to insomnia."

"What happened to you over there?"

"Long story." Another pause. "I'm sorry I wasn't here when your mom died."

She'd let him get away with evading talking about his time in the service for now. "It was right before you came home."

"We didn't see eye to eye but I never wished Barb ill."

"I'd like to think she'd say the same thing about you, but I don't think she had it in her."

"Maybe not. Still, for all her faults, she brought you into the world, so that's saying something. I can't bring myself to hate her."

"Why are you being like this?" she choked.

"What?"

"Nice."

"Has it ever occurred to you that I'm not an asshole?" He was using his joking tone, but that didn't mean he wasn't serious.

"Honestly, no." And she meant it. "But you know me, I'm a sucker for your asshole." She froze, wishing the uncomfortable mattress would open up and swallow her whole. "Okay, hang on, that came out way wrong."

"Still putting your foot in your mouth." He chuckled before breaking into a yawn. "You don't have to sleep with me."

"I know." Her edges pressed his, the tension of two tectonic plates, years of pent-up stress, small seismic waves. She inched to the wall; panic building, desperate to limit the friction.

He fidgeted with a frayed corner of the blanket. "Sorry the blizzard messed up your house and business. I can tell that you've worked hard on both."

She fought for a calm tone. "Guess I forgot the real golden rule. Want to make God laugh? Tell him your plans.

He made a movement like he was going to touch her, to put his arm around her shoulders and kiss her nose.

She flinched, unable to bear the magnitude of his lips on her skin. If he slid over her, she'd go off the Richter scale. The whole house would wake up to the Big One, and not the geologic version. "Sleep tight." She rolled away, unable to bear another second of this bittersweet intimacy. "Try any funny stuff and I'll end you faster than you can say Ebenezer Scrooge."

Blood whooshed through her ears. Her palms damp. With a single tug he moved her onto her back and crawled on top so they were belly to belly. He kept the bulk of his weight on his elbows so as not to crush her, but it didn't matter. She still couldn't breathe. The earth rocked.

"Get off—"

"What if what I want isn't funny? What if it is the most serious I've ever been about anything in my goddamn life."

"I can't do this," she whispered over a rising panic.

"Because you don't want me?" There was challenge in his tone, and a subtle note of vulnerability.

Stupid man. Didn't he know he'd always been it for her? If he'd returned and chased her down she would have been caught. But damn if she'd go to him after being left. He'd taken so much that he didn't get her pride in the bargain.

"Answer me." The desperate thud of his heartbeat punctuated the growling command.

"Don't tell me what to do," she hissed, hating getting

backed into a corner. It would be so easy to lie, to tell him what he seemed desperate and terrified to hear. That she didn't want him. That their past was dead and buried in a six-foot-deep concrete-lined vault.

But she was sick of wanting and never getting. She was tired of night after night alone with nothing but her imagination and hand.

The attic had grown colder during the long night but here under the goose-down comforter, they generated their own heat.

"Know something? Didn't think I wanted anything for Christmas." His laugh was incredulous. "But I was kidding myself. I want you. Never stopped."

"That's enough. No more." His words pierced her, and the pain had the potential to become an addicting pleasure.

"All I want to do is kiss you until we've forgotten our names, but that's not how this is going to go."

Bossy. He was always so bossy. And God how she loved it. "And I suppose you're about to tell me how it'll be?"

"First off, I don't want to kiss you to forget. I want to kiss you to remember." He leaned lower, and her belly twitched, the butterflies inside giving birth to the next generation. "But I won't do a damn thing until you beg me."

"I'd slap you but that would be animal abuse."

His chuckle echoed through her as he rolled off her. Goose bumps broke out down her arm, protesting the temperature change even as her brain tried to steer back on course, regain captaincy of the ship.

"The letter."

"What about it."

She nudged his foot with her toe. "Tell me what it said."

He went and nudged her right back. "It wasn't Shakespeare."

He wanted to joke this away. That wasn't happening. "You thought I ignored it."

"Yeah. In the end, I did." The outline of his broad chest rose and fell, but any exhalation was silent. "But if I'd stuck around Brightwater, you'd have saddled your future to a loser."

"You were never a loser."

"Class clown. Broke. No trade. I'd hardly ever been out of the Sierras. Just that one spring break with Archer to Vegas. When you lost the baby it was the hardest thing that had ever happened to me, but it was a kick in the ass. I had to get out and make something of myself. And if what we had was real, you'd wait." He turned. "That's what I said. More or less."

"You asked me to wait for you?" Her voice cracked. "You should have talked to me. It wasn't right that you made decisions about our future alone."

"Yep. You're right." He shoved his hands behind his head. "Can't tell you how many nights I wished on a star."

She bit the inside of her cheek, toes curling. "For what?"

"To build a time machine, go back, and give myself a hard kick in the ass. I didn't mean to hurt you, but you know what the road to hell is paved with."

She sniffled. "For the record, I don't think you're a coward. That was a terrible thing for me to say."

"No need to apologize. Tonight you rescued me. Don't think I won't forget it."

She rubbed her hands over her upper arms. He hurt and she wanted to help, but putting herself out there wasn't scary, it was killer-clown-movie terrifying. "Go to sleep now, Kit. I'm right here." Emotion made her whisper tight. "It's not long until morning."

And as she kept the midnight watch, his breath slowed and her body trembled.

There was a good chance it plotted a mutiny.

Chapter Eight

KIT WOKE TO an engine starting up, or a chain saw. Nope. He turned his head, his mouth tugging into a grin.

Goldie still snored.

Her blonde hair was mussed, a tangle of it stuck to her flushed cheek, and a hint of drool gleamed in the corner of her mouth. She was the most goddamn beautiful creature that he'd ever seen. Did she still wake like a captive tiger that'd been fed a vegan diet?

He sighed long and low. She'd done him a solid when he'd had a nightmare, most likely brought on by the harrowing flashback after the car crash. He owed her a good deed in kind. No doubt a cup of hot coffee in bed would help tame the beautiful beast.

He slid out from the covers, climbed down the ladder, and padded across the floor, opening the attic stairs as quietly as possible. Male voices rose up from the landing below.

"Hear the thump in the attic last night?" That was Sawyer.

"Maybe they finished each other off?" Wilder.

"Or fucked each other's brains out." Archer.

The three amigos blocked his path to the second floor, gossiping like old biddies at a quilting bee. He grinned to himself, not flexing a muscle.

"Get a chance to check out the *Bugle Online* yet?" Archer continued. "The bets are rolling in."

Sawyer made a grunt of disapproval. "I don't think Annie will approve of you hijacking the comments section of her article."

"All news is good news for a paper," Archer shot back.

"What the hell are you two talking about?" Wilder growled.

"This morning Annie posted an article on tips for riding out the storm," Sawyer said. His fiancée was the editor-in-chief of the *Brightwater Bugle*, and was hard at work transforming the once dying small-town paper into one of the West's premier lifestyle magazines. "Then Archer had to chime in his two cents to announce that one way everyone could keep entertained was to bet on how long it would take before Kit and Goldie killed each other while stranded here at Hidden Rock."

"A joke," Archer said. "Until it wasn't. Now it's like Vegas."

"People are really betting?" Wilder sounded incredulous.

"The pot is up to eighty bucks."

"Try hundred and twenty," Sawyer answered. "I checked."

"No shit," Wilder sounded interested. "And where is this again?"

"Comments section in Annie's *Bugle* article this morning. All of Brightwater is snowed in. People are seeking cheap entertainment to avoid going stir crazy," Sawyer said. "But if the pot keeps climbing that's going to be a lot of Christmas presents under someone's tree."

"Holy crap, it's at three hundred dollars," a voice whispered behind him.

He whirled, and Goldie was sitting on the end of the bunk bed, her shapely legs dangling over the side as she ogled her phone screen. "What?" She glanced up and arched a brow. "You thought I could sleep with those three carrying on like a herd of wild buffalo? The whole Kane family is genetically programmed to yell-talk. None of you know the meaning of indoor voices with the possible exception of Sawyer."

Kit shrugged. "I'm not about to argue with the truth. But I am confused."

She pressed a finger to her lips and beckoned him over. "Don't let them hear you."

"Why?" he whispered, nevertheless shutting the door and tiptoeing back to her.

"Because I have an idea."

As a kid, his favorite holiday movie was *How the Grinch Stole Christmas*. There'd been a part when, as the Grinch concocted a plan to steal Christmas from the Whos, he'd contorted his face into a self-satisfied smile.

Goldie wore its twin right now.

"Archer thinks this is funny. Joke's on him. I'll win this bet and recoup some revenue stolen by this stupid storm." She pointed at the window that offered no view, only a whiteout. "Here, take a look." She passed over her phone. "I'm going to win," she announced decisively.

"How?"

"Make a fake account and bet on Christmas"

His jaw fell open. "Have you lost your mind?"

"We're going to make a pretend profile and bet that we get along until Christmas." She jumped off the bed and snatched the phone from his hand. "I'm going to win the pot and pay for a plumber so I don't spend the next three months boiling snow in my garage to have fresh water."

"Hold up, there's a 'we'?"

"Time to dust off your manners." She poked a finger into his chest. "You owe me one for old time's sake. We're convincing this town that we're sugar, spice, and everything nice. A regular Christmas miracle."

"So I'm going to be . . ." He swallowed hard.

"The man of my dreams." She smiled sweetly. "Even if it's in *your* dreams. Now let's roll, buster." She stalked to the door. "You are about to make me pancakes."

"Hey, hey, hey, not so fast."

She whirled, her sexy mouth pursing. "What?"

He bit the corner of his lip in an effort to remain serious. Ten years seemed to melt away; their fighting did feel a hell of a lot like foreplay. "You're keeping a hundred percent of the profits? I don't think so. I'll help you, but that doesn't mean I'm not going to make you work for it."

She narrowed her eyes. "What's your expected cut?"

"Fifty-fifty seems fair."

"Eighty-twenty."

"That's highway robbery. Sixty-forty split or no dice."

"What do you need money for?"

"Fast cars and loose women. Maybe a black Lab puppy. I've been speaking to a breeder from Bishop for the last few months." Always shying away from the responsibility at the last moment.

She snorted. "Seventy-five-twenty-five and pancakes for breakfast."

"Once or forever?"

"Once." She dropped her chin, leveling a death stare. "Now."

"Deal."

"Surprised you wanted to make a deal with the devil," she said archly.

"You know me, I'm full of surprises"

"Whatever." And as she sashayed past, he took the moment to appreciate her ass.

Because no one was more surprised than he was by what was happening inside him.

Something shifted last night when Goldie crawled into his bed, and despite having every reason not to, decided to give him a gift he hadn't had in recent memory . . . peace.

She might be a feisty hellcat but she was also his eye in

the storm, and he'd rather fight with her than make nice with anyone else.

A genuine grin stretched ear to ear. For the first time since coming home, he felt like maybe, just maybe, he could chase a dream.

Chapter Nine

"This is delicious." Goldie scooped up a final forkful of pancakes onto her fork.

"Flour, water, egg, a dash of baking soda, and a sprinkle of cheer," Kit bent to peck her cheek, but she turned too fast and their lips grazed, the shock of it zapping them apart.

He whipped back, his face unreadable.

So he still chewed cinnamon gum. The familiar flavor made her mouth water like Pavlov's dog. She'd gone so far as to remove cinnamon rolls off the menu at the Baker's Dozen way back when she'd first taken over the café. There'd been complaints. It was one of the few things she could do decently, but her stony frown usually checked the complainer in an instant.

She gritted her teeth, avoiding Annie and Edie's thunderstruck stares. Any explanation about this kiss—half kiss? Sort of kiss?—had to be swallowed whole. If she squeaked any of the dozen expletives dancing across her tongue, she and Kit's lovey-dovey gig would be up before they'd even started. Instead she sat on her hands, hoping to hide the trembling and to avoid doing anything stupid like reaching to yank him back.

This was an act. Just a silly act where they had to pretend to be friendly, but no need to overdo it.

Wilder walked into the kitchen doorway, bouncing baby Austen against his hip. "I think she's getting a cold. We're letting Mama have a chance to grab some well-deserved shuteye."

Her phone buzzed with a text. It was an unknown number.

(442) 555-8551: Set up our fake account on the Brightwater Bugle

GOLDIE: Who is this?

(442) 555-8551: Do you like pina coladas and getting caught in snowstorms?

She swiveled her head to where Kit leaned on the counter, keeping watch over the griddle. He casually picked up his phone and hit a few keys.

(442) 555-8551: Don't look over

She dropped her head. I wasn't

(442) 555-8551: On a scale of 1–10 how hard is it to restrain yourself around me?

GOLDIE: Ignoring this. How did you get my number?

(442) 555-8551: I was in covert ops. I have my ways. Also you have the same number from high school. I've got it memorized.

GOLDIE: I'm sort of touched.

(442) 555-8551: If you wanted to touch me I wouldn't complain

GOLDIE: Ignoring this too. Did you place a bet?

(442) 555-8551: Affirmative. Said we'd make it all the way to Christmas Day ;)

GOLDIE: Is that a winky face?

(442) 555-8551: ;)

GOLDIE: Whatever. I'm going to look

GOLDIE: Wait, is this for real? The pot is up to $880? How is that even possible? And who are these people. I don't recognize a lot of the names, weird

I don't see your bet. Someone else made one for December 25th too, boo! Pinky Glitterballs???????

(442) 555-8551: ;)

GOLDIE: . . . wut

(442) 555-8551: I searched for Christmas names on the Internet. Found a meme for "What's Your Sassy Elf Name." Chose the first letter of my name and combined it with your birthday month. Boom. Operation: Pinky Glitterballs.

GOLDIE: You're so getting a lump of coal

(442) 555-8551: Incoming. Edie's about to ask what you're doing. Tell her you're researching snore remedies

"Whatcha doing?" Edie plopped in a chair across the table, gathering her long red hair up into a messy bun.

"Researching snore remedies," Goldie blurted.

Across the kitchen Kit masked his laughter with a coughing fit.

Her cheeks flamed, even as an unwilling giggle bubbled in her own throat. She was going to straight-up murder him, right as soon as she got her revenge.

"You snore?" Edie wrinkled her brow.

"No, but my temporary roommate?" Goldie made

sure that anyone on the first floor could hear. "There's another story." She gave him a subtle toast with her coffee mug.

"Kit's a snorer?" Edie asked with a giggle.

"Picture Chewbacca gargling with mouthwash," Goldie quipped. "Now, if we've got the day ahead of us, what should we do to pass the time?"

Her phone vibrated.

(555) 428-8551: You're going down.

GOLDIE: Not unless you start talking a little nicer ;)

"Do you need cough syrup over there?" Edie glanced to where Kit was doubling over. "Austen's under the weather. Maybe there's a cold going around."

"I'm good," he wheezed, punching his chest.

She turned her attention back to Goldie. "I've got a homemade gingerbread in the pantry. I'll set up a gingerbread house–making station at the dining room table later."

Another text buzz.

She ignored it as Edie frowned.

"Who keeps calling you?"

Goldie shrugged. Let him stew.

"Come on, dish. Is it a guy on the side? You know Tommy at the Village Tap keeps asking about you."

She hadn't the slightest interest in hearing more, and besides, Edie was closer than she knew to the truth. Better to say nothing and let assumptions fall where they may.

Sawyer's dog Maverick wandered into the kitchen and Kit bent to pet him, affording her a glorious view of his Wrangler-clad ass. He'd borrowed a pair from Archer, and the rugged cowboy look suited him. Back in the day, he'd pick up odd jobs around the ranches here in the valley. Heat flooded her cheeks as her arousal fanned into a flame. Darn it! She was supposed to be playing nice, not panting after the guy.

"So you and . . ." Edie whispered and cocked her head in Kit's direction. "Rooming went okay? I see you didn't murder each other."

"It was fine."

"Like old times?" Edie arched a brow.

"No." Goldie jumped to her feet, almost knocking back the seat. In old times, they wouldn't have slept at all and the bunk bed would have broken. They'd always been enthusiastic.

Not that Edie—or anyone—needed to know the nitty-gritty.

"I'll help set out the gingerbread."

The windowpanes rattled, buffeted by another gust. Snowdrifts were everywhere. The mountains were blocked by a canvas of white.

"The roads are going to take forever to get plowed," Edie said. "I don't have a clue when I'm going to get Haute Coffee back in business."

"Hopefully sooner rather than later." Goldie tried not to think about her shop, all the flowers waiting, waiting for her to get back and finish the job. "People will be rioting in the streets if they don't get your eggnog lattes."

Edie mustered small smile. "Those are good aren't they? The peppermint mocha is selling well too."

Goldie tried to keep a worried look off her face but to no avail.

"How are things at Thistle Do?"

"It's going to be more like Thistle Dud if I can't get my orders out."

"Storm is half over," Edie said a trifle absently, glancing to the back door. "Plenty of time before Christmas."

Goldie didn't have the heart to say that one of the Christmas-themed weddings was scheduled for Sunday. How was she going to finish everything in time? And if she flopped on a wedding, word would get out and no one would ever want her and she'd have given up Mother's legacy, and for what?

No. Stop. Failure wasn't going to be an option.

She'd make it happen. She turned back to Edie. Her friend's cheeks were a near match for the weather outside.

"Hey." She reached over and touched Edie's hand. "What's up?"

"It's coming down hard." A worried expression crossed Edie's face. "Archer went out to feed the cows." She rechecked her wristwatch. "He should have been back by now."

As if on cue, the back door slammed opened. "Freckles, I'm home, baby!" Archer tumbled in with a whoop, hurling a giant snowball at Kit's head.

Kit's reaction was cat quick; he turned and dove, but it still exploded across his back in a white mess.

"That shit's cold, man," Kit howled, jumping to his

feet and glancing around for any sort of retaliation. The bowl of pancake batter rested on the counter. He jumped forward and *thwack!*

A broom blocked his path.

"Fool of a Kane." Grandma jammed the handle into Archer's middle. "You might own Hidden Rock Ranch now but don't forget that this was my home before you were a twinkle in the good Lord's eye. And if there is one thing I can't abide it's a mess. Look at you, boots on in the kitchen. Did your mama, rest her soul, birth you in a barn?"

Archer looked chagrined. "I—"

"No, she didn't." Grandma finished. "Someday I'll be buried on the hill, and you can wear boots in the bathtub while I roll in my grave. But until then, listen and listen good." She grabbed Archer's ear and yanked it close. "Don't think you're too big for me to beat your bottom."

"Thought that was Edie's job," Kit wisecracked, his smile beating a hasty retreat as Grandma whirled around, broom high.

"As for you, Kitridge, I'll remind you that there are children on the premises. My grandbabies. And unless you want your filthy mouth washed out with a bar of soap, I'll ask you to watch your p's and q's." She lowered the broom. "Now strip."

Kit blinked. "Ma'am."

"Did I stutter?" Grandma snapped. "Strip off that wet shirt and fork it here. I'm about to stick on a load of laundry and you're not sitting on the furniture sopping wet."

Kit blinked again.

"Do what she said, man." Archer rubbed his ear with a wince. "Just do what she said."

"Glad to see you have some sense, son." She pursed her mouth. "Now go kiss your wife, she was worried."

Edie scrambled over to give Archer a quick hug, but Goldie's gaze was riveted on the man in the middle of the room, the one peeling off his shirt and revealing a torso both familiar and strange.

Last night, it had made her tongue-tied, but in the light of the day, her mouth watered. His muscles were tense, coiled like a spring, each one defined and steel-taut.

That's when she saw it. Something she hadn't noticed in the shadows.

A scar slashed low across his torso, right below his ribs, an ugly line that traveled diagonally down his abdomen, cleaving the dark fur of his happy trail.

No one else reacted.

Of course not, why would they? They'd known all about Kit and his wounds.

But this was news to her. A gut shot? Rage started in the flexed balls of her feet and sent a shock wave up her thighs to churn though her stomach.

She might be sick.

Someone had shot Kit. Tried to kill him.

She was ready to turn to Edie and ask her friend to hold her earrings because she was ready to put the smackdown.

No one messed with the people she loved.

The truth doused her overheating temper in a crushing wave of realization.

The people she loved.

Kit.

She still loved Kit.

Not in the fond but regretful way one might pine for an old flame, but with a wildfire-caliber blaze.

He was *hers.*

So what was she going to do about it?

KIT TURNED ON the shower, stuck his hand into the spray, and winced at the icy blast. This many people in an old house meant that it was going to take a few minutes to make it hot.

His reflection stared back from the mirror.

Goldie had watched him leave the kitchen with a furious expression stamped on her delicate features. He couldn't guess how he'd set her off now.

He winced, his scar aching, the way it always did in the morning. He ran a finger over it, his daily reminder that he'd fucked up. That he let people down.

Now he was here trapped with another reminder.

The door creaked open.

He snatched for a towel. "Hey, I'm in—"

A body rushed him, pressing a hand to his mouth before back kicking the door shut.

Goldie?

"What are you—"

"Hush. No one knows I'm here," she whispered. "I evaded capture like Rambo."

Goldie was here.

And he was stripped bare.

Literally.

She registered the fact at the same moment if the stain creeping across her cheeks was any indication. And then she did something he hadn't dreamed of.

Liar.

He'd dreamed it night after night, just never thought it would be possible.

"Looks like you're at attention, soldier." She dropped her hand from his mouth, trailed it down over his Adam's apple, lower, over his tat, to his scar, lightly following it to his V-lined muscle, and in a gesture so intimate and familiar, circled the root of his cock. It had been forever since she'd done this, and yet it could have been five minutes.

"In recruit training," he whispered, needing her to hear this, "I kept your senior picture in my footlocker, took it all the way to Afghanistan. My glimpse of heaven when the world had gone to hell."

They crashed together, a tangle of limbs, of lips and tongues. Her kiss was hungry, hot and wet. Good thing because he was starved.

"It's been you." He clung to her, a drowning man with a life ring. "It's always been you."

Chapter Ten

Kit was everything she remembered. Thick. Hard. Masculine. She drew her hand down, down, down, the thick vein along his shaft pumping under her palm. The first time she'd ever touched him, doubt had tampered with the moment–the fear that he'd never fit. Thank God she wasn't seventeen again. She was older and wiser. The same size that daunted her all those years ago now tempted her onward.

"You're wicked," he rasped.

Her lips pricked. She hadn't realized she'd sunk her top teeth into her lower lip.

"This?" she murmured. "This is nothing." She shrugged off Edie's bathrobe and dropped to her knees on the tiles. "*This* is wicked."

She angled him to her mouth, sheathing him in a deft swallow. Oh, he fit all right. She'd take him to insanity, and ride along shotgun. As she drew back, the only thing keeping her gaze from his were the two hard cut lines of muscle on either side of his abdomen, rigid with tension.

She worked him up and down a few more times, tentative, getting used to the swirl across the head, the dash of salt, the tang of desire. He'd always loved the way she'd pass over the slit with the flat of her tongue while gripping the root.

His firm grip on the back of her head hinted his silent fight for control.

Silly Kit.

Didn't he know? She ran this show.

She eased her free hand between his legs, and this time when sucking him to the hilt, she skimmed his sac.

Whatever fragile hold Kit had mustered snapped. He savaged her mouth with greedy thrusts, meeting her mounting hunger stroke for stroke. Her panties were slick as her inner muscles flexed in a clench of lust.

He jerked, and victory shot through her. She'd conquer this man who cut her control, and took him again, deeper, deep as she could.

"No!" He gripped her under the arms and scooped her up.

"WHAT THE HELL are you—?" Goldie's gray eyes shone like silver as Kit crushed her mouth with an urgent kiss, hooking his thumbs into her underwear and tearing them down in a single tug.

"I don't have protection." He never carried it. Didn't have a need.

She kicked her panties off her ankles and grinned. “Good thing I don’t need protecting.”

His world boiled to three little words.

In.

Her.

Now.

His hands migrated to her ass, and with a quick lift and pivot he drove her against the wall. His dick sank in and he swallowed a groan, pausing to savor the wet heat. She’d always gotten so hot sucking him, one of the five thousand secret details he’d loved.

Love.

Need.

The two feelings surged, left his chest roiling, and his heart wild. Maybe he should slow down. Light candles. Sprinkle rose petals. Play Barry Manilow or some shit.

Her nails bit into his shoulders. Later he’d wear these marks, the half-moons of her own need carved into his skin. “Now,” she ordered, her gaze lost in his.

He didn’t know where they were going, what this would mean, but knew now, after ten long years, he was home.

Her eyes opened fractionally with every inch. When he couldn’t go deeper, when he’d held nothing back, they paused, sweat-slicked belly to belly.

“Shit, I haven’t gotten your shirt off,” he ground out, noting for the first time her top was still in place. This was regular amateur hour.

She reached and peeled it off with a single unselfconscious motion. “Happy?”

Her round, pale breasts rose and fell with her ragged breath, the rosebud nipples dusky with desire.

Very.

"Hello old friends," he growled, bending to nip one, let the pebbled flesh skim his lower lip.

"Not too old I hope." She gave a teasing gasp as he withdrew to the tip, then returned.

"I've missed these girls." He turned his attentions over to the other. No good letting one get lonely.

For ten years something had been wrong with him. He was a guy. Sex. Love. They didn't have to go hand in hand. After it was clear he and Goldie were done, plenty of women, fellow soldiers and civilians alike, had made it clear he never had to sleep alone.

But he'd never been tempted. Not once. The idea had made him sick. He was broken, defective even. Surely he should want a woman to warm his bed, if only for a night.

Or maybe he was a different beast.

The kind that mate for life.

He'd only ever had Goldie and he only ever wanted her. Anything else wouldn't be fair. No one deserves to be a cheap substitution.

Her inner muscles gripped his as her gorgeous mouth, the one that got her into so much trouble, went slack.

She was tight but getting tighter. Outside the storm shook the house with its ferocity. Good. Need bore down and he slammed her harder, relishing her bit-back yelp.

She panted. "You love filling me like this?"

A shudder ran through him. This was his girl, sweaty, sweet and a little dirty. The fact he hasn't come at the first touch of in her hand was its own Christmas miracle. To hear her whispering exactly what he was doing to her, how wet she was, how big he felt, dragged him to the edge.

But he'd be damned if he went alone.

He switched the rhythm and instead of a relentless pound, slowed, ensuring he kept a glide on her slick clit, showing no mercy.

Neither of them was in the mood for taking prisoners. They were burning down the barriers that had divided them in one blinding inferno. Her heels dug into the small of his back, urging him on until at last he was there, nothing left to give, and he hadn't gotten there alone.

She flung back her neck and came with him, and they drowned their cries in kisses. What he held in his arms was more precious than any treasure. He'd found his way back to Goldie, the love of his goddamn life.

Chapter Eleven

Goldie crept from the bathroom, sore yet smiling. Thank God the coast was clear because she was walking crooked. As she tiptoed past the closed door where Wilder and Quinn must be staying, there came the sound of Austen whimpering, the baby's soft cries muffling her parents' worried voices.

"Why were you showering with Kit?"

She whirled to see Atticus standing in the hallway, dressed in a Wonder Woman costume, a child-sized Thor helmet perched on his head.

"I, ahem, needed a toothbrush." She tied her robe tighter and thought fast. The memory of what just happened was too new, too fragile for the world; like a violet or orchid, it needed shade and secrecy, not the direct sun of public scrutiny.

It was one thing to not kill each other to win a bet.

It was a whole other kettle of fish to fuck each other's brains out in the upstairs hall bathroom.

The boy gave a sage nod. "Sometimes my mom needs Sawyer's help washing her back and I watch PBS Kids."

Goldie slow blinked. She was sure to a high margin of error that Annie and Sawyer would *not* want their son sharing their bathroom antics. "Hey." She cleared her throat. "It happens. So, uh, what's Santa bringing you this year?"

He shrugged. "Got to write him a list. Want to help?"

She froze. How old was Atticus? Not quite as old as her own child would have been. He or she would have been ten this year. She bit the inside of her cheek. A stupid impulse to compare this big, bright-eyed boy to a pregnancy that ended at eleven weeks, but it still came as instinctively as breathing.

And so did the pain.

She'd opened her heart, body, and soul to the man who'd led her into hell. She swallowed hard, the copper taste in her mouth a sign she'd bit too hard. This time would be different. He was back, her mountain man. She didn't have to be her mother's daughter, brimming with resentment and negativity, willing to sacrifice her child's happiness because misery loves company. Kit had made mistakes in the past, but nobody was perfect. *She* wasn't, and still, good things could happen for her.

Correction.

Good things *were* happening all around. She had a job she woke up excited for, caring friends, and a man who might help her faith in love become bigger than her fear.

He'd lift her up. And she'd lift him right back, hold him safe against his inner storm with her own two hands.

"Why are you staring?" Atticus asked.

She cleared her throat. "I wonder if a little boy or girl that I once knew would have turned out as great as you."

Atticus cocked his head. "What happened to them?"

This got too heavy too fast. The lightness she'd felt leaving the bathroom transforming to lead.

"They got lost."

"It's okay." Atticus reached out and took her hand. "Bet you'll find each other again someday."

If she blinked fast enough, maybe she could keep away the tears. How she'd missed the little spirit snuffed from her body, from her life. Maybe it felt the same way, and someday, wherever it was, it would return.

"Are you crying sad or happy tears?" Atticus asked "Mommy says there are both."

"Annie is a smart lady." Goldie sniffled, regrouping. "Hey, let me go get dressed and we'll write that letter."

KIT CAME DOWNSTAIRS, relieved the living room was empty except for Wilder, sitting in the rocking chair with Austen, next to the fire. He ducked his head, unsure of the expression on his face. What happened between him and Goldie felt like a dream, but if that was true, then for once, he didn't want to wake up.

"Her fever is hundred and two," Wilder didn't drag his gaze from his daughter's small face. "We gave her

Children's Tylenol an hour ago, but it's not making any difference."

Kit walked closer, a helpless feeling taking hold as he peered at the child wrapped in a blanket, her tiny face drawn tight. "Jesus. Can you get the doctor on the line?"

Wilder nodded at the ceiling. "Quinn's upstairs trying now. Annie and Edie are with her." He glanced to the window. "Fucking storm." His eyes narrowed beneath his thick black brows as his gaze swung back to lock on Kit's face. "What's up with you?"

"What do you mean?"

"Dunno. You look different."

"Like a man in love?" Archer cooed, sauntering from the kitchen. He lifted the massive sandwich from his plate. "Want one?"

"You cook?" Kit ignored the first comment. It was never clear when Archer was shit-talking just to shit-talk or had dug up a factual bone. "Thought you mooched off your wife's skills."

"What do I do to deserve such insults?' Archer leaned against the fireplace and pressed a hand to his heart. "When it comes to fixing a manwich, I'm the chef of the family. Pastrami, check. Turkey, check. Roast beef, check. Bacon, check. Pepper jack, check. Provolone, check. Lettuce, onion, tomato, mustard, and mayo. Check. Check. Check. Check. And check."

Kit chuckled. "I'd pay good money to watch you stuff that sucker into your face."

"Yeah, well, I'd pay good money to see you and Goldie . . ."

"What?" He kept his face ignorant.

"All I'm saying is that it's something, seeing you two playing so nice." Archer said. "I hope it—"

Sawyer burst through the front door, the scarf around his face muffling his expletive. "I wanted to see if I could get to my place. We have a bottle of children's ibuprofen. Went into the barn to get the snow machine keys and the damn door's blown open. Red's out."

"Shit." All trace of laughter snuffed from Archer's face. The guy joked, but took ranch operations deadly serious. Red, an eight-year-old Poco Rojo, was his favorite trail horse. "We've got to find her."

"Hang on." Kit said. "My jacket's upstairs."

"What do you need your jacket for?" Atticus froze halfway down the stairs. "I wrote my letter to Santa. Want to hear it, Sawyer?" he asked.

"I do, champ, but how about later? We've got a horse to go find."

"What?" Annie crowded in behind him, Grandma at her heels.

Sawyer explained the situation in short, clipped tones. Archer zipped into his jacket.

"Don't go. The risk's too high." Grandma gripped the banister. "It's a horse. You're my boys."

"Red always heads toward the west fence," Archer said. "That's where she'll be. We'll take the three snow machines and if she's not there, return home."

A stair creaked. Goldie stood on the landing, hands slack, her beautiful face tight with alarm.

Chapter Twelve

"I HAVE TO help," Kit spoke to Goldie, uncomfortably aware that the house had gone silent. Everyone held their breath, wondering if at last he and she were going to throw down, have one of their infamous fights.

"We'll be fine," Sawyer said. "The storm isn't as strong today. I'd never put anyone in my family in danger."

Kit suspected that while Sawyer was looking at Goldie, he addressed Atticus and Annie, who wore identical frowns.

"We'll be gone fifteen minutes, twenty tops." Archer added. "Someone tell Edie. She's with Quinn. And all of you, stop looking so worried. We got this."

Kit nodded. "I'll grab my things. Be out in a minute."

He slipped up the stairs, giving Goldie a tight smile as he passed. If she wanted Pinky Glitterballs to win the bet, she wouldn't fight with him.

She worried. He got it. But he had a responsibility

to help his cousins, his best friends, practically his own brothers. He wasn't going to let them down.

He laced his tactical boots when she came into the attic.

"I'm sorry," she whispered, twisting her hands. "I know you wanted to go."

He stood, grabbing his knit hat. "Sawyer's right, the storm's letting up, and we won't go far."

"No. You won't." She folded her arms.

He lowered his chin. "What's that supposed to mean?"

"I told Archer and Sawyer in no uncertain terms that you aren't putting a single boot outside. They left."

Two snow machine engines fired up outside the window, roaring away.

"What the hell!" His temper flared. "Damn it, Goldie. That wasn't your call to make."

"Really?" She cocked a brow, holding firm. "Because the way I see it, you owe me one or two."

"You can't hold our past over my head. It will block out any good we'll ever have."

She nodded. "I get that, I do. But explain how I'm supposed to risk losing you before we've even had a second chance?"

He took her into his arms. "You won't. But—" His voice cracked. "You gotta understand, you know my nightmare?"

She rested a hand on his cheek. "What happened?"

"When I dream, I'm always there, the same place—eight miles from the Pakistani border. We had teams of Afghan troops and U.S. soldiers driving to set up an outpost near a village." A muscle tightened in his jaw. "I led men into a killing zone, signed off on shitty intel and we got ambushed. The terrain—craggy ravines and steep mountains peppered with caves—was made for guerrilla warfare. Six Americans and twelve Afghan allies were pinned down and wounded.

"My friend . . ." He forced himself to say his name. "Daniel Youngblood died. So did two others. I let them down. And all those years ago, I let *you* down too. I didn't mean to, but I was an eighteen-year-old dumbass. I can't let down any more people."

Tears sheened her eyes. "I hear you, I do. I *really* do." She gave her head a little shake. "But I can't take a chance, not when we've found our way back together."

Downstairs, Quinn screamed.

GOLDIE AND KIT rushed into the living room. Grandma stood by the Christmas tree gripping Quinn's shoulders. "It's going to be okay, honey. It's all going to be okay," she repeated, even as her mouth pursed, worry deepening the lines in her face.

"No, no, no." Quinn pressed her hands over to her face. "No more sitting, I can't do this. I won't do this. What if she . . . no!" She bunched her hands into two fists, ground them into her temples. "I'm getting help for my baby if I have to crawl."

"Like hell you are," Wilder growled, striding into the room, his dark hair standing on end, his gaze wild. "Let me think. I got to think."

"What's going on?" Goldie's heart was in her mouth. Quinn's terrified screams still ringing in her ears.

Wilder stared at the bundle in his arms. "Austen had a seizure."

"The fever," Quinn muttered. "We can't get it down."

"Have you spoken to a doctor?" Kit asked in a low voice, tension radiating from him.

Quinn nodded, a sob bubbling in her throat. "He can't reach us here. The roads haven't been plowed."

"Right. Damn." Kit shook his head. "And the clinic is back in town."

"The clinic? No! He's at home." Wilder's gaze landed on Kit's as the thought occurred to them at the same time.

"Shit, Doc's place is three miles south." Kit nodded. "The other side of Five Diamonds Farm."

"Sawyer and Archer took off on two of the snow machines," Wilder said. "That leaves one for me."

"No!" Quinn's voice was shrill, her eyes bright through her black-framed glasses. "You cannot leave. What if something happens? To her? To you? No. Wilder. No!"

"There, there." Grandma held her close.

Kit turned to Goldie. Could he hear the scream inside her head? Every bone in her body echoed with the word "no," but her tongue remained silent.

"It's their baby, Cookie." His gaze pleaded for her understanding. "I can't let them down."

"Neither of us can." She closed her eyes and drew a shaky breath. "Go."

"I'm on it." Kit yanked down his hat, moving into action. "Don't worry, Quinn. Wilder. I swear on everything that I hold dear I'll get the doctor back for your baby."

"I'll walk you out." Goldie squared her shoulders, preparing to bear the weight of waiting.

The air was sweet in the kitchen, full of chocolate and brown sugar. Edie looked up, brandishing a spatula. "What can I say? I'm a worrier." She fought for a smile. "And when I worry, I bake." Seeing their tense expressions, she bit the corner of her lip. "You know what, I forgot a thing that I need in my room, this important . . . you know . . . *thing*."

They waited until she bolted and then Kit reached out and took her hand. "Get over here." He tugged her close and pressed a kiss to the top of her head. "Be my Tough Cookie," he murmured, as the wind grew in ferocity. "I'll need your strength."

She jutted out her chin. "I try."

"I'm coming back, you know." He brushed her lips in a last lingering kiss. "Back in the living room, I swore to Wilder and Quinn on all I hold dear. And that's you." And, as if unable to look in her eyes after that confession, he turned, head down, pushed open the back door, and stepped into the howling abyss.

Chapter Thirteen

AUSTEN CONVULSED AGAIN.

Quinn wept by fire, light flickering off her damp cheeks. The lights of the tree were out. The phones dead. In the hour after Sawyer, Archer, and Kit had left Hidden Rock, the storm had doubled down. Power lines must be down. The cell tower damaged.

Edie and Annie, both white-faced, stood by the window while Margot attempted to read Atticus the final Harry Potter book. A plate of brownies sat untouched on the coffee table.

"Hey, you read that sentence already," he protested.

"Why don't you take over solo for a while, honey?" Margot passed him the book and nibbled her thumbnail.

"Nah." The boy set it down and wandered off.

Wilder held Austen in a pink towel. He and Grandma Kane had plunged the baby in a cold bath in an attempt to stop her soaring temperature and seizures. She barely nursed. She wasn't even crying. Her half-open eyes listlessly watched the far wall.

The grandfather clock by the stairs chimed four. It had been an hour.

Goldie felt a tug. She glanced down and Atticus was beside her. "I changed my list to Santa," he whispered. He'd crossed out ~~Lego~~, ~~a trip to the Wizarding World of Harry Potter in Florida~~, ~~See a hockey game with Margot~~, and ~~Rey doll from Star Wars~~. All it said was "Baby better. Sawyer home safe. Kit and Archer too."

Boots clomped outside. Two sets.

All heads turned.

"Christ on a cracker," Archer tripped over the doorway, bracing Sawyer upright. "Sorry, Grandma. I know how you hate boots in the house, but here's a time when you're going to have to make an exception."

"What happened?" Annie cried as she and Margot raced forward to help him into a seat beside the fire.

"Horse bolted." Sawyer's face was tight with pain. "The engine noise must have spooked her. Lost my glove getting her back."

"Your poor hand!" Annie held his white fingers between hers and pressed down.

"That's frostbite, sure as I'm looking at it," Grandma said in a dour voice. "I'll warm a bowl of water, not too hot, not too cold. You'll need to soak it."

Goldie ruffled Atticus's hair. "Looks like Santa heard your wishes."

"Almost." He beamed before his smile faded. "What about Kit?"

The question of the hour. "He'll be here any second," Goldie tried to project a confidence she didn't feel.

"I'll fix a pot of peppermint tea," Margot beelined to the kitchen.

"We need something a stronger," Archer called after her before looking around. "Why all the long faces? I know we're late, but we made it back in one piece."

"Kit's out there. He went to fetch Doc." Wilder told them about Austen's rising fever and febrile seizures.

"He'll be back soon," Sawyer said, and it took Goldie a minute to realize that he spoke directly to her, his handsome, stoic face the picture of utter confidence.

Wasn't hard to see why Annie had rearranged all her life plans for this steady, kind man.

On they waited.

The sun set behind the storm clouds. Light faded to darkness.

The clock struck five. Grandma and Margot lit candles. Austen nursed a little. Threw most of it up.

Six o' clock.

No one asked for dinner. Small talk ceased. Archer, Sawyer, and Wilder conferred in the corner.

Goldie caught bits and pieces of their sentences.

"Should have been back by now."

"Wait another twenty, then we go."

"Not enough gas."

She gritted her teeth. If Kit wasn't back in twenty, she'd ride out herself."

Her throat closed. No use pretending. She'd never make it far. And what if he was thrown from the vehicle?

Or struck a fence buried beneath a deep drift? Worse, crashed into barbed wire?

Kit Kane, you swore. You swore on me.

She let him go, trusting that this time he'd return to her. That at last, after all this time, they'd be ready to reap and sow a future together. If he didn't make it, the future would be barren, cracked, and uninhabitable.

She rose, unable to sit, unable to stand the torture of patience another moment. On the top of the tree perched a silver star, the edges a little battered, the glitter missing here and there. But she needed to put her faith in Kit, to send it out into that storm for her, for the baby, for Quinn and Wilder.

"Please," she whispered to the star. She'd lost any capacity for an eloquent speech. All that she had was that simple word.

"Please."

She needed a Christmas miracle.

What a joke. The memory of Mother's sneering tone lanced her thoughts. Why should anything go her way? What made her so special?

Kit believed she was worth loving. He'd *sworn* on her.

A low noise cut through the storm. She balled her hands into first. Were weather gods playing tricks?

"That's him." Wilder glanced up, with razor-sharp focus. "That's Kit."

Her mouth went dry. Everything playing out as if in a blur. Kit and the doctor staggered through the door. She'd have sworn she didn't take a single step, she'd flown into his arms.

"You're okay!"

"Safe and sound." He kissed her on the forehead, telling the assembly how he'd made it out to Doc's place fast, but on the way back hit trouble. They'd become disoriented in the storm.

"We reached Five Diamonds and broke in through the back door to warm up. I'll replace the windowpane soon as storm ends," Kit said to Annie, not releasing his grip on Goldie's shoulders. Dr. Keen removed an IV from his backpack and moved to the couch to examine Austen.

"It's not a big deal." Annie's eyes shone. "We're just glad to see you home safe."

"Hear, hear." Edie added. "Let me spike the eggnog. The power might be out but we need a toast."

Dr. Keen removed his stethoscope with a smile. "Austen's breathing and heart rate are within the high end of normal. Let's get her upstairs. I'll administer antibiotics and an IV for dehydration, but I predict she'll be back to her usual happy self by Christmas." Wilder and Quinn embraced while Grandma burst into tears.

"Oh, suck an egg, the lot of you." She yanked a hankie from her cardigan pocket and gave her nose a loud blow. "We're family. One hurts, we all bleed."

"Love you, Grandma," Archer reached under her arms and twirled her in a giddy spin.

"Eggnog's ready," Edie called over the laughter.

Quinn, Wilder, Austen, and Dr. Keen walked upstairs while everyone else migrated to the kitchen.

Everyone, that is, except for Kit.

The ends of his hair were damp, the thick chestnut

waves curling around the angular planes of his cheekbones.

"You okay?" he asked, running a hand down her cheek.

Her lip quivered, but she'd been brave. She'd faced the dark and held fast.

"Deep down, I knew you'd make it."

The skin near his eyes crinkled as his grin stretched wide. "That right?" he asked, stepping forward.

She hooked her hands around his neck, brought his head down near her. "A few snowflakes weren't going to stop you."

His brow arched. "More than a few."

She took a shuddering sigh and shrugged. "My legs will still be shaking on New Year's. But on the plus side, I dug deep and found faith. I *knew* that you'd come back to me."

"I could feel you with me the entire way. Even when I had a scare or two."

"*Two*?"

"None of that matters now." He tugged a lock of her hair. "I love you, sweet girl. Always have."

"Love you too, always will."

As their lips pressed, the tree lit up, hundreds of multicolored lights. "Joy to the World" resounded from the stereo. The power was back on.

"I knew it, I knew it!" Grandma Kane burst into the room, raising her eggnog as she gave them a victorious smile. "Archer, Sawyer, get in here and tell me, am I a genius, or am I a genius?"

The two men stood behind her, trading bemused looks.

"What're you talking about?" Goldie asked as Kit hugged her to his chest with a chuckle.

"The bet." Grandma shrugged smugly. "These two boys owe me fifty bucks. Each. And I don't mean Monopoly money. I want greenbacks."

"Aw, man." Archer dug in his wallet.

"It was her idea." Sawyer shrugged. "To set you guys up. Rig the Bugle article to look like people were making bets."

Grandma winked at Kit. "You going to tell them or should I?"

"Fine, I will." His chuckle turned into outright laughter. "We came up with it together, Grandma and me, last night over mulled wine."

"What?" Goldie gasped.

He tilted up her chin. "I needed you to give us a chance. Figured if you were more invested in *not* fighting with me, we could use the storm to figure things out. The guys unwittingly helped. Made a bunch of fake accounts after Grandma bet them a hundred bucks it would get us together."

She couldn't believe her ears. "So that conversation on the landing below the attic this morning was a setup for me?"

"And us." Archer whistled under his breath. "Damn, Kit. You're diabolical."

"We masterminded the whole thing." Grandma Kane's giggle was almost girlish. "I told those three to go wait until Kit opened the door."

Kit guffawed. "But they didn't know I was the one pulling the strings, a regular Godfather."

"Is your mafia nickname Pinky Glitterballs?" Goldie said dryly, even as she hugged him again. Once she'd started, it was impossible to stop. He was here. He was safe. Nothing else mattered.

"No regrets. I made the bet for Christmas." He picked her up and swung her around. "But you fell for me fast."

"Guess I'd never gotten back up after the first time." She tweaked the tip of his nose, laughing too hard to care how good he and Grandma Kane had gotten her. She hitched her legs around his waist, Brightwater better brace for some serious PDA.

"Hey, get a room," Archer called as they leaned in for another kiss.

"Don't need one." Kit winked at her. "We have ourselves an attic."

Epilogue

Marigold tied the champagne-colored silk ribbon around the bouquet of pink peonies, yellow roses, ferns, and trailing clematis. "The perfect 'spring is almost here' bouquet." She frowned at the cockeyed bow. "Wait a sec, a few minor adjustments and aha, now you're wedding-worthy for our Annie."

"And good thing too," Kit stopped tugged at his gray tie to check his watch. "The ceremony's in twenty."

"Oh my God, is that the time?" She plucked the bottle of water from next to the cash register and drank deep. "Right. We have to get a move on. Wait, where's my journal. I have a checklist for the reception. I need to—"

"Chill." Kit took her by the shoulders and planted a kiss on her forehead. She sank into him, savoring a moment to trace her fingers over his biceps, evident even through the suit jacket. Big, strong arms able to fix a cottage damaged by a broken water pipe, and tapering to clever fingers delicate enough to handle roses when pitching in to help her meet every single Christmas order after that blizzard.

A warm snuffling heat crossed the back of her knees and she yelped. "Daisy!"

"Looks like the little girl wants your attention." Archer bent to gather up the wiggly black Lab puppy, who rewarded the effort with a wet slurp across his cheek.

"You have her leash?" She reviewed her mental checklist.

He gestured to the pink leash coiled by the sink. "Yes, ma'am."

"Oh!" She held up a finger. "What about the birdseed?"

"Done." He lifted the brown paper bag.

"The champagne?"

"Grandma Kane wanted to contribute. She's thrilled Annie and Sawyer aren't living in sin anymore."

Goldie's laugh cut off quick. "Wait, oh no. The flower girl basket for Austen!" She surveyed the store. "Where the heck did I put that?"

"Since Quinn's going to be carrying it along with the baby, she stopped by an hour ago to pick it up. Now come on, let's go." It was a two-minute walk to the courthouse. Annie and Sawyer were getting hitched in a low-key civil ceremony, followed by a reception in the old barn at the Five Diamonds.

Goldie's stomach lurched, and this time not from excitement. Her palms slicked as her tongue prickled. *Not again.*

"I need a quick bathroom break," she murmured.

"Wait." She took a deep breath as the roiling subsided. "No. Crisis avoided."

Two lines creased between Kit's brows. "Sure you're okay?"

She beamed. "I've never been happier." Not since the two lines on the pregnancy test confirmed her suspicions. A Christmas present she and Kit would have the rest of their lives. Picking up Annie's bouquet, she walked to the door and turned, resting her hand low on her belly.

It took a minute for her gesture to sink in. He gulped even as a broad smile creased his face. "Serious, sweet girl?"

She nodded and held out her hand.

He took it and pressed his lips to the ring, the one he slipped on her finger on New Year's Eve.

"Excited?" she asked with a giddy laugh.

He scooped her up and walked her over the shop's threshold and into the sunlight. His ear-to-ear smile the perfect answer. "Our future won't be calm, but it sure will be bright."

Snowed in at Copper Ridge Lodge

BY MAISEY YATES

To everyone who needs a little Christmas magic.
May your days be merry and bright!

Chapter One

Mia Landry had fought tooth and nail to get up the mountain. Because nothing, nothing was going to stop her from spending Christmas with her best friend's family.

The Graysons were the closest thing to a functional family she had ever known. She'd started spending holidays with them in Copper Ridge, Oregon, back when she was a kid. Her mother had never understood that.

Why she opted to go out into the middle of nowhere and spend summer on a farm when she could spend it at their family home in New England was beyond her mother. But her mother was always grateful to extend the time between her daughter's visits. So she hadn't looked into it deeply.

If she'd known Mia had spent the Fourth of July with grass stains on her knees, dirt on her bare feet, and pie on her face, that she'd spent Christmas sledding down mountainsides and wandering through the woods behind the farm, freezing rain dripping from the trees and sliding down the back of her coat, then Mia imagined her mother wouldn't have been quite so relaxed about it.

But that was where the distance worked in Mia's favor.

Trying to gear up to face the cold wind, Mia opened the door on the rental car and shrieked when sleet blew straight into her eyes. She swore, then got out of the car, doing her best not to slip on the icy driveway, bracing herself on the door as she slammed it shut.

She leaned against the car, surveying the grounds. Everything up here was white. She had spent several Christmases in Copper Ridge over the years, but typically she stayed down in town with the Graysons. This year, Joshua, the youngest Grayson brother, had insisted that they converge on a lodge up in the mountains east of the town.

All well and good, except, apparently, prone to snowstorms.

She had heard something about that on the radio. Something about the storm of the century blowing through the western United States, but, given that she had spent the past two years living in Portland and they used the word "snowpocalypse" to denote the presence of three flakes on the ground, she was somewhat inured to dramatic proclamations of weather.

She could certainly see the attraction to spending Christmas up in the Copper Mountain Range. It was like a Christmas card. Only the thinnest sliver of green peeking out from beneath the blanket of snow on each evergreen bough. The lodge itself was nowhere near as rustic as Mia had imagined.

It was closed in by trees, constructed of honey-colored logs, a broad river rock chimney rising up from the middle of the green, steep-pitched roof. In spite of the fact that its basic ingredients were rustic by their very nature, the structure itself was almost elegant in a way.

She supposed that reflected the change in the family's economic status. Her best friend, Faith, was quickly becoming one of the most famous architects in the country. The company that she ran with her brothers was spearheaded by Isaiah's brilliant business mind and her other brother Joshua's PR skills.

Only the middle brother, Devlin, wasn't involved in the firm at all. Which really didn't surprise Mia at all. Devlin was . . . Well, he was uniquely Devlin. Sometimes she was completely certain he did things just to be in opposition to what everyone else was doing.

All this money at his family's disposal now. But as far as Devlin was concerned, that didn't give him a right to it. And it didn't give him a sudden desire to go work in the glass and steel building his siblings had in Seattle. No. Instead, he had opted to continue on with a life of ranching. Not what his mother and father had wanted, which Mia knew because his mother had confided in her the last time they had visited.

Mia always felt a little bit twitchy whenever Devlin was brought up, especially in the presence of his parents. Like they could see down into her thoughts. Her thoughts that she tried really hard to control. But it was inevitable. His name came up and her cheeks started to feel warm.

Not just because she felt . . . well, protective of him in a way, though that was part of it. She was proud of his ranching spread in Copper Ridge, and of all he'd accomplished. But also because she had a case of the long-standing hots for him that could never, ever become anything.

She cared too much about the Grayson family to compromise her place with them by doing something as ridiculous as making a move on Devlin. And anyway, he was immune to her.

She pushed those thoughts to the side as she did a controlled slide to the trunk of her car and popped it open. She reached inside, grabbing hold of her suitcase, but as she did, her feet slipped forward, her shins butting up against the bumper, stopping her from falling on her butt, but still leaving her in a precarious position.

She swore again, tugging on the suitcase, putting one hand down on the bumper and pulling hard. Then, suddenly, it was like the suitcase didn't weigh anything at all.

"Careful," came a low, masculine voice from behind her. And that was when she realized she wasn't the only one holding the suitcase.

She jerked back, and found herself falling again, but just as quickly found herself braced against a hard, hot wall.

She was no longer holding her suitcase, and she was being propped up by a strong body and an equally strong arm.

"Hi there, chipmunk."

Oh, that voice. That nickname. Given to her at a time when her cheeks had been much rounder, and her braces had yet to do their good work on her teeth. Only one person still called her that.

She looked up, her heart slamming into her breastbone. "Devlin. You're here already."

DEVLIN GRAYSON LOOKED down at the petite bundle of irritation he currently held in his arms. He could honestly say that of all the times he had ever thought of getting his hands on Mia Landry, this was not quite the position he imagined them in.

Usually sleek, she seemed a bit more askew than normal. Her dark brown bob flopped forward into her eyes, one end of her scarf trailing much lower than the rest. And, when he had approached the car, he had heard her curse, and he was pretty sure he had never heard a swearword come out of that prim, proper mouth of hers.

Yeah, the low-class Grayson family had done their part to turn the cosseted rich girl into a redneck, but he hadn't realized they'd gotten quite that far.

That made him wonder about other ways he might corrupt her. But, as was his habit, he simply gritted his teeth until the rising heat passed. Then he released his hold on her, setting her firmly on her feet and keeping the suitcase in his possession.

"How were the roads?" he asked, walking ahead of her and making his way toward the lodge.

"Horrifying. How long have you been here?"

"I came in last night, and it looks like it's a good thing too." He looked around at the snow that was starting to fall faster, piling up on the ground.

"Is anyone else here?" He did not miss the hopeful note in her voice.

"Nope," he tossed back, keeping his tone purposefully cheerful.

"Perfect," she muttered, her footsteps audible behind him as they made their way up the porch.

"But I'm here, and you can be grateful for that. Since I saved you from falling into a snowbank, and also have a fire going." He opened the front door and pushed the suitcase in, then stood there, holding the door open for her.

She walked in behind him, stepping into the entryway and brushing snowflakes off her shoulders and arms before removing her coat. "I am grateful for you, Devlin. Did I not say that?"

"No," he said.

"Well, thank you for keeping me from falling into a snowbank."

"You're very welcome. Are you going to fly back East for actual Christmas?" It was currently a couple of weeks until the blessed event, but because of everybody's schedules they were having their festivities a little bit early.

His mother and father didn't care if their children had other plans. No, they insisted that they all spend certain holidays together, even if they had to move the holiday. But then, that summed up his parents. Caring and involved to a fault.

"No. Likely I will be sitting in my apartment eating Chinese take-out. But that's preferable to going back to my parents' house for the holidays."

"They're still married, huh?" He didn't know the full story of Mia's home life, but he had absorbed a fair amount from comments she made over the years, and from things his sister, Faith, had said.

It seemed to him that she had lived in something of a nightmare. Nothing abusive, but the kind of distant disapproval that could drive you nuts eventually. Death by a thousand cuts.

When he had first met her, she had been thirteen years old. Pale and drawn, with large eyes, and almost shaking with nerves. Over the years, he had watched her open up, watched her grow in confidence. And she had grown from a girl into a woman. Regrettably, his body had noticed that change with a hell of a lot of enthusiasm.

But there was no way he was ever going to go there. She was eight years younger than he and more than eight times sweeter. She'd gone to a private school for smart kids, like his sister. Gone to college and graduated. She read books for fun. She needed some guy who could handle her with care, who could give her forever. Give her the kind of life she was accustomed to. Something soft, something genteel. She lived in the damn city.

He was never going to be that man for her. He'd barely dragged his ass through school, his dyslexia making reading a form of torture so great he would honestly rather do hard manual labor than submit himself to reading a novel. They had nothing in common. They never would.

So he was hardly going to put his hands on her and risk causing more damage than her upbringing already had. Not going to indulge himself, and his attraction to her, when he knew that it wasn't going to go anywhere.

"Yes," Mia said, bringing his focus back to the present. "Still wandering around the same giant house avoiding each other as much as they can and flinging extremely arch barbs at each other whenever possible. The usual."

He chose his words carefully. "All families fight, I guess."

"I prefer the Grayson brand of fighting. Where you and your brothers either punch each other or flip each other off, then get over it."

"Now," he said, "in fairness, I haven't punched Joshua in at least a year."

She snorted. "Sure."

He watched her face carefully when he mentioned Joshua. Joshua was the kind of man a woman like Mia should be with. His brother was smart, owned a suit, and had several million in the bank. Yeah, he was the kind of guy she deserved.

And he had often wondered if Mia might set her sights on him, considering she was close to being a member of the family anyway, and a relationship between the two of them would make that connection more binding.

But he didn't see anything telling in her expression at the mention of Joshua's name.

"Come on," he said, grabbing hold of the suitcase, needing to get out of this closed-in space, "you can choose your bedroom."

"I get to choose?" she asked, trailing behind him as he carried her suitcase up the sweeping staircase.

"Sure. As long as it's not the room I chose."

This time, he did see a reaction on her face. Her cheeks turned bright pink, those large eyes glittering. And he felt a response deep down in his gut, a tightening, followed by a feeling that was a lot like hunger.

"Why would I choose the room you chose?" she asked, the words coming out quickly, prickly.

This was how his interactions with Mia always went. Eventually, something happened to create this crackle between them, and she got irritated. As if she could see through him, see all the dirty fantasies he had about her. Judging by her reaction, she didn't like it.

Lucky for her, he was never going to act on it.

"To be contrary," he said, moving resolutely down the hall. He pushed open one of the doors. "Here you'll find a stately room with a reindeer comforter. Can't beat that." He moved down farther, kicking open another door. "And here you have . . . Well, damn, there are Christmas lights around the bed."

"I'll take the very festive door number two," she said, brushing past him and grabbing hold of her suitcase handle, tugging it toward her.

As she did so, her fingers brushed against his, sending a lightning bolt of heat through his body. Damn it, he had no idea how she was able to affect him like this. She was . . . She was sweet. And if there was one thing Devlin Grayson was not, it was sweet.

He'd slept with more women than he could count,

and the fact that Mia Landry persisted in being his most cherished, most forbidden fantasy when he had once slept with a woman who could tie a cherry stem with her tongue, and was able to demonstrate the practical application of that on his body, was beyond a joke.

His pocket vibrated, and he reached inside to pull out his phone, grateful for the interruption. "Hello?"

"It's Joshua."

"What's up?"

"Nothing," his younger brother said, his voice sounding rough and exhausted. "Other than the fact that we're stuck down in town. Faith is stranded at the airport in Seattle, and can't fly into Portland because of the fog, and the road up to the lodge has now been closed until conditions improve."

"What?" He looked over at Mia, who had released her hold on her bag and was standing there staring at him like she was trying to decipher the muffled sounds she could hear coming through the phone.

"Isaiah and I are in town with Mom and Dad, who are very unhappy, Faith is still in Washington, and we can't get up to the cabin." Joshua repeated the information as if Devlin was stupid. Which was par for the damn course, really.

"Well, why the hell don't they just plow the road?"

"It's a low priority. It's not a regular route. They've got all snowplows on deck dealing with roads that lead up to people's houses, or run through towns. Do you have Mia's number by any chance, or should I have Faith call her and tell her not to start driving in?"

He looked over at Mia. "I'll handle it," he said, not quite sure why he didn't make it known that Mia was there. "And, hey, when you get here I'll have the fire going for you."

"Great. I will appreciate that. If Mom doesn't worry my ear off before then."

"Better you than me," Devlin said, and he meant it.

His brother ended the call with some choice words, and Devlin smiled, then frowned as the full implication of the situation sank in.

"That was Joshua," he said. "They can't make it up. The road is closed."

"So they're stuck in Copper Ridge?"

"Seems like it."

Mia blinked slowly. "And that means . . . Well, that means that we're stuck up here."

Yes, they were. That meant that he was snowed in, alone, with Mia Landry.

Chapter Two

MIA COULDN'T QUITE process the implications of what Devlin had just said. At least, not quickly. Not without her mind taking some very strange detours.

They were stuck here. Alone. Together. Well, she supposed you couldn't actually be alone *with* someone. Then you were just with someone.

But when that someone was Devlin Grayson it was problematic to say the least.

She should think of him like family. She really should; it was how she thought of everyone else in the Grayson family. Joshua, Isaiah, Faith. But never Devlin.

Not from the first moment she had seen that green-eyed, sandy-haired boy with dirt on his face, and broad shoulders and muscular forearms from all the work he did outdoors.

He had made her heart flutter then, made her stomach

twist. But he had done his best to shove her back at a distance and keep her there since that moment.

Oh, he was friendly in his way. But he was also crude, blunt, and not in any way interested in coddling her.

He was also . . . Well, Faith had told her more than once about the kinds of exploits her brother got up to. He was a manwhore, for lack of a more sophisticated term. Mia wholeheartedly disapproved of that kind of behavior. Basically, she disapproved of him in general. His language, his tattoos, his muscles, and the fact that no matter how hard she tried, she was never going to be immune to them.

"So, we're stuck here?" She knew that she sounded a little desperate, possibly breathless also, which she didn't mean to, but she did. "Alone. Just the two of us."

"You sound like I just told you I'm carrying a deadly disease."

"Well, I don't know your life, Devlin."

He laughed and started to drag her suitcase into the bedroom. She took two big steps backward, realizing that that put the two of them in the small space together. "What are you doing?" she asked.

"Helping with your bag," he said, lifting it up in one fluid motion and depositing it in the center of the bed. "The word you're looking for is thanks."

"Do we have food?" she asked, suddenly remembering that Christmas dinner had been in possession of the remaining Graysons back in Copper Ridge.

He frowned, deep grooves bracketing either side of

his lips. That should . . . Well, it shouldn't be sexy. But it was. "There's some. I ate in town before coming up, but there was cereal for breakfast, and milk. I think whoever rents out the lodge put some basics in here."

"Good. Because I would hate to be forced to consume your body if things get Donner party up in here."

He lifted a brow. "You are not the first woman who has talked about devouring me, but you might be the first one to mean it literally."

Heat washed through her. Because that conjured up images of putting her mouth on him. On his neck, maybe his bare chest. His lips.

She hadn't kissed a man in a long time. And the last time she had, the experience had been something of an unmitigated disaster. Panic had set in the moment his hands had wandered from a secure position at the center of her back and begun migrating downward.

She was pretty sure she had hit him. Yeah, it was bad.

Though, when she thought about kissing Devlin, panic was not the immediate response.

Still, she never knew when panic like that would strike. It was an old enemy, her anxiety. One that she had learned a lot of tricks to master along the way, but one that she imagined would be with her in some form or another for the rest of her life. It helped, knowing what it was. Knowing that the vague, unsettled feeling that would press itself over her chest sometimes was coming from inside her, rather than external forces. But that didn't make it go away.

She shook her head, redirecting herself to the present. "Come on. Let's forage."

She walked past him, taking the stairs two at a time as she made her way to the ground floor. Then she realized she didn't know which way the kitchen was. She took a moment to admire the grand living room, with floor-to-ceiling windows that looked out over the mountainside. It was a blanket of white out there, the sky an endless wall of gray that seemed to be encroaching on them.

The whole space was decorated with garlands, wound with deep red velvet ribbon; white Christmas lights; and a Christmas tree with coordinating ornaments. There was a red sled propped against the wall, lit up like the rest of the decorations, clearly a prop more than anything practical.

"Well, they don't go halfway," she said, looking around.

"The owners of the lodge, or my brothers and sister?"

"Both," she decided. "Which way to the kitchen?"

"Due north," he said.

He pointed in that direction, and the sleeve on his sweater rode up, giving her a glimpse of the ink that was hidden beneath the fabric. She wondered if he had gotten any new tattoos since she had seen him in short sleeves last summer. And then she gave herself a mental slap, because she should not be wondering about Devlin's tattoos.

She was not the kind of woman who was into tattoos. She lived a quiet life. She had a cat. She had an apartment.

She often ate cereal for dinner. She had the flexibility to work from home for the graphic design company that employed her, and she often exercised that flexibility in her pajamas.

Simple. Soft. Cozy.

All things that Devlin Grayson most certainly was not.

He was complicated, hard, and . . . Well, he might be cozy. It was likely that were she to rest her head on that broad, sweater-covered chest, he would be a bit cozy.

Suddenly, her hands itched to stroke the fabric of his sweater. She curled those wayward fingers into fists and balled them up resolutely at her side.

The kitchen was no less grand, and no less decorated. Lights wound around everything, making all of the stainless steel appliances sparkle. "That is the most festive refrigerator I've ever seen," she said.

"I'm going to reserve my judgment on that." He walked over to it, opening up the door. "Okay. There's beer. So, festive works for me as a descriptor."

"Men. Everything is not about beer. I want to know if there's food."

He frowned, peering deeper inside the fridge. "Not much. There's a loaf of bread back there. Some cheese. Butter. So, basically everything we need for kick-ass grilled cheese. Oh, and there's Coke."

"All right, you work on the sandwiches, I'm going to hunt down some tomato soup."

He pulled a face. "Why would you do that?"

She rolled her eyes. "Devlin, we are not animals. Opposable thumbs, and the use of them to dip our sandwiches in soup, is what separates us from our four-legged counterparts."

"Guess I'm an animal, then," he said, a wicked smile curving his lips upward. She didn't know why she thought of the smile as wicked. She imagined he didn't think of it that way. But something inside her registered it as such. No matter how sternly she lectured herself.

"Then use your thumbs to hold the spatula, and maybe I won't judge you too much."

Her search turned out to be fruitful. After digging through a few cupboards she found a dusty can of soup and some saltine crackers. She set about heating the soup on the stove.

Suddenly, Devlin was next to her, with two sandwiches in a pan that he placed on the burner next to hers. He looked at her and grinned, his elbow brushing up against hers as he adjusted the heat on the stovetop.

This was . . . Well, this was a strange sort of intimacy.

Anytime she had been with Devlin before, she had had his family around, distracting from the general fluttery feeling she felt. Right now, there was no distraction. Right now, they were somehow cooking together like they were . . . a couple or something.

She swallowed hard, stirring the soup lazily, then taking a step back. "I'll check on it again in a second," she mumbled.

Devlin didn't hear her, or if he did, he didn't consider it worthy of a response. She leaned back against the island, watching as he stood there, all broad-shouldered and narrow-waisted, filling up the space in a way that bordered on indecent.

Right now, with her defenses lowered, she had to admit that—suitable or not, her theoretical type or not—Devlin was the sexiest man she had ever seen.

The only man who had the ability to drive her to sexual fantasy. At least without an accompanying skin-crawling bout of anxiety.

Well, there was anxiety. About what it would mean to her connection with the family. About the fact that he would obviously reject any kind of advance she made. But the anxiety wasn't about the . . . the intimacy. The nudity. The touching.

She had hang-ups. Serious hang-ups.

She had never talked to anybody about it. Not even Faith. She hadn't wanted to tell her friend that she had made it all the way through college without ever having sex with anyone. Without ever even seriously making out with anyone.

If it had been a conscious choice, that would have been one thing. She would never have been embarrassed by that. But it wasn't. She wanted to. Her body was willing . . . Her brain just couldn't quite deal.

She hadn't actually talked to a therapist or anything, but she had watched enough crap therapy on TV that she was pretty sure she had figured out why. Her family wasn't physically affectionate. At all. And when it came to self-expression . . . Well, that wasn't even a thing. It was all brittle, repressed silence. And anything that pushed her outside of being controlled made her feel panicky. Anxious.

Well, there was very little control involved in arousal. And when she felt her body heating up, when any kind of noises she hadn't given herself express permission to make came out of her, she just shut down.

Everything worked fine when she was by herself, however. In that she was able to orgasm just fine as long as there was no audience.

Which put a damper on the whole sex thing.

Right at the moment, watching Devlin cook, she felt . . . Well, she was starving. Not just for the sandwiches.

"Is something on your mind or are you going to stand there burning holes into my back with your eyes?"

She startled, clutching her hands to her chest. Like something in her blue blood was genetically predisposed to look for pearls to clutch, even though she knew there were none there.

He was staring at her hard, and she felt herself blushing. And in that moment she saw a glint of something in his eyes, some kind of knowledge that made her feel . . . angry. He was standing there looking at her like he knew something about her that she didn't.

It was every horrible, socially anxious moment she'd had with men rolled into one. That he could see she thought he was hot. That he could also see she couldn't handle him. And that she was a sad, twenty-three-year-old virgin who got sweaty at the mere thought of kissing a man's lips.

"I'm just . . . thinking about . . ." She struggled to force out words. "Sandwiches."

"Hmmm," he said, a very masculine kind of sound that rumbled in his chest. And seemed to resonate inside her. A sound that was as knowing as that look. A sound that said he didn't believe her. "Sandwiches are a pretty compelling topic."

"Very practical food, the sandwich," she said. "A fulfiller of many . . . needs." She nearly choked on that last word.

"Oh yeah," he agreed. "I like sandwiches all the time. Morning sandwiches. Those I particularly like. But a little bit of a late-night sandwich is good too."

She couldn't tell if they had officially gone straight into double entendre territory, or if it just felt like that to her because her thoughts had been prurient.

"I really haven't had as much experience with sandwiches as I would like." She said that to test where they were at, what exactly he thought they were talking about.

He whipped around to face her, something in his expression intense. And she regretted all the choices she had made that had led to this moment. Because she had written a check that, quite simply, her inexperienced ass was not prepared to cash.

"Really?"

"I've never tried rye bread," she said, trying to cover herself now. "And I've never tried bánh mi. They have those everywhere in Portland, and I've still never tried it."

"Are you literally talking about sandwiches right now, or has this taken a very strange turn?"

"That depends," she said, swallowing hard. It really did. It depended on whether he had known she was checking him out. Because that was kind of the hinge of the whole sandwiches-as-sex metaphor.

He picked up the pan, turning to face her, sliding the spatula beneath one sandwich and flipping it. "Depends on what?"

"Whether or not *you're* talking about sandwiches?"

He pressed the spatula beneath the second sandwich, then flipped it too. "Well, I'm cooking sandwiches."

"Yes," she said, "you are. Which is why it is not . . . it is not unreasonable for me to have been thinking about sandwiches in the first place."

Something in his expression hardened, his eyes getting a little too sharp. She felt like they had pierced her façade. Like he could see inside her. See all the things she tried so hard to keep hidden. "Come clean with me, Mia. Were you looking at my ass?"

Her whole face felt like it had been pushed into a wood stove. "I . . . I was not." She hadn't been. She had just been looking at him and ruminating about sex. That was completely different. Now, she had looked at his butt before. But this was not that moment.

"You're very red."

"And you're very rude." She shut the burner off and left her spoon in the pan. "I don't know very many men who would broach such a topic." She sniffed, and then felt immediately irritated with herself. She really couldn't play the part of prude better if she tried.

"Right," he said, "but you know me. Manners, all that,

never bothered me much. But I do want to know if you were checking me out."

"That is . . . that is hardly the best topic for us to be on considering we are snowed in."

"Well, that all depends."

"Depends on what?"

"On whether or not you want to do something about it. Because I had a look in the game closet and there aren't very many board games. So we might need another activity to occupy us tonight."

Chapter Three

HE HAD ONLY meant to tease her a little bit. He hadn't meant to take it so far. But she was stammering, and she was blushing, and it was the first time he had ever gotten the feeling that Mia might not be immune to him after all.

But it had now gone a hell of a lot farther than he had intended it to. Sure, giving her a hard time was something that he did, but it didn't usually have a sexual undertone. Correction, it never did. Because he was far too aware of his own inappropriate attraction to her, and he had never wanted to take things into that territory.

The way she had been looking at him just now . . . Unless she was looking at the sandwich. Who knew? Maybe she had a serious affinity for cheese.

However, in his experience, illicit thoughts of cheddar didn't make women blush like that.

"I . . . I . . . I brought a book," she said finally. "I will be entertained. Also, I know so many Christmas carols. We could sing. We would never run out of songs."

She was nervous, her gestures becoming broad and somehow timid at the same time. There was something mouselike about them.

And suddenly, a switch flipped inside him. All of the control he had exercised for the past ten years crumbling like a house of sand. Until this moment he had held himself back, in part because he had never wanted to push her into something. Had never wanted to be the one to instigate.

But she wanted him. He could see it. As suddenly and clearly as if she had written it across her face. Oh, she might not fully realize it, but she did.

And, now that he had seen it, he couldn't go back to the way things had been before.

"I don't want to sing songs."

"Because you want to . . . eat grilled cheese?"

"I want to see something." He was a crazy bastard, there really was no other explanation for what he was about to do. If Mia sent out an SOS to his family, telling them what he had done, then they would probably ostracize him and keep her in the fold. But it was a risk he was going to have to take. A risk brought on by the spark he had seen in those beautiful brown eyes of hers when he had caught her looking at him like he was what she wanted to have for dinner.

He set the pan down on the counter, and then he closed the distance between them. She backed up, her bottom butting up against the island, hands gripping the edge of the counter tightly. He made her nervous, and that should make him feel like a dick.

Instead, he just felt like his whole body, every damn cell, his skin, his bones, were bleeding the word "finally." He had wanted Mia Landry for so damn long, and in every other area of his life he didn't know the meaning of the word "restraint."

He worked hard, he played hard, he fucked hard.

But never her. Ever. Because she had been off-limits. Because she was too soft. Because she was too sweet. But now, all those things that she was very much too much of were the very reasons he wasn't going to resist anymore.

He reached out, curling his hand behind her neck and drawing her forward. He wasn't as gentle as he should have been, he knew that, but he couldn't modify either. He was shaking. Damn it, he couldn't remember the last time a woman had made him shake. Maybe back when he'd been a sixteen-year-old virgin getting busy in the back of a truck.

But he wasn't sixteen. And he sure as hell wasn't a virgin.

"What are you—"

He didn't let her finish that sentence. Instead, he brought his lips down onto hers, and the world exploded behind his eyelids.

She was sweet, just as sweet as he had thought she would be. Her lips soft, impossibly soft. Maybe all lips were this soft, maybe all kisses felt like a long, slow lick from his mouth down to his cock. But if they did, he didn't remember. He couldn't. Couldn't remember any other kiss but this, couldn't remember any woman besides her.

She wasn't skilled. She didn't return the kiss. She just stood there. She didn't put her arms around him, didn't touch him in any way. But she didn't make her mouth tight, didn't move to pull away from him. He angled his head, sliding his tongue against the seam of her lips, and she reacted. Her hips jerking forward, away from the counter, a gasp escaping, allowing him deeper entry.

Still, she didn't put her hands on him. He wanted those hands on him.

Then it hit him suddenly that not only had he made a move on his little sister's best friend, the one woman he had always been so determined he wouldn't touch, he had done so when they were trapped. Trapped and alone. Great.

If his aim had been to scare her, he had probably accomplished it.

He pulled away from her, which was the hardest damn thing he had ever done, his breath being pulled from his lungs in great handfuls.

"What just happened?" she asked, her hands still gripping the edge of the counter, her knuckles white.

"Don't worry," he said, taking a step away from her, his voice sounding a lot more cut up than he meant it to. "I'm not going to force myself on you or anything."

She frowned. "I didn't think you would."

"Well, we're stuck here."

"Now that you mention that, I can see why you felt

the need to clarify." She blinked, then swallowed audibly, nodding her head slowly. "You kissed me."

"Yes," he said, "I did."

"You've never kissed me before. And, you've never seemed like you wanted to kiss me before."

"Yeah well, I'm mysterious and shit."

"Not usually. Usually, you're about as subtle as . . . well, anything that isn't subtle. I can't metaphor right now. My brain is scrambled."

"My kiss scrambled your brain, chipmunk?"

His gut tightened while he waited for the answer, and he called himself ten kinds of fool for worrying either way. It was Mia. And there was nothing in the world he could do about that damn attraction that sat low in his gut, that damn well of feelings for her that existed in his heart. Nothing at all.

"Actually, it didn't scare me." She looked like she was full of wonderment.

"It didn't . . . scare you?"

"No. It wasn't . . . I didn't feel . . . I wasn't afraid. Your lips touched mine, and I felt . . . I felt a lot. I felt it down low and, you know . . . it turned me on. But I didn't . . ." She was blushing furiously now, and if he had any kind of compassion he would probably stop her, change the subject, let it go.

But he was a bastard.

"It turned you on?" He wanted to hear her say it again.

"Yes. You're a . . . Well, you're a very good kisser. And you should be, given your level of experience."

Something about that hit him square in the chest,

made him feel something hot and sick that reminded him a lot of shame, or at least shame as he had always imagined it might feel. "Sure. Do something enough and you are likely to reach a certain level of proficiency. And I've never had any complaints," he said.

"That's very interesting. All of this is very interesting."

"Mia," he said, "you have that look in your eye like the time you and Faith decided you were going to sneak out and go to that college party in the old McIntyre barn when the two of you were fifteen."

She scowled. "I'm not fifteen. Also, you told on us."

"Damn straight."

"And then *you* went."

"Yeah, well, I was old enough to drink." He shook his head. "And that is a fantastic reminder of why I should not have kissed you."

"Hey, I'm old enough to drink now," she said, and his dick was more than happy to take that as solid reasoning.

"Are you propositioning me, chipmunk? Because you should know that if you come near me again, it's not going to stop as a kiss. I don't want a bite of the sandwich, I want the whole sandwich. I'm a guy, that's how it works." That wasn't it. It wasn't at all. It wasn't just because he was a man, and she was a woman, and they were snowed in. It wasn't just because sex was more fun than board games—though it was. It was because of her. Because of her, and because of him. Because of all those feelings he had never quite been able to exorcise, no matter how much he knew they needed to be.

"What if I was?" She released her hold on the counter, straightening her diminutive frame and staring him down.

It was the strangest damn thing. To look at her and see the girl she had been, that quiet, withdrawn teenager who had blossomed in the Oregon coastal air during the months she spent with his family, right along with the woman she was now.

And that was the thing. She was a woman now. With a woman's needs, a woman's experience. If she wanted sex, who was he to protect her from it? Yeah, he had this idea that she deserved more than he could give, but was that really his decision to make?

His penis rationale was really on point tonight. He would give it that.

"If you are, you had better be certain."

She nodded. "I think I am. Devlin . . . I need you to take my virginity."

Chapter Four

She kind of wished she could go back in time, stuff her grilled cheese into her mouth quickly to keep those words from escaping, then swallow them down along with her sandwich. But it was too late. The words had tumbled out. Just like the kiss had happened. Just like she had admitted to liking it. All of those things had happened, and now she was just standing there in the kitchen of this beautiful lodge, with the snow falling outside and twinkle lights doing their twinkly things all around them while her proposition hung in the air.

Devlin was just staring at her. His green eyes were unreadable, but they glinted with that same predatory light they had taken on when he had begun to move toward her earlier. That same sharpness that she had seen just before his head had descended and his mouth had met hers.

That kiss had been a revelation. Heat had exploded

inside her. More intense than any she had ever known. And there had been no panic. None at all.

Because . . . because it was Devlin. So for some reason it had felt okay. Right, even, that he should kiss her.

It made her wonder. It made her wonder if all she needed was a man she trusted. A man she knew. Yes, she and Devlin didn't always see eye to eye. Yes, there were things about him that were a mystery. And often he was a bit more of a slightly cranky acquaintance to her than a friend. But still, she trusted him. When he had said that he wouldn't force himself on her. she had almost laughed, because she trusted him that much.

So much that even with the kiss, being snowed in with him, she knew that he wouldn't take advantage of her. Unless she asked him to. Which she had just done.

"You what?" Devlin asked, finally speaking after what had seemed like minutes of silence, when she was sure it had only been seconds.

"When I said I hadn't tried very many sandwiches, what I meant was that I'm a virgin." *Wow, way to make it worse.* "And please, don't say anything to anyone about that. Because nobody knows. Not even Faith."

"Trust me, I'm not going to say anything to anyone about this, ever."

Of course not. Because it would be complicated. Oh, what had she been thinking? Now they had kissed, now she had told him she was a virgin, and she had asked him to help her deal with it. This man who she was going to have to see after this. No matter what happened. But then, that was okay, wasn't it?

He was the kind of guy who had relationships that were physical only. The kind of guy who was well-equipped to deal with that. Running into people he'd hooked up with before. Hell, he hooked up in a small town that he lived in, so pretty much that was his life.

And there was something romantic about that. Losing her virginity to someone she knew. Someone she would always have good feelings for. Someone she'd *always* had feelings for.

Or maybe she was just jumbled up because she was turned on, and for the first time that didn't mean fighting the urge to run away.

"Well, perfect. Because here we are snowed in, and there's nobody else here. And . . . and apparently we have chemistry."

Well, she had always known she'd had some kind of sick fascination with him, she just didn't know it went both ways. Or maybe it didn't. Maybe he had just been messing with her. For the first time since the kiss, a bit of anxiety tap-danced around in her stomach. "We do, right? You kissing me meant that . . . meant that you think I'm pretty?" Wow, that could not have sounded more pathetic if she'd tried.

The familiar, sick sensation began to overtake her. She took a deep breath in through her nose and let it out slowly. But then Devlin was moving toward her again, this time bracketing her cheeks with both of his hands and leaning in to press a quick, hard kiss to her lips. "That," he said, pulling away, his breathing ragged, "is an understatement."

She couldn't quite believe it. That Devlin Grayson, known bad boy and spreader of his masculine charms, thought she was pretty. That he was attracted to her. That the kiss had done something to him.

"I don't want you to take my virginity if you don't really want me," she mumbled, feeling embarrassed still.

"Mia," he said, "feel this." He grabbed her wrist, pulled her hand forward, and pressed it against the front of his jeans. "Men can't fake that. I want you."

Her whole face lit up like wildfire, but she wasn't afraid. Instead, she pressed more deeply against him, testing the weight and length of him through the denim. "Oh," she said, "oh my."

"It's not a good idea," he said.

"Maybe not," she said. "But if it's not you, I don't know who it's going to be. I tried . . ." She swallowed hard, her throat dry. "I have tried, but every time a guy gets close enough I panic. And with you . . . it didn't feel scary. This doesn't feel scary."

"So," he said slowly, "what you're saying is . . . I'm the fuzzy blanket of sexual experiences?" He didn't sound overly happy about that characterization.

"No. I didn't say that."

He advanced on her, a predatory gleam in his eye. "Let's get one thing straight, Mia. You're safe with me. No matter what. Whether you change your mind about this at the last minute, or you want to go full speed ahead, I promise you I'm going to keep you safe. But I'm not a teddy bear. You sleep with me tonight, and you're not going to end up peacefully cuddled next to me. There's nothing soft about me." He tightened his hold on her wrist, pressed her palm more firmly against his length, and then drew her hand up to his stomach, across the flat planes of his ab muscles, and up to his well-defined chest. "And just because you're a virgin, because you never met a man who made the kissing good enough to make all that other stuff fade into the background, I'm not going to take it easy on you. I'm going to demand a lot. But I'm going to give you a lot. And if you're all right with that . . . Then yes, we'll do this. But if you're expecting me to turn the lights off and let you leave your nightgown on while I dispense with things quickly and easily, you have the wrong guy."

Heat swept over her, along with a strange sense of relief. And still, there was no fear. This was the right choice. He was the right man. She knew it, with a kind of bone-deep certainty she had never imagined feeling in this moment. Part of her had always believed it would happen with extreme awkwardness, or with some nice guy who had opted to stick around even though it had taken her months to get over her issues with physical intimacy.

This was . . . Well, it was spontaneous, and exciting. A combination she hadn't imagined she could have. And it was with Devlin. Who was something of a fantasy, even though it had always been difficult for her to admit that, even to herself.

Another thing she had never told her best friend, obviously. That she harbored secret daydreams of watching Devlin pour a bucket of water over his head, and seeing all the water trail down his muscles. She had come close to that once. They had been horsing around with a hose and mud in the thick of the summer when Mia had been fourteen, and Devlin had come and thrown dirt them, then hosed himself off, shirtless, right in front of them.

He had only had a couple of tattoos then, but still, watching the water sluice over the ink, over his muscles, over his skin, had been a very formative kind of experience for her.

Maybe that was the heart of the issue. She had yet to find a man who made her feel like watching Devlin Grayson hose himself off had made her feel at fourteen. Except now. Except when he'd kissed her.

That had been better than those fluttery feelings that had taken root inside her back then. Possibly because she was a grown-up now, and she knew exactly what they meant. What she wanted.

They meant she wanted him.

"I promise you," she said, "the feelings that I have right now are not fuzzy blanket feelings."

"Good to know," he said, drawing her up more firmly against him so that she could feel every hardened inch.

Her knees went weak, but that had nothing to do with fear.

He gripped her chin between his thumb and forefinger, tilting her face upward. But he didn't close the distance between them. No. Instead, he just looked at her. And she had no choice but to look right back. To fully take on board the fact that this was Devlin. That she was about to kiss Devlin. About to do a whole lot more with him than that.

She would see him naked. And he would see her too. That freaked her out a little bit. But the counterbalance of being able to count each and every one of his tattoos, to finally have a chance to trace the lines of those incredible muscles . . . Yeah, that was worth any fear.

So maybe it was more than familiarity at play here. Maybe it was just the need to have something stronger as an incentive.

"This is my Christmas present," she said absently, fingertips trailing over his chest, his sweater soft, the muscles beneath hard.

"Is that so?"

"Yes," she responded, looking at his lips for a long moment before directing her gaze up to his. "And it couldn't have been planned more perfectly."

"No. Can't take credit for the weather."

She smiled. "Santa sent me a snowstorm." She stretched up onto her toes and this time she was the one who initiated the kiss. She was the one who pressed her lips against his. And oh, it was as glorious as the last. If not more so.

His mouth was firm and certain, his tongue slick against hers as he delved between her lips and tasted her like she was his very favorite dessert. Or the forgotten grilled cheese that was still sitting on the counter, perhaps.

He groaned, angling his head, pressing both palms between her shoulder blades and holding her tightly. No, definitely dessert. This was definitely a dessert kiss, not a grilled cheese kiss.

She had a feeling it was going to be dessert sex, not grilled cheese sex. And most certainly not fuzzy blanket sex.

But that was all right. For the first time in her life, Mia felt ready for that. To step outside her comfort zone. To be wild. To have hot and adventurous, instead of safe and secluded.

And this was the perfect chance. Completely isolated from the world. No chance of interruption. And no way for them to leave to get . . . anywhere. Anywhere at all. Like . . . a store. For . . .

She wrenched herself away from him. "Oh no!"

"What's that?" he asked, his chest heaving up and down with all the effort it was taking him to breathe. She related.

"Condoms," she said. "We are totally snowed in. Which means we can't leave to go get condoms. And I didn't bring any with me. I mean, why would I? *Virgin*."

A slow smile spread over his face. Then he chuckled. "Don't worry. I'm carrying."

"Condoms?"

"Of course."

"You . . . you brought condoms to the family Christmas weekend?"

"Look, you never know what's going to happen. Distressed motorist. One of my brothers could have brought a girlfriend who got tired of them over the course of the week . . ."

"Devlin! You're . . . shameless."

"Yes. And stop acting like it's a bad thing, Mia. You

want sex and I happen to have condoms, and a dick with a very loose grasp on morality. If anything, you should be acting grateful."

She couldn't help it. She laughed. Then, she covered her mouth, feeling suddenly self-conscious. "I'm sorry. I shouldn't laugh."

"Why shouldn't you laugh?"

"Because we're . . . Well, we're talking sex. We're about to have sex."

"As long as you don't laugh when I take my pants off, we're fine."

Some of her bravado suddenly drained. "I won't." She knew she wouldn't be laughing. Likely, she would be beset by virginal nerves.

As if he sensed her sudden trepidation, he curved his arm around her waist, sifting his fingers through her hair, kissing her a bit more gently this time. And then she found herself being swept up off the ground, held against his chest.

She blinked rapidly, reflexively curling her fingers around his T-shirt. "What are you doing?"

"Women love this stuff."

He swept her out of the kitchen, back toward the staircase, and she looped both arms around his neck, hanging on tightly, her heart thundering rapidly, an answering pulse beating between her legs. "We do?" She couldn't deny that she pretty much did, but she disliked the idea that he considered her reaction a foregone conclusion based on his previous experience.

Disliked it in a way that felt almost like jealousy.

Which was ridiculous. Since she was about to benefit from his vast range of experience, she should be grateful for those other women, not irritated at them. Still, she was in fact waffling between irritation and arousal.

He kissed her. Not tentative. Hard and firm while he continued to walk them both up the stairs. Then, his lips still pressed to hers, he whispered against them, "Yes, you do."

She couldn't argue at all that time.

Somehow, she had gone from the kitchen to the threshold of her bedroom with Devlin in record time, and she wasn't sure if she was ready. Her heart was doing cartwheels, and she was pretty sure if it gained enough momentum it was going to go straight up her throat and out of her mouth. She was nervous. But she was excited. And it was the excitement that kept her there. The excitement that kept her rooted to the spot when he set her down and grabbed hold of the suitcase he had left on the bed earlier.

He picked it up and dropped it on the floor none too gently.

"Hey!" she said. "I have breakables in there."

"I will replace them." He advanced on her. "I will replace every last one of them. But I can't bother with being careful just now."

He looked almost regretful when he said those words, and when he reached out, tracing the line of her jaw with his fingertips, the look intensified.

"Sorry," he said, his voice a thin rasp.

She didn't have a chance to ask what he was sorry for,

because he was kissing her again. And this time, he didn't keep his hands still. They moved down her waist, all the way down to her butt, and he growled as he cupped her there, then he slid them back up again, one large hand covering her breast.

She arched into his touch, following instinct rather than any kind of deep, feminine knowledge. He slid his thumb over one tightened nipple, then pinched her gently. She felt an answering arrow of pleasure pierce her at her core and she let out a hoarse cry of need in response.

That sound echoed in the empty room, and she waited. Waited for the shame that was usually associated with such a loss of control. She didn't feel it. It didn't come.

"You're magic," she said, knowing that she sounded as dazed as she felt.

"No," he said, angling his head and kissing her neck, that unexpected contact on such a sensitive part of her body making her shiver. "I'm just a man. And I might not be able to read for shit, I might see letters backward, but when it comes to women? I know what I'm doing."

"But you don't . . . you don't know all the right places on me," she said, mostly just to score points, to remind him that she wasn't just a faceless woman in a line of many. She wasn't sure why. It shouldn't matter. She should be happy to be one in a faceless line. Because what was happening between her and Devlin wasn't going to go any further than this snowstorm.

Wasn't going to last any longer than the flurries that were fluttering down on the landscape. When the snowplows were available, or the snow melted, or the roads were salted, whatever came first, this would be over.

So it shouldn't matter to her whether this was just generic sex for him. And yet, she found that it did. Because it wasn't for her. And it never would be. It was her first time, and it would always be her first time. Devlin Grayson would always be the first man to do this, the one who made it possible for her to be with anyone who came after. He would always matter. This would always matter.

She hadn't mattered to very many people in the world. Not even to her own parents. Was it so wrong to want to matter?

"You're right," he said, lifting his head. "I don't. I don't know all the right places on your body. But you're going to help me learn."

"I don't know what I'm doing."

"I do. But you're going to have to show me what feels good for you." He pushed his fingertips up beneath the edges of her sweater, his hot, rough hands making contact with the delicate skin beneath. She didn't have a moment to protest before he wrenched the garment up over her head, then reached back and unhooked her bra.

Cold air washed over her skin, and her nipples tightened, not just from the chill in the air. And he was . . . he was just looking at her. Looking at her like she was a marvel, a wonder, not just another woman he was seeing topless.

It made her want to cry, but if she cried he was definitely going to run out of the room.

"Touch me," she said, the words broken, ragged.

"You don't have to ask me twice." He reached out, cupping her again, this time without layers of fabric between them. He skimmed his thumb over her nipple and she shuddered, a wave of pleasure racking her body, arrowing down to that sensitive place between her thighs.

He reversed their positions, walking her backward toward the bed, kissing her deeply as he laid her down on top of the soft mattress. She opened her eyes, looked up, saw him surrounded by a halo provided by the Christmas lights that were draped all around the bed.

"The rest," he said, leaning forward and touching the button on her jeans.

"No," she said, shaking her head. "You first. You're my Christmas present."

He straightened, and then a slow smile spread over his lips. "Do you want to unwrap me yourself?"

She shook her head again. "No. I expect you to be a self-unwrapping Christmas present."

For a moment, she thought she saw a grave emotion flicker across his face. But it was gone before she could process it. And then he just smiled again. He reached down, grabbed the hem of his shirt, and pulled it slowly upward.

With each flex of his body, his ab muscles shifted, and before the shirt was halfway up, she counted her first tattoo. She couldn't quite tell what it was, the dark shape extending to his ribs around from his back. Then there was another one on his pectoral muscle, and when the sweater came off all the way, it revealed the full sleeve tattoos on both arms.

The way the swirls of ink and color accentuated his muscles made her throat tight. Made her mouth dry.

"Merry Christmas indeed," she said, not quite sure how she managed to speak the words.

And as soon as she did, she blushed. And he smiled.

"You don't have to be embarrassed. But I do think the blush is kind of pretty."

"Well, as long as I'm kind of pretty."

He leaned forward, bracing both hands on either side of her hips, pressing into the mattress, his eyes intense on hers. "Not kind of. Absolutely"—he leaned down, kissing her stomach—"incredible, heart-stopping beauty." He undid the button on her jeans, drawing the zipper down slowly, and she didn't have it in her to protest, and tell him that he promised to take off all his clothes before he saw to the business of removing hers.

She was way too fascinated with what he was doing to protest at all.

Way too invested in what he might do next. It turned out he was going to wrap those strong hands around the waistband of her panties, drawing them and her jeans down her legs, leaving her completely naked in front of him. She started to breathe quickly, shallow, ineffective breaths that made her dizzy.

He leaned his head forward again, kissing her just beneath her belly button before moving up slightly, tracing a circle around it with the tip of his tongue. And she got dizzy for an entirely different reason. If she was nervous, it was drowned with anticipation, with an intense need that was overtaking everything. Common sense, embarrassment, control.

"So very," he said, pressing a kiss to her inner thigh as he pushed her legs open slowly, "pretty."

Pinpricks of heat washed over her skin as she realized just how exposed she was to him now. Just how close he was to her. And then he pressed strong, firm fingers between her thighs, drawing that dampness that had built there up and over that sensitive bundle of nerves.

She gasped, her hips arching up off the bed. She reached out, grabbing hold of his wrist, not sure if she wanted to pull him away, or make his touch firmer. Not sure if desire was going to win out over embarrassment.

He flexed his wrist, pressing the heel of his palm harder into that place where she ached for him as he slid one finger deep inside her. Her mouth fell open on a silent scream that built in her chest but couldn't quite make its way out.

She arched her back, let her neck relax as she let go. Of everything. Of her need to control the situation. Of her desire to keep herself from being embarrassed. It didn't matter that he knew how much she wanted him. Didn't matter that he could feel for himself how wet she was. In fact, it was a good thing. Because he liked it. She could feel it in the attention he gave to her body. In the low, satisfied sounds he made as he continued to explore her.

Suddenly, he gripped her hips hard, drawing her forward as he dropped down to his knees on the edge of the bed. She was open to him, completely vulnerable, and trapped in his hold.

She lifted her head and opened her eyes slowly, transfixed by the sight of his head down there. By his arms wrapped around her very pale legs, his tanned skin, and the dark ink over the top of it standing out in intense contrast.

And then, he lowered his head. And stars exploded behind her eyes. He kissed her, right there. Followed by a long, slow glide of his tongue over her slick flesh. She was going to do . . . something. Protest maybe, because there was no way she could allow this to happen. There was no way she could keep any semblance of control while he did that.

She was sure that she reached down with the intent of stopping him, but it turned into her twining her fingers through his hair, not holding on strong enough to direct his movements. Oh no. She wanted him to show her. Everything she had said to him about her knowing her own body, about him not knowing what to do, because he didn't know her body at . . . Well, that all went right out the window. Because, damn it all, he knew what he was doing.

Knew places to touch, to lick and suck that she never would have guessed she would want licked or sucked.

And, when he added his fingers, when he pressed two deep inside her, stretching her gently while he continued to torment her with his talented tongue, fire exploded behind her eyes, blending with the beautiful glow of the Christmas lights in the room. Or maybe the glow was coming from inside her. Her eyes were closed, so it had to be.

But she had lost her sense of everything. Of time, of space. Of tomorrow. Of what it would be like when this was over, when she had to face the fact that Devlin Grayson had done that to her, and that she had liked it.

Then he pushed himself away from her, rising up into a standing position, his hands hovering over the buckle on his belt, currently keeping his low-slung jeans from falling to the floor. She was ready for them to fall to the floor. There were no nerves. Not now. She was floating on a cloud of pleasure, and she didn't ever want to come down.

And right now, she didn't have to. Right now, this was happening. And there was so much more to go.

She kept her focus rapt on him as he slowly undid his belt, followed by the closure on his jeans. Bit her lip as he drew the zipper down slowly, as he pushed his pants and underwear down his legs.

She let out a slow, jagged breath. "Oh my."

"Is that a compliment?" he asked.

"Very much yes," she said.

He was beautiful. It seemed strange to think of someone wholly masculine like Devlin as beautiful. But there really was no other word for it. His thighs were thickly muscled, his stomach washboard flat. And really, she was only fixating on those things to keep herself from focusing on . . .

Well, on the very most masculine part of him. Which

was thick, and long, and mostly a whole lot more man than she had imagined.

But hey, that was supposed to be a good thing. She was sure that were she a more experienced woman, she would appreciate the great gift that was before her. And visually, she did. Physically, she had a slight concern.

Except then he was back on the bed, back between her thighs, his arms wrapped tightly around her as he kissed her deep and long, his chest hair brushing up against her nipples, making her ache. And she wasn't so concerned anymore.

She was just lost. In this. In him. She remained wrapped in a sensual fog when he moved away, reaching for something off the bed. When she heard the sound of tearing plastic. She opened her eyes partway, just enough to watch as he rolled the protection on over his thick length. There was something erotic about that, and she had never thought something so practical could be considered erotic.

When he moved back over her body, the blunt head of his arousal probing the entrance to her body, tears pricked at her eyes and she had to squeeze them shut to keep them from building.

As he filled her, stretched her, as he became the first person to ever be inside her, it wasn't fear that she felt. It was an overwhelming, all-encompassing emotion that built from her chest and moved outward. That made her feel full in ways that extended far beyond the physical.

And when he was fully inside her, her indrawn breath

caught on a sob and she lowered her forehead against his shoulder, hoping to disguise the emotion that was threatening to drown her.

She hadn't anticipated this. Anxiety, yes. Pleasure, yes. Even pain. Yes, she had anticipated pain. But not this. Not this sense of connection. Not the sense that when he withdrew from her body she would be empty in a profound way that she had never been before.

And most certainly, she had not anticipated the overwhelming sense that this was Devlin inside her. Devlin, whom she had always wanted, no matter how much she had tried not to. Devlin, who had always driven her just a little bit crazy in ways she hadn't wanted to analyze.

Devlin Grayson. The only man she had ever truly wanted. Because of course that was why his kiss hadn't given her anxiety. Because of course no other man had ever been half so compelling. It was he. It had always been he.

And as he rocked forward, a deep, piercing need joining with the intense emotion that was surrounding her heart, she feared it always would be.

That there would never be anyone else, that there would never be anything else. But this wasn't the road to being able to banish the anxiety she felt with other men. Rather, it was the confirmation that there would never be another one.

She gripped his shoulders, letting her fingertips trail down his back, over all that fine musculature. And she tried to focus on the physical. Tried to erase that sense of connection that was on the verge of overwhelming her.

Because he felt so good. And even though the sensation of being filled by him was foreign, even though there was a little bit of pain with it, it was also the fulfillment of every desire aroused by his kiss.

She flexed her hips against his, meeting his every thrust with her own. She screwed her eyes shut, kissing his shoulder, kissing his neck, kissing his jaw before moving back to his lips.

Devlin's lips.

Devlin's body.

Devlin. Devlin. Devlin.

No matter how hard she tried to blot it out, his name was a tattoo on her soul with each and every thrust inside her. As he quickened his pace, as he lost his control, she felt her own beginning to slip. She didn't even want to hold on to it. All she wanted to do was hold on to him.

This was so real. It was so raw. It was, quite possibly, the most real she had ever been. With her legs wrapped around his narrow hips, urging him on as he moved deep within her, as hoarse cries of pleasure escaped her lips, as she moved with him and against him like a greedy thing, as she gave in to the desire that was roaring inside her.

And even with all that, she could never forget it was he. Because this could only ever happen with him. It wasn't only about desire. Wasn't only about feeling safe. He was right; there was no fuzzy blanket here.

It was about feelings. It was about whatever this deep, unending emotion that was roaring through her like a thunderstorm meant.

And then he stiffened above her, trembling, a fractured

apology on his lips as he lowered his head and pressed his forehead against hers. His hips surged forward, hard, and it was that motion that sent her over the edge. An explosion of stars behind her eyelids as her orgasm rocked her.

And then she just clung to him. And he didn't make a move to leave her.

She had done it. She had lost her virginity to her best friend's older brother.

But, as she looked up at him, at the pure exhaustion on his face, that replete, deep pleasure so easy to read in his expression, she feared she might have lost something else too.

This was supposed to be her Christmas present. But she feared she had given Devlin something in return.

She was very afraid that she had given her heart to Devlin Grayson. And she didn't know if she would ever get it back.

Chapter Five

"I REALLY WANT a sandwich."

Those muffled, sleepy words pierced through the fog that had encroached on Devlin's brain.

"The fact that you can talk, and are talking about sandwiches, means that I may have gone wrong somewhere," he said.

He brushed Mia's hair out of her eyes, searching her expression to see if he could tell what she was thinking.

She shook her head, a shy smile on her lips. "You didn't do anything wrong. But we did abandon a perfectly good grilled cheese."

"For sex."

Her smile widened, and this time, it wasn't so shy. "Yeah. Sex. I had sex."

"Smug," he said, tightening his hold on her and rolling them so that he was on his back, and she was lying on top of him. "I like it."

It wasn't the only thing he liked. He smoothed his palm down her back, the indent in her spine, up to the rounded globe of her ass. He squeezed her, then gave her a slight pat, and she squeaked in response. "I like that too," he said.

"Yes," she responded. "I can see that."

"You like it too. You like me."

"Maybe." For some reason, that admission twisted something in his chest. For some reason, all of him felt twisted up by her. By what had just happened.

No doubt he was going to hell for this. For taking Mia Landry's virginity. Yeah, it had been all well and good to justify it. To acknowledge the fact that she was a grown-ass woman and didn't need his protection. Except he knew her. He knew her well enough to know all the things she had been through. All the things she deserved.

And in contrast to that, he knew everything he was. And everything he could never be.

He shoved the dark thoughts aside. It didn't matter. Not now. Now, they were still alone. Now, they were both still naked.

"Come on," he said, adjusting their positions and sitting up, still holding her. "Let's go get a sandwich. I just have to go to the bathroom for a second."

"I'll get dressed."

"You damn well will not."

"I think I should."

He stood up, backing toward the bathroom. "You are going to stay naked, Mia. Because until the storm lifts, the rest of the world doesn't exist. And as long as the rest of the world doesn't exist . . . there's only you and me. And I want you naked."

He went into the bathroom and made quick disposal of the condom before returning. He'd half expected to see her covered up when he returned, but she wasn't. Instead, she was still sitting on the edge of the bed, gloriously naked. And all those Christmas lights behind her made her look like a beautiful fallen angel.

Thank God he had all night with her.

He extended his hand, because, hell, if they were the only two people in the world, then the rest of everything didn't exist. And that meant tonight he could play at being what she deserved. For a few hours at least he could be the man she needed.

And if that meant being a gentleman just for a while, he would be a fucking gentleman.

At least, until the next time he had her.

She reached out, taking his hand, her delicate fingers curling around his. And he felt like he'd been punched in the chest.

He ignored that feeling. He reached behind her and took the quilt off the bed, slinging it over his shoulder. "Just in case."

"I thought you said there would be no fuzzy blankets."

He took the blanket off his shoulder then wrapped it around hers, and swept her back up into his arms. She didn't protest at all. Instead, she wrapped her arms around his neck, holding on to him. And the way she looked at him . . . Well, no one had ever looked at him like that in his life.

Like she expected things. And like she expected he could accomplish them.

"No," he said, "I said I wasn't a fuzzy blanket, chipmunk. Fuzzy blankets are a must, if you don't want your lover's body to get chilly in a snowstorm. And I don't."

Her expression changed to one of wonderment. "Am I your lover?"

"For now."

He carried her downstairs, and when they got there, he deemed the grilled cheese beyond salvageable, and the tomato soup a gelatinous mess.

So they settled on cold cheese sandwiches and Diet Cokes, taking them in front of the fire, where he spread the blanket he had brought downstairs.

Mia sat there, her hair flopped into her face, the firelight casting an orange glow over her skin, highlighting those delicate, high cheekbones and those soft, perfect lips.

Even the way she ate a cheese sandwich fascinated him, and he couldn't for the life of him figure out why.

Why she had always fascinated him. Yeah, at first, it had felt a lot like protectiveness. Because it was clear when he first met her that her home life sucked. That something inside her had been crushed. And it had only been natural to want to rebuild that.

That hadn't meant taking it easy on her. She was Faith's friend, so that had meant giving her grief the same as he had her younger sister. But she hadn't ever seemed to mind that. She had always liked the attention. And the more he had learned about her life at home, the less surprised he had been by that.

"Do you ever go back to visit your parents?" he asked.

"Sometimes," she said quietly, taking another bite of her sandwich. "But I try to avoid it when I can. Of course, I can't always avoid it. Sometimes the guilt trip isn't worth the avoidance."

"Your mother?"

She nodded. "She doesn't really want me there. She finds me as useless now as she did back when I was a kid, and yet she feels like I owe her, I guess."

"For what?"

"The parade of neuroses that she gave me? No, I suppose for ruining her body by bringing me into the world?"

"I mean, my parents aren't perfect, Mia, but that's something else altogether."

A smile touched her lips. "Your parents always seemed pretty perfect to me."

"I don't know, I guess in some ways they are."

"Going to your house was always . . . so different. And I went ahead and let my mother imagine that the farm you guys lived on was some kind of big ranch spread. Because I knew she would never understand why I wanted to spend my time in that tiny little house. But it was so . . . noisy." She smiled when she said that. "And I didn't feel like I had to walk on my tiptoes." When she looked up at him again, her eyes were shining bright. "I found my voice there. I learned more about myself, about the world . . . About how dirt felt underneath bare feet, and about how salt water makes your hair stiff, and the sun can burn your skin. I learned that Christmas wasn't about immaculate decorations and a big dinner surrounded by people you don't know, but are trying to impress. But that it was about being together. I learned all of that from your family. I guess it's kind of fitting that I learned about sex from you."

Something about that settled sour in his stomach. And it shouldn't have. Because that was their agreement. He was supposed to take her virginity, because she felt safe with him. So of course in a way he was her teacher. And he had no call being irritated by that. That she saw this as an extension of the function the rest of his family had served all these years.

He should just be glad that she had someone. That she'd had them. Instead, he was jealous. Jealous of his family. Of the fact that she had the same connection with all of them, or so it seemed. That she didn't feel any more strongly about him than she did about any of the others.

That if she had been snowed in with Joshua or Isaiah she would have just as easily asked them to take her virginity instead of him.

Because she felt safe with them. *All* of them. If anything, it only confirmed that he was lower than Joshua and Isaiah, really. He was here. He was the one who had done this. They were too good. Too smart, too rational.

He was . . . well, all he'd ever been. The underachiever. The one whose parents constantly lowered their expectations, then had to readjust when he slid beneath them.

He gritted his teeth. "Yeah," he said, "real fitting. Though you probably would have been better off with one of the more accomplished of the Grayson brothers."

She frowned. "What do you mean?"

"Oh, come on. I'm not exactly the overachiever in the family. My sister is a wunderkind architect taking the world by storm, and Joshua and Isaiah have combined their business sense to make our entire family insanely wealthy. Me? I'm a dyslexic cowboy, if you want to romanticize it. A glorified farmer if you don't. I don't have a lot, but what I have, I work with my own hands. Still, it's not the life my mom and dad wanted for me. Not even a little bit. They thought we could do more, be more. That if I wanted to I could fight harder and transcend all the learning disability stuff. And it is a constant disappointment and surprise to them that I didn't. But some people aren't meant for more. I'm one of them."

She looked wounded, and he regretted everything he had said. Regretted that he might have affected her view of his parents, because she deserved to feel about them the way that she did. Hell, they deserved it. They really were great people. It wasn't their fault that he didn't want the kind of life his siblings had gone out and gotten for themselves.

It wasn't their fault for having big dreams for their children.

He supposed it wasn't his fault for not sharing those dreams either.

"I've never thought what you did was any less than what Joshua or Isaiah did. Faith is . . . Well, nothing about Faith is normal. She's exceptional. And she always has been. None of us should compare ourselves to Faith."

He snorted. "It's true. When she got accepted to that fancy private school on that scholarship . . . Well, none of us knew what to think. She was the first person in the family to fly on a plane."

"She's amazing. But . . . do you want to do something else? Do you want to be part of the architectural firm? Do you want to sell off your ranch and move to a city?"

"No," he said. "A firm hell no, actually."

"Then you aren't falling short. The only way you could possibly be falling short is if you wish you were doing something else, but you didn't have the guts to go after it." It was ironic that she was the one saying that. But, professionally, there was nothing he had ever held himself back from. He loved his ranch. He loved what he did. He loved to work the land.

But when it came to her . . . Well, he had spent the better part of the last decade holding himself back.

"You shouldn't always go for everything you want," he said, his voice rough.

"You don't think so?"

"No," he said. "Sometimes that's selfish."

"Isn't selfish okay sometimes? I mean, I spent most of my childhood operating under the desperate need to keep my parents happy. So that I never had to have their attention on me. So that I wouldn't upset them. Wouldn't it have been better if I would have been a little bit selfish a little bit earlier?"

"You would never have been the one that was selfish. They were. They are."

"I think . . . I was so afraid to let my guard down. To lose my control. Because at home I had to be so buttoned up all the time. So quiet. So ridiculously . . . careful. And it was such a habit that losing control, making noise . . . It was difficult for me. The only place I could ever find enough peace to do it was at your family farm. Was in Copper Ridge. And I guess it makes sense that the easiest place for me to do it . . . with a man . . . was with you."

He gritted his teeth. "Right. And I bet it would've been the same for Joshua. The same for Isaiah?"

"No," she said, decisive, firm. She set her plate down, brushing a stray crumb from the side of her mouth. Then she leaned in, planting both of her hands on his thighs and sliding them upward before kissing him. "No," she repeated.

"Why not?" He grabbed hold of her wrists, pulling her closer, looping her arms around his neck. "You feel safe with my family."

"Because . . . because . . . when it comes to this, it was only ever you. I've always thought . . . Well, you always made me . . . I've always thought you were hot, okay?"

It wasn't exactly an admission of long-held feelings, but he would take it. "Really?"

"And of course . . . your brothers look like you. So, objectively, I suppose they're handsome. But they aren't you."

That meant more to him, did more to him, than he wanted to admit. That for some reason Mia thought he was more, when everyone else thought he was less. And sure, maybe she wanted him for sex. Maybe that was his edge. The fact that he was more basic. But whatever. He'd spent years honing the skill, so he'd take the advantage when he could.

"Tell me what you like about me," he said, surprised at the roughness of his own voice.

"I'm not sure where to begin," she said, smiling slightly. "I really like your tattoos."

"Well, who knew. Mia Landry has a bad-boy fantasy."

"A little bit. But maybe because it's so different to me. Well, you know what a good girl I've been," she said, rolling her eyes. "What I've always liked about you is the fact that you just did what you wanted. You're just . . . you. I know it was always hard for you. To grow up in a family that put emphasis on education like they did. To grow up with parents who saw school as the ticket out when you struggled. To do something you feel your parents don't approve of. But the fact is, no matter how hard it was, you did what you wanted to do. You're happy. I've always thought it was . . . amazing the way that you did that on your own."

"I don't know. I'm not sure there's anything amazing about being a stubborn cuss who doesn't do what he's told. Nothing amazing about not going the extra mile and fighting an impediment. Hell, if I'd become a writer or won a spelling bee or some shit I could have gone viral on the Internet. People like it when you overcome, not when you coast."

"You're not coasting," she said, "and trust me. From someone who wasn't a stubborn enough cuss for a very long time, it isn't nothing to go after what you want when everyone is telling you no."

"What did your parents want you to be?"

"A senator's wife? I don't know. But yeah, probably

something that could benefit them in some way. So, not what I'm doing now. Not graphic design in Portland."

"I think you're strong," he said, cupping her cheek. "I want you to know that. I don't see you as some weak, defeated little girl. You were, when I met you. You were like a horse that had her spirit broken, and it killed me. Made me want to kill whoever had done that to you."

He shouldn't be saying this, and her reaction, her abrupt departure from his touch, her downcast eyes confirmed it. But he had already started, and it was too late to go back.

He shifted his hold, gripping her thumb and forefinger and tilting her face up, forcing her to meet his gaze. "You're not. You hear me, Mia? Your parents are the ones that were wrong. For making you ever feel like you couldn't shout. For making you feel like you had to be quiet, like you couldn't be yourself. It was them, not you, the whole time. And now you can be as loud as you want."

She flung herself forward, knocking them both backward, sending the cheese plate clattering to the side. "Okay," she said, "then give me a reason to be loud."

Chapter Six

WHEN MIA WOKE up the fire was dying, and a bright white light was filtering through the window outside, casting a bluish tint onto everything that wasn't touched by the cooling embers.

She sat up, suddenly realizing that it was morning, that she was naked, in the living room with Devlin. And that they were on the floor.

They had spent the entire night making love, and this morning, in the cold light of day . . . well . . . she wanted more.

She smiled, then rolled over. Her phone was off to the side, lit up, and she could see a scroll of text messages on the screen. It flashed for a moment, then went dark. She reached out, taking the phone from its spot on the floor and unlocking it.

And then she swore.

"Wake up," she said, smacking Devlin's bare shoulder. "They're on their way."

"What?" His voice sounded sleep clouded, and under any other circumstances she would have paused to reflect on how sexy that was. The fact that she was with him when he was first waking up, how rough and gravelly his voice was.

"The roads got plowed, and everybody is on their way. I have a text from Faith, and a couple from your mother."

"Shit. From when?"

"Almost an hour ago. So . . ."

She heard the sound of an engine and her heart dropped into her stomach. She scrambled up, clutching the blanket to her chest as she scampered to the window and looked out the front door.

"Are they here?"

"Yes," she said, grabbing the bottom of the blanket and gathering it up so that she could move quickly with it wrapped around her. Then she started up the stairs. As fast as she could make it.

"There's no point in making a quick getaway unless we get rid of the evidence." He indicated the plates and the condom wrappers on the floor.

"For all they know you had a romantic evening alone."

"Yeah," he said, "except me and my right hand don't need condoms."

"Ever the charmer, Devlin," she said, continuing on up the stairs. "You and the condom wrappers are on your own."

"What about equality?"

"Chivalry!" Then she hurried into the bedroom as quickly as possible, closing the door behind her. Devlin's clothes were still in there, so she shoved them underneath the bed, then grabbed her own clothes and started to pull them on as quickly as possible.

A moment later, Devlin came into the bedroom. "What are you doing?" she asked.

"Getting my clothes," he said. "Where are my clothes?"

"You could have gone into your room," she hissed, getting down on her hands and knees and yanking the articles of clothing she'd just stuffed under the bed back out.

"This way you get a show," he said, tugging his jeans on slowly, then pulling his shirt over his head. And, she had to admit it was a pretty compelling show.

A show she did not have time to enjoy.

"Okay," she said, shaking her head and doing her best to shake off all the sexy feelings that lingered inside her. "Get out."

He smiled, then complied, leaving the bedroom and closing the door behind him. He took a few steps away from the door, and that was when she heard the front door open. Her knees went weak, and she sat on the edge of the bed, holding on to the edge of the mattress. They had almost been caught. And if they were caught . . .

She blinked. She wasn't really sure. What would it mean? Of course she didn't want to announce to the world that she had just had sex. That was a little bit embarrassing. But she had a feeling the biggest reason they were avoiding a confrontation was because then the family might have expectations.

They were supposed to have no expectations. None at all beyond him taking her virginity. Getting her over the hump, so to speak. Which, all things considered, was a bad word choice. Or maybe a good one. But the thing was, she wasn't over *him*. She didn't know if she wanted to be.

She pushed up from the bed on shaky legs. Well, she wasn't going to go making any announcements. Not to the family at large. But she did need to have a talk with Devlin.

For a moment, she imagined it. Being with him. Standing with him in front of the Christmas tree down in the living room, his arms wrapped around her.

Okay, so her fantasy was a little bit Stepfordian. And Devlin would never be that.

She frowned. Devlin would never be a lot of things. He was . . . Well, he was Devlin. He was rough, he had been with a lot of women. For all she knew, he wasn't looking to settle down ever. Least of all with a recently deflowered virgin who didn't know what she was doing.

At least he didn't see her as a kid anymore. That, she was fairly confident in.

She took a deep breath and opened the door, pasting a smile on her face and turning toward the bottom of the stairs. Faith was standing there, removing her outer layers, shaking snow out of her strawberry blond hair.

"You made it!"

Faith looked up, an answering smile on her face. "I did! I didn't realize you were here already."

"Yeah," she said, "I got here yesterday." She realized belatedly that she and Devlin hadn't really agreed on a story. But she was going with the truth. Hopefully, he hadn't told anyone anything different in the few moments she had taken to get ahold of herself in her room.

"Oh," Faith said, "yikes. Hopefully everyone's okay?"

"Why wouldn't we be?"

"Well," she said, "I know that Devlin likes to mess with you. And you tend to snarl back."

Mia blinked, thinking back to last night. Yeah, Devlin had messed with her pretty efficiently. But she hadn't snarled so much as . . . screamed. She felt her face heat, and she did her best to redirect her thoughts. "It was fine. Devlin and I are adults, we can handle ourselves."

Devlin handled her like a pro. But she wouldn't say that either. Or think it. She was going to stop thinking these things any moment.

Isaiah, the oldest Grayson, walked in then, wearing a suit and tie, snow on the shoulder suggesting he hadn't been wearing an overcoat in spite of the weather. It spoke volumes about him, the fact that he looked like a polished businessman on the outside, but was still a hardy country boy underneath.

"Hi Mia," he said, reaching out and drawing her in for a slight hug. It was strange, because Isaiah was handsome. There was no question. Square-jawed and polished, he looked a lot more like the kind of man her family would have expected her to marry.

But he didn't make her heart do somersaults. He didn't

make her body ache. She didn't want a man who worked in a high-rise and lived in a penthouse. Her happiest days had never been in places like that. She had always been happiest in Copper Ridge. And she wondered then why she had chosen to move to Portland instead of going to the place that she loved most.

She was so stunned by that thought that she froze. She had moved herself all the way to Oregon from the East Coast, but then hadn't taken that final step. She had kept herself on the outskirts of the place she loved.

She felt like it was a metaphor for how she'd handled Devlin.

Forcing herself to try and think of him as a brother, or at least family in some regard. Keeping herself close to the entire Grayson family, and always keeping a close watch on Devlin, but never taking what she wanted. Adjacent to the thing that would bring her most happiness, but never right in it.

It was quite a profound moment to have standing in the entryway of a cabin, surrounded by other people. But she supposed you couldn't be too picky about personal revelations.

"Hi," she said, realizing she hadn't returned the greeting, and that it looked a little bit weird.

"Mom is already in the kitchen starting dinner. She was appalled by the state of the pantry. She was pretty sure Devlin might have starved to death. I don't think she knew you were here though," Mia said.

"Devlin probably didn't say," Mia said, "which is very

like him. To forget that I'm here." She gritted her teeth as she said that. She didn't really like lying to her friend.

"Joshua isn't here yet," Faith said. "He's down in town gathering a supply of emergency rations. Because you know how he is. The living embodiment of a Boy Scout, he is intent on making sure we're in want for nothing should we end up unintentionally off grid."

"Well," Mia said, "I suppose I appreciate that."

She took a deep breath, looking around, hoping to catch sight of Devlin. But she didn't see him. She wandered away from the entryway, moving farther into the lodge. She saw Devlin standing out on the deck, the snow falling on his broad shoulders. He was leaning against the railing, and she couldn't help but admire his physique.

And his butt. She really liked his butt.

"Excuse me," she mumbled, walking out of the room and making her way out to the deck. She should have grabbed a coat, because it was freezing, but she hadn't thought about practicalities like that. All she had thought about was making her way to Devlin.

"Hi," she said, stomping through the snow, making sure she didn't slip on the slick wood.

He turned to look at her, arching a brow. "What's up, Mia?"

"I wanted to see you."

"I bet you could have seen me through the window."

Well, he was back to being his difficult self. He certainly wasn't the same man who had confided all that stuff to her in front of the fireplace, completely naked last night while they had eaten their sandwiches. Then devoured each other. He was trying to get back to the way things had been before, and she should take that as the warning that it was. But she didn't want to.

She was tired of not having what she wanted.

She had already said so to Devlin, just last night. There was no shame in not being a millionaire. There was no shame in living a modest life. The only shame was not going after what you wanted.

And the very hypocritical thing was that she had never gone after what she herself wanted. Not really. She had allowed fear to hold her back. Had allowed anxiety to win. Well, she wasn't doing that. Not anymore.

"Yes," she said, "I could see through the window. And in fact, so can everyone. So, what I'm going to say to you, I'm going to keep brief, and I'm going to not put my hands all over you."

"I was with you until the part where you said you weren't going to put your hands on me."

That warmed her, low and deep. Gave her a little spark of hope that what she was about to say might actually be well received. "Maybe I will later."

"I don't know if that's a good idea with a full house, Mia."

"Well," she said, clasping her hands in front of her and picking at her thumb. She wasn't so aware of the cold now. She felt hot. Anxiety rolling over her in waves. Sweat breaking out on the back of her neck. But she wasn't going to give in. She wasn't going to hide. She was going to make herself heard. "I figure maybe it doesn't matter if everybody knows. If everyone is here. Because . . . because I don't want it to be one night, Devlin."

He straightened, his entire body going tense. "What?"

"Because I love you."

Chapter Seven

Well, hell and damn. He hadn't imagined that things might go this way. Of all the ways he imagined their morning-after talk might go, all the reasons it was wrong, all the reasons it was dangerous and he should never touch her, he certainly hadn't imagined it was because she would think she was in love with him.

She knew him too well for that. Or at least, she should.

Or maybe that was the problem. Maybe, regardless of what she said, she had him confused with his family. With the feelings that she had for them. The nostalgia that was wrapped up in her time spent on the farm.

Now, all of that was bound up in sex. She had been a virgin, and she probably had feelings she couldn't sort through. He could barely remember being a virgin himself, but he was pretty sure even he'd had some strange feelings associated with the loss of it. With the fact that he'd finally had an orgasm with something other than his own hand.

But it wasn't what she thought it was. That was for sure.

"You don't love me," he said, turning away from her, looking out at the snow-covered trees.

"Yes I do, you insulting ass."

"No," he said, "Mia, you don't. You're attracted to me. Our chemistry is hot. But that's not love."

"Yeah, I'm pretty clear on that, actually, Devlin. Considering I've lived a lot of my life with the absence of love, I'm pretty sure I know what it feels like when it's there."

"That doesn't make any sense, chipmunk. Sorry. That only means you're more likely to be confused by all of it."

She took a step forward, and she pushed against his shoulder, clearly not caring that his entire family was likely watching this exchange from inside. "You condescending jackass. Don't tell me what I feel. Don't. I'm brave enough to stand here and tell you that I think the two of us have been in denial about our feelings for each other for a long time. I know I was. That's what I've been doing my entire adult life. Denying myself what I really want. Because I've been afraid. I was never afraid of my parents' attention, not really. I mean, they never hit me. They never hurt me in that way. What I was afraid of was letting them know how much I wanted that attention and being denied it. I've always been so afraid of that. So afraid of loving people more than they loved me. Of wanting somebody more than they wanted me."

Her eyes clouded with tears and he ached to comfort

her, to wipe away the tear that streamed down her cheek. A tear that he had caused. But he wouldn't, because in the end it was a kindness for him to keep his distance.

"I've always done this," she said, her words getting thick, "given myself little tastes of my dreams, without fully going for them. Why do you think I live in an apartment in Portland when what I want more than anything is to be by the ocean. What I want more than anything is to live on a farm surrounded by mountains where the clouds hang low in the sky and the mist wraps around your skin like a cold blanket. That was the happiest time of my life, the summers, the Christmases spent on your family farm. And yet I did my best to keep it a memory, to preserve it, to protect it, to protect myself. And I did the same thing with you. I kept you close, but not as close as I wanted you."

Heat streaked through him, anger that shocked him. "I think you hit the nail on the head right there. What you want is a ticket back to childhood. To happier times. And you're trying to use me to get there."

"If I was trying to use you to get back to my childhood I hardly would have spent the entire evening naked with you."

"Right. Well, tell yourself whatever you want, but what I think is that you're looking for a ticket into a permanent position in this family."

She drew back, looking stricken. "Don't. Don't accuse me of using you. I would never do that to you, Devlin."

"Oh, I don't think you do it on purpose. I'm sure you don't even realize what you're doing. But how can you be sure that's not what this is?"

"Because you're right. If I had wanted that I would have set my sights on one of your brothers. Why not? They're nicer. They're easier to talk to. They don't make me work quite so hard for the attention. Why wouldn't I have gone with the easier one? You are the most inconvenient person to have feelings for, Devlin, and yet I do. Don't tell me that I'm choosing it to make my life easier. Saying this, feeling this, is the opposite of easy. It's the hardest thing I've ever done, and don't you dare reduce it to nothing. Don't you dare reduce me."

"Don't accuse me of doing the same things your parents did to you just because I can't give you what you want." He knew he was the jackass she'd accused him of being, but at this point he didn't care. At this point, he needed this conversation over with. Because Mia had to realize that it was never going to be like that for the two of them. He couldn't stand there and indulge the fantasy. Because it was too tempting. Too tempting to say great and let her love him with the full force of all that sweetness he'd always coveted for himself.

But he wasn't for her. And he wouldn't be able to stand her disappointment when she realized that. No, it was better to end it now. Better to end it now while she could imagine that maybe things might have been good, than be with her and destroy any good feeling she might have ever had for him.

He was a disappointment to everybody, but he couldn't stand being a disappointment to her.

"Don't be a coward, Devlin," she said, her voice vibrating with rage. "Don't you want more for yourself? Don't you want more for us?"

"Oh, right," he ground out, "Now I need to want more for myself. Now when you don't like my choices. That isn't happening, chipmunk. But if it helps, here's the *more* than I want. I want more for you than some strange wish fulfillment that's never going to give you what you think. I want more for me than a wife who just wants my last name. Who just wants a secure position in life because she could never get it from her own parents."

He could have punched his own face for that. And Mia drew back as though he had hit hers. He hated himself for it. But then, hating his own self was never that far of a step for him.

"It would be best if we didn't talk about this again, Mia," he said.

She nodded, the motion jerky. "Okay. I'm not exactly tempted to bring it up again. But at least I won't have regrets. At least I won't have to wonder what might've happened if I were brave. Because I was. And you're the one who's afraid. I'm not going to let you take this from me. I'm not going to let you silence me. Not going to be quiet. Not again." Another tear dropped down her pale cheek and it did something to him. Made his heart shatter in his chest, ground into the rest of his organs like glass, made each and every breath painful.

It was no less than he deserved.

"It's not about bravery, chipmunk. It's about whether or not I love you like that. And I don't." The words sat sour on his tongue, and he wondered if that was what a lie tasted like. He had never thought of it in those terms. Of loving Mia. Because he had never allowed himself that kind of hope.

He wasn't going to do it now.

Mia nodded wordlessly, backing off the front deck and going back into the house. He could see her, just barely, through the reflection on the windows. Watched her as she walked quickly up the stairs and into her bedroom.

He gritted his teeth. He wasn't going to stay. He couldn't stay. Not after that. Mia was the one who fit here, with his family. Mia was the one who loved Christmas. The only reason he was here . . .

Well, damn. The only reason he had ever been here was for her. He realized that now, standing there out on the deck. That the only reason he came every year, the only reason that he went to every damn holiday event, that he went to every Fourth of July barbecue was because of her.

But he was the Grinch who had just stolen Christmas from himself.

And so there was no reason left to stay.

Chapter Eight

MIA HEARD A knock on her bedroom door, and she hoped—even though she shouldn't—that it was Devlin.

"Come in."

The door opened, but it wasn't Devlin. Instead, Faith walked through, looking concerned. "What happened out there with Devlin? He left."

"What?"

"Yeah," Faith said, moving over to the bed where Mia was sitting and taking a seat beside her. "He just said that he had to go and he got into his truck and drove back to Copper Ridge. He didn't explain why. But it was right after you two had a fight outside."

Mia's face got hot. "You saw that?"

"Yeah," Faith said. "We're nosy, and we all watched. But Devlin was tight-lipped about it."

"Of course he was. He was being an ass."

Faith looked at her hard. "Are you ever going to talk to me about the fact that you're in love with my brother?"

Mia felt like she'd been struck right in the chest. "What?"

"I mean, seriously. I think you've been in love with him since we were fifteen. But you've never said anything about it. And now . . . I find out that you were snowed in with him overnight. Which he kind of lied about, by the way. I heard him telling my parents that you got here right before they did. And then you had that fight out on the deck. So I'm going to go ahead and stand by my assessment that you're in love with my brother. And . . . I'm guessing that something happened between you two last night."

Mia's fingertips prickled. "I . . . Yes. Okay. I . . . I might have feelings for Devlin. But I didn't keep it from you on purpose. I mean in that . . . I think you wouldn't ever want to know that I had feelings for your brother?"

"You are correct in that assessment. I really don't want to know details about you and Devlin, except that I do want both of you to be happy. And what I'm seeing right now is that neither of you are happy. Does he have feelings for you too?"

Mia stammered. "I mean . . . he's not immune to me . . . physically. But apparently he doesn't have any kind of emotional feelings for me at all. Which is why he stormed off. Because I said that I loved him and he . . ." The words caught in her throat, cut off by a sob that she couldn't hold back. "Anyway, he doesn't feel the same way. And I imagine he thought it would be best if he left so that I wouldn't pour hot cider over his head tonight when we passed stockings around."

"I might have done it for you," Faith said, "so I guess it is a good thing that he left."

"You don't have to do that."

"For what it's worth . . . none of my brothers are very good at talking about their feelings. I know that Isaiah and Joshua seem a little more well-adjusted and open than Devlin, but that's all a lie. They just have better front-of-house manners than he does. But that's a side effect of them being in business. Our dad is like that too. He's a good man. And of course he loves us, of course he loves you, but you know it's almost impossible for him to say. For all that Devlin and our dad don't get along, the real issue is that they're actually the same person."

Mia nodded. "Yeah, I kind of get that. Devlin feels . . . like your parents don't approve of what he's done with his life. Mostly because it's what they did with theirs."

"Of course. And they have this idea that we need to do more. But Devlin isn't that person. He wanted the ranch. Something he could build all on his own. And I think what he wants he wants, with all of himself. Of course he would rather die than say that. I think he wants nothing more than to have you on his ranch with him. But I also think admitting that is next to impossible for him. Because he wants it so much." Faith shook her head. "That's a funny thing. I love what I do. It's amazing that my career as an architect has taken off the way that it has. And I'm lucky to have brothers who are so good at managing the business end. I get to focus on the part that I love. Creating a building in my mind, drawing, watching it become something real and tangible from that initial design phase. But the rest of it, the thing that my parents think about success, that's just accumulating money. And as nice as it is, as much as it has changed things for all of us it's not the same as passion."

Mia swallowed hard. "Everything Devlin does is his passion."

"Absolutely," Faith responded. "But sometimes I worry that he doesn't think he deserves what he wants."

"Yeah," Mia said.

The idea that Devlin felt deeper, not less, than other people resonated with her. It was one of the things that had always drawn her to him, really. Yes, he expressed it in a wholly testosterone-filtered way, but Devlin had never bothered to modify himself. Had never made himself into anyone's image but his own.

And all that desire he had, he'd been told was aiming short. He'd been told what he wanted wasn't living up to his full potential, and that was all wrapped up in his dyslexia and how he felt about it.

And it made sense to her that his life was full only of essentials. Of his ranch, and whatever dreams he had for that. Oh, how she wanted to know his dreams. How she wanted to be a part of them.

"I imagine," Faith said, "that taking a risk on anything is hard for him. Especially something he feels passionately about. He's had to fight to get our parents to accept what he's chosen. And he's . . . really fought hard. Because I think for a man like Devlin, there is no such thing as option number two. He wants what he wants, and nothing else. If that doesn't pan out, he wouldn't know what to do."

"Well, there's every chance that what he wants isn't me."

Faith leaned against Mia. "I suppose so. But I was observant enough to realize that you wanted him. Let's just say I observed a few things about him too."

"I have a feeling it's going to take a miracle for all of this to work out."

Her friend wrapped her arm around her shoulders and squeezed her tight. "Then I guess it's a good thing it's Christmas."

Chapter Nine

The roads were clear in Copper Ridge, and the storm that raged in the mountains certainly hadn't affected the crowd at Ace's bar. Devlin could do without the crowd. But he was glad that his favorite bartender was in residence to hand out alcohol. Because Devlin needed a strong dose.

He walked up to the counter and tapped the hard surface. "Give me something good," he said, sitting down on the stool and leaning back.

"Happy holidays to you too," Ace said, smiling.

"Yeah," he said, "Merry Christmas."

"That would have been a lot more convincing if you didn't sound like you were talking about having a terrible disease."

Devlin nearly laughed. He did have a terrible disease. Feelings. "I will take the drink and no commentary. Something that will make me forget. And then I'll walk home in the cold."

"As long as you don't forget not to walk into the ocean. Which in your current state you look like you might be in danger of doing."

"I'll keep that under advisement. Right now it just sounds like a good idea."

Ace shrugged, then turned and started mixing what looked like a pretty potent concoction. Which was exactly what Devlin was here for. Not commentary.

"I thought I might find you here."

Devlin turned to see his younger brother, Joshua, standing there, wearing a suit and looking like a smug prick. Which was basically his default position. "What the hell are you doing here? Aren't you supposed to be up at the cabin?"

"I stayed behind because I'm scouting out some property. Which Mom and Isaiah don't know yet, so you can't tell them. I said that I needed to make sure we had enough supplies, a generator and stuff. And, I did that. But, I also looked at a ranch spread about five miles down south."

"Are you getting out of the business?"

"No, looking at relocating and expanding, actually. But, early stages. And you know Mom will lose her mind if she thinks that we're all considering moving back. And in case things fall through, I don't want that kind of trouble."

"Fair enough," Devlin said.

"Speaking of Mom, though. She told me that you lit out of the lodge like a bat out of hell. And that you made Mia cry."

"Yeah," he said, knowing that that was never going to pass as a sufficient response. But still, a man had to try.

"No explanation?"

"I don't suppose you would arm wrestle and see if I have to answer?" He always could beat his younger brother at arm wrestling. Though, looking at him now, he figured he would have a lot more of a fight on his hands.

"No. Mia is like a sister to me. When she's hurt, I'm concerned. However, I'm well aware that she's not like a sister to you."

"What?"

"Come on, dumbass. Don't play stupider than you are. You have the hots for her, and you always have. I mean, since she was legal."

Devlin was hardly going to deny it, especially when there was complete truth to what his brother was saying. There was no way he could mount a convincing argument against it, especially when he felt like he could still smell Mia on his skin. "Well. She's hot."

"Maybe. But it doesn't affect me. Don't act like it doesn't mean something to you. Especially not after that."

"After what?"

"The fight the two of you had in plain view of the entire family. I don't know what's holding you back . . ."

He snorted. "You don't know?" Ace handed his drink over the bar and Devlin took it with a nod, knocking back half of it, then turning again to his brother. "She's . . . Well, she was born what the three of you have made yourselves into. She has nothing in common with me. Nothing to do with me at all. You think she's going to be happy living on a ranch with me? You think she's going to be happy if we have a bad year and struggle to pay the bills?"

"Money doesn't make you happy. Trust me on that. And, if you can't trust me, trust her. She lived in a house with a shitload of money and no happiness. I think she's the last person to harbor fantasies about mansions being the key to eternal joy."

"Still," he said. "I'm not . . . I'm not the kind of guy that she deserves."

"Oh, you mean because you're not man enough to take the chance?" Joshua reached out, grabbed hold of Devlin's drink, lifted it to his lips, and downed the last half. "Yeah, you're right about that, I guess."

"I paid for that."

"Sorry. Cowards don't deserve alcohol."

"Wrong. Cowards are the ones who deserve alcohol the most. Because we have to drink to forget what cowards we are."

"You don't deserve to forget it."

"What? You think that she's going to be happy with me here? With a guy who barely graduated high school? She's . . . brilliant. She's like you. She's not like me."

"She doesn't want me, Devlin. She wants you."

"She thinks she does. You think that she's going to be happy with my choices when our own mother and father don't think they're good enough?"

Joshua slammed his hands down on the bar. "Mom and Dad are just that. They're your mother and father. And yeah, they had this idea that they wanted us to live life differently than they did. They wanted us to not struggle. But that's parent stuff. This is love stuff. If you find a woman who wants to be with you, who wants to submit herself to all this, to the hard stuff, the life stuff, why wouldn't you take it?"

"Says my very single younger brother."

"Hey, if I found a woman willing to overlook all of my flaws . . . I think I would be smart enough to take it."

"With the size of your bank account you'll be fine."

Joshua's smile turned rueful. "Millions of dollars and about ten kinds of fucked up. Trust me, you have a lot more to offer. But Devlin . . . the only who thinks you being dyslexic is an issue is you. So maybe think about that."

"Screw you."

"You're welcome. And if you hurt Mia . . . I really will kill you."

Then Joshua clapped him on the back and got up off the bar stool, making his way back to the door. And leaving Devlin there alone, and only about half as drunk as he had wanted to be.

And for some reason, Mia's words kept echoing through his mind. About his life. About how there was nothing to be ashamed of as long as it was the life he wanted. That it wasn't underachieving if it was his dream.

She believed it. She really did. Even if he couldn't.

But either way, without her, it was nothing.

He was still afraid. Afraid that she wouldn't actually like the life he'd built when she got to living in it. Afraid that she might have somehow romanticized what had happened between them. Made it into something it wasn't, made him into something he wasn't. Try to recapture times past instead of actually wanting a future.

But the fact was, if he didn't make absolutely sure, if he didn't fight for those things, if he didn't drop all his pride, all his fear, and tell her that he loved her too . . . then he really was a damn coward.

No. Hell no. Devlin Grayson was a lot of things. But he wasn't a damn coward.

And he was in love with Mia Landry.

Chapter Ten

MIA WAS ATTEMPTING to be less morose over a cup of hot chocolate with marshmallows. It was difficult to be morose while drinking hot chocolate with marshmallows, but she was doing an admirable job, it had to be said.

She sighed heavily, taking a sip of the sweet, hot beverage and looking up at the tree glistening in front of the floor-to-ceiling windows. Beyond which she had experienced intense heartbreak only a few hours ago.

Faith was the only member of the Grayson family she had talked to about it, but she had a feeling everyone else had picked up on the reality of the situation. Anyway, if Faith's reaction was anything to go by, she had not been very subtle when it came to her feelings for Devlin.

In fact, she had a feeling the entire situation was comically transparent. Or maybe it would be, when she felt like she could laugh about anything again. Someday maybe she would feel that way. It was hard to imagine now.

The front door to the lodge opened, bringing with it a flurry of cold air. Mia jerked in her seat and turned to see Devlin standing there, the snow falling behind him.

"You're back." It was such a stupid response. But it was the only one she could think of. Mostly because her heart was pounding so hard in her head she couldn't think straight.

"I'm back."

His parents were watching them both closely, and so were Isaiah and Faith. But nobody said anything. Which added to the kind of surreal quality of it all. The Graysons were nothing if not vocal, usually.

"Good," she said, taking a sip of hot chocolate and looking back at the tree. Because until he said why he was back, she wasn't going to get up and make an idiot out of herself. She had already done that.

"Mia," he said, his voice firm, intense. Enough that she turned back to look at him, in spite of her desire not to. "I'm back for you."

Suddenly, she became very aware that every eye in the room was on her.

"Well," she said, taking another sip. "Well." She set her cup of hot chocolate down on the coffee table. "If you'll excuse us."

She stood up, then walked over to the stairs, making her way up slowly, trying to look . . . well, dignified instead of terrified. But Devlin was following closely behind her, and she was pretty sure she was shaking from the inside out. And it wasn't just because they had an audience.

She walked into her bedroom, and he followed, closing the door firmly behind them. "I'm a coward," he said, as soon as they were ensconced in the room.

"I did tell you that," she said, her lips feeling slightly numb now.

"You did. But my head is particularly hard, so I needed to hear it more than once."

"Well, I can't argue with that."

He just stood there, his hands clenched at his sides. He looked decidedly at a loss, her strong, confident Devlin who was normally nothing if not decisive and completely certain about what he was doing. And there he was, looking lost. For her.

"You're part of a world that I will probably never fully understand," he said. "I'm never going to be able to talk about books with you. I'll go watch the movie. I'm never going to be the kind of guy my brothers are. And sometimes I wonder if that's a failure. I wonder if I could have tried harder to be that person, even though it doesn't come easy to me. But I always found more happiness working with my hands then working at a computer. Always found it easier to go do something physical than sit and try to read when I can't make the words sit still on the page."

"I'm not sure very many people would ever think that choosing a life ranching is taking the easy way out. Least of all me. Didn't ever occur to you that it's those differences between you and me that I appreciate so much?"

He shook his head. "No. Because it feels a shortcoming, and I'm not sure how you can appreciate a shortcoming."

"What you do isn't second best. And for you, it isn't a second choice. You love it, don't you?"

He nodded. "I do."

"If you loved having a corporate job, then I believe that is absolutely what you would have. If it was what you wanted, you would have moved heaven and earth to make it happen, dyslexia or not. You're not the kind of man that takes second best, Devlin. And it's a shame you were ever made to feel like that's what you were doing. Your father might have fallen into ranching, but you love it. You're cowboy down to your blood because you love the land. And that has nothing to do with anything else. You do work hard. And you've taught me so much."

"Sex stuff," he said, lifting a shoulder.

"Stop that. You are the one who helped me find my voice, Devlin. Something you've been showing me for the past ten years. That path you took, the one you keep being afraid was lesser? The way you went and did that because it was what you wanted . . . That was the thing that started me on my own path too. The way that you took what you wanted without giving a damn what anyone thought . . . or at least looking like you didn't . . . It inspired me to do the same thing. How could you ever think you weren't as smart as your brothers? That you aren't as smart as I am? We're different. Your strengths reinforce my weaknesses, and I hope that mine do the same for you. That's love, in my mind. My parents were the same. Cut from the exact same cloth. And all they did was intensify all the terrible toxic things in each other. That's not a marriage I could ever have. It isn't what I want."

"You want me? You want me and my tiny little house and my muddy fields?"

"Well, and your tattoos and your muscles. But yes, those other things too. Because it's you, Devlin. It's always been you."

He took a step toward her, cupping her cheek, sliding his thumb slowly over her cheekbone. "And if I can't discuss the books you read?"

"I'll just summarize them for you. Or we'll go see the movie."

"I love you, chipmunk. I think I have for a long time. But what you saw as bravery all those years was just hardheadedness. I've been afraid this whole time. And I was afraid to want you. Because I was afraid you would see that. But right now . . . I want you more than I want to be safe. So I want you to know that I love you. That I want you, forever. Even though I'm shaking in my boots."

Mia's heart swelled up in her chest, her lungs burning, joy filling her so full she was sure that she might burst with it. She wrapped her arms around his neck and kissed him. And when she pulled away they were both breathing hard. "I love you. And you know what? Knowing that you were afraid while you went and did all of that . . . it only makes me love you more. It only makes me more confident in the fact that you are the right man for me. Because I'm never going to get rid of all of the fear and anxiety inside of me, Devlin. It lives there. But you make me think that it isn't a failure. As long as I don't let it win."

"Damn straight," he said, his voice rough. "Love has to win."

"It always will," she responded, holding his face in her hands, "because our love is stronger than fear. I think if we've proven anything over the past twenty-four hours it's that."

He bent down, picking her up—he seemed to really like doing that—and deposited them both on the center of the bed.

"Devlin! Your entire family is downstairs."

"I don't care." He nuzzled her neck, then kissed her. "It's Christmas, or, at least, it's our Christmas celebration. And you're my present."

"I thought you were supposed to be mine?"

"No," he said, kissing her long and deep, "from the start, you were most definitely mine."

Keep reading for a sneak peek at the next Montana Men novel from *New York Times* best-selling author Jennifer Ryan,

HIS COWBOY HEART

Bound by honor and by love . . .
That's a Montana Man

Ford Kendrick has often dreamed of the day that Jamie Keller would come home to Montana. After high school, she needed to leave—and he, duty-bound to rescue his family's ranch, pushed her to go. The army made Jamie a hero, but Ford still sees the gorgeous, loving woman who lit up his whole world.

Every day since she left, Jamie has longed for Ford. One glimpse confirms it: the sexy, dangerous-looking cowboy left a hole in her heart that nothing else can fill. Yet the battle scars she bears—inside and out—won't let her trust anyone enough to get close.

Ford wants to bring Jamie back to the life they dreamed of building. But locked somewhere in her memories is a dark truth that threatens her safety. It's a battle Ford won't let her fight alone, not when he's determined to keep her by his side, now and always . . .

I'M FLYING. NOPE. Arms out wide, a bullet slammed into her chest and sent her falling backward off the side of the armored vehicle. Another bullet ripped through her side. One more through her left thigh like a blazing lightning bolt. She hit the ground on her shoulders before her ass smacked the pavement and her head bounced, ripping off her helmet as she slid across the ground on her burned back. She gasped for a breath that felt like sucking in fire that seared its way through every cell in her body.

She stared up at the dark figure who had sprayed bullets everywhere, staring down at her with the automatic weapon pointed at her heart. The need to stop him and a deep sense of failure overwhelmed the pain.

She sat bolt upright, gun in hand pointed at the closed bedroom door in her grandparents' old house, breathing hard, sweat rolling down the side of her face, and cussing herself out for blurring her present reality and the past again.

This was good ol' Montana, not some insurgent-infested town in Afghanistan.

Fucking nightmares.

She dropped her hand and smacked the gun on her knee. The small pain helped to fade the last of the nightmare, the echo of pain that mixed with the real pain throbbing through her body, and settled her in reality. She focused on the door again and the three bullet holes she'd put in it the last week she'd been living here after her family kicked her out of their house, because they couldn't deal with her erratic behavior, short temper, and potentially lethal insanity.

"At least I didn't shoot this time."

Small victory, but her shrink said those small victories would build until she found herself firmly rooted in the here and now, with the war and what happened a distant memory. Yeah, well, she didn't know what happened to her. Not all of it. Despite the scars on her body that told the story, the details were still missing from her black mind.

Her phone trilled with a text. She grabbed it off the nightstand and swiped the screen, noting the three missed calls from her old friend and the accompanying voice mails waiting along with the text he'd sent.

TOBIN: Call me. I miss you.

Yeah, I miss me too.

She tossed the phone back on the table next to the crispy dead fern. Tobin sent it to cheer her up. It didn't. She didn't feel bad for neglecting to water it.

She tried not to feel much of anything these days.

If she let herself feel one thing, she'd have to feel everything, and that felt like drowning.

So she turned up the numb and shut down her heart.

Light filled the room through the slit in the curtains she kept shut. She squinted and raised her hand to her forehead and rubbed the headache pounding behind her eyes, not from a bad night of sleep but another night drinking herself into oblivion, hoping to keep the nightmares away. It didn't work. Never did. She needed to stop dulling the pain and find a way to make it stop.

She fell back onto her pillow, hoping to relax and figure out how to make it all go away, then it hit her all at once and she sat bolt upright again. Shit. She checked the clock. Overslept, again.

How that always happened when she barely slept at all eluded her.

She rolled out of bed with a loud groan for the pain in her whole aching body, grabbed the uniform she hoped to never wear again, and put it on anyway. She'd promised she'd do this. A few pain pills would help her get through it. She only hoped she didn't make a complete fool of herself in public, in front of the whole town, and hopefully not in front of the one man nothing and no one could erase from her screwed-up mind—or her broken heart, it seemed.

She tossed the phone back on the table next to the crispy dead fern. Tobin sent it to cheer her up. It didn't. She didn't feel bad for neglecting to water it.

She tried not to feel much of anything these days.

If she let herself feel one thing, she'd have to feel everything, and that felt like drowning.

So she turned up the numb and shut down her heart.

Light filled the room through the slit in the curtains she kept shut. She squinted and raised her hand to her forehead and rubbed the headache pounding behind her eyes, not from a bad night of sleep but another night drinking herself into oblivion, hoping to keep the nightmares away. It didn't work. Never did. She needed to stop dulling the pain and find a way to make it stop.

She fell back onto her pillow, hoping to relax and figure out how to make it all go away, then it hit her all at once and she sat bolt upright again. Shit. She checked the clock. Overslept, again.

How that always happened when she barely slept at all eluded her.

She rolled out of bed with a loud groan for the pain in her whole aching body, grabbed the uniform she hoped to never wear again, and put it on anyway. She'd promised she'd do this. A few pain pills would help her get through it. She only hoped she didn't make a complete fool of herself in public, in front of the whole town, and especially not in front of the one man nothing and no one could erase from her screwed-up mind—or her broken heart, it seemed.

More sizzling Copper Ridge novels are coming soon from Maisey Yates and HQN!

Read on for a sneak peek of

SLOW BURN COWBOY,

where a lifelong friendship begins to heat up into something more . . .

Lane knew that Finn was mad at her. It happened. They had known each other for a long time, and initially they'd known each other in the capacity of her being his friend's irritating younger sister.

But as they'd eased into adulthood, and into a real friendship in their own right, rarely had Finn ever looked at her like he wanted to drown her in the ocean. About now, he was looking vaguely murderous.

When she said her good-byes to everyone and headed for the door, she wasn't surprised when Finn followed her outside. He closed the door hard behind them and let out a long, slow breath. "Are you going to apologize?"

"Me?" she all but squeaked. "You were being a jerk."

"I'm sorry if you don't understand my family dynamic, which consists mainly of my brothers and me calling each other names while we try not to punch each other in the face. But it's definitely not for you to lecture me about. What was that stunt you pulled?"

She threw her arms wide, the cool night air washing over her bare limbs. "Oh, do you mean cooking you a delicious dinner? How dare I?"

"If you think you're going to railroad me by going through my brothers—"

"Are you serious right now?" Anger spiked inside her. "You honestly think that I was trying to manipulate you?"

"Can you *honestly* say that you weren't?"

She almost exploded with denial, then stopped herself, chewing on the words for a moment.

"I thought so," he said, rocking back on his heels.

"You know me," she said, instead of denying it outright. "I wasn't really trying to manipulate you. I promise."

"The situation with them . . . I cannot believe that they think they're going to stay here and take ownership of this ranch. It's mine."

She wanted to reach out and touch him, but she remembered what had happened when she'd done that the night before. It had left her fingertips feeling tingly.

Instead, she did her best to make her face sympathetic. "I don't know what to tell you. Except that life changes, and people suck."

Typically, Finn was the steady rock of the two of them. He was a cowboy, for heaven's sake. Riding around his property on a horse with a big hat. Doing all the work, day in day out.

But right now, he seemed on the verge of cracking,

and when she had looked at someone and seen a stalwart for so long it was a little bit jarring.

Then she felt like a jerk, because of course he was having a hard time. He'd lost his grandfather, and now he was expected to share the property he'd put blood, sweat, and tears into. Finn didn't share well. And he didn't unclench easily.

"I'm sorry," she said finally, because she probably did owe him an apology.

"I know."

He turned to look at her, his expression deadly serious. There was something in his face just then, the glint of his dark eyes and the set of his square jaw, that made something respond inside her.

She wanted to do something. To close the distance between them.

Put her arms around him, maybe.

She could only imagine how he would react if she tried to hug him after he shared his feelings. He would probably have a straight-up allergic reaction.

So she just stayed where she was, curling her fingers into fists.

"They won't stay," Finn said. "My brothers."

"Maybe not."

"You don't believe that."

She closed her eyes for a moment, let the sounds of the night sink into her skin, all the way down to her bones. There was a faint dampness to the air, a tinge of salt and pine on the breeze.

"No," she said eventually. "I don't. Mostly because I don't see why anybody would ever want to leave this place."

"The ranch, or Copper Ridge in general?"

"I meant the town in general. But I have to admit that this house has a leg up on my little cabin. You better be careful, or I'm going to want to move in too."

"I'm much more likely to move in with you," he said flatly. "I mean, if my house gets any more crowded."

She laughed, and for some reason it sounded a little more nervous than she felt. "There may be fewer people in my house, but it's small. Tiny. We would have to share a bed."

For some reason, that comment seemed to land in a weird spot. It hit heavy between them, like a sad, popped balloon that had fallen back down to earth. And they both just sort of stood there, staring at it . . .

Go back to where it all began in the very first Brightwater novel from Lia Riley,

LAST FIRST KISS

A kiss is just the beginning . . .

Pinterest Perfect. Or so Annie Carson's life appears on her popular blog. Reality is . . . messier. Especially when it lands her back in one-cow town Brightwater, California, and back in the path of the gorgeous six-foot-four reason she left. Sawyer Kane may fill out those Wranglers, but she won't be distracted from her task. Annie just needs the summer to spruce up and sell her family's farm so she and her young son can start a new life in the big city. Simple, easy, perfect.

Sawyer has always regretted letting the first girl he loved slip away. He won't make the same mistake twice, but can he convince beautiful, wary Annie to trust her heart again when she's been given every reason not to? And as a single kiss turns to so much more, can Annie give up her idea of perfect for a forever that's blissfully real?

Go back to where it all began in the very first Brightwater novel from Lori Riley

LAST FIRST KISS

That is just the beginning . . .

Flawless. Perfect. Or so Annie Clark's life appears on her popular blog. Reality is [illegible] messier. Especially when it lands her back in her own town, Brightwater, California, and back in the path of the gorgeous [illegible] she left. Sawyer Kane may fill out those Wranglers, but she won't be distracted from her task: Annie just needs the summer to [illegible] up and sell her family's [illegible] so she and her young son can start a new life in the big city. Simple, easy, perfect.

Sawyer has always regretted letting the first girl he loved slip away. He won't make the same mistake twice. But can he convince beautiful, wary [illegible] to trust her heart again when she's been given every reason not to? And can a single kiss change so much more, can Annie give up her idea of perfect for a forever that's blissfully real?

THE KNOCK CAME as the last ice cube melted into her scotch.

What the . . . ? Annie Carson slammed against the chair, adrenal system upgrading from zoned out to Defcon 1. The vintage pig cookie jar stared back from the Formica counter with a vaguely panicked expression. Nothing arrived after midnight except lovers and trouble.

Annie didn't have a lover. And the biggest trouble she had tonight was trying to finish this blog post while forgetting all the reasons she fled from here in the first place. On the surface, Brightwater boasted a quaint Ye Olde West appeal. Nestled under the shadow of Mount Oh-Be-Joyful's fourteen-thousand-foot peak, the historic main street boasted a working saddlery instead of Starbucks, the barbershop offered complimentary sideburn trims, and tractors caused the only traffic jams.

Then there were the cowboys. Some women—fine,

most women—would consider the local ranchers to be six kinds of swoon-worthy, but she'd learned her lesson ten years ago.

If you meet a cute guy wearing a Stetson, run in the opposite direction.

The next knock rattled the front door's hinges; whoever was out there meant business. Annie sneezed before drawing a shaky breath. Drinking wasn't a personal forte, but chamomile tea didn't do much to blunt the first-night-back-in-my-one-cow-hometown blues, even with extra honey.

Maybe if she took her time, whoever was out there would go away.

She closed her laptop's lid, stood, and walked to the sink, setting the tumbler under the leaky tap. Water drip, drip, dripped into the brown dregs. Dad's radio above the fridge, tuned to a Fresno classical station, piped in Mozart's Requiem on the scratchy speakers, hopefully due to coincidence rather than cosmic foreshadowing.

More knocking.

This could very well be an innocent mistake. Someone had confused directions, taken a wrong turn, driven up a quarter-mile driveway to an out-of-the-way farmhouse . . . to where she sat wearing a "Kiss Me, I'm Scottish" apron with a sleeping five-year-old upstairs.

She hadn't missed Gregor in months. Her ex-husband might be a metrosexual philosophy professor, but at least he stood higher than five feet in socks. Why oh why had she enrolled in yoga instead of kickboxing last summer in Portland? No way would a sun salutation cut the mustard against a crazy-eyed bunny boiler. An alarmed buzz replaced the hollow feeling in her chest. Brightwater was a sleepy, safe backwater. Had it grown more dangerous since she tore out of here on her eighteenth birthday? Meth labs? Cattle thieves? Area 51 wasn't too far away, so throw in possible alien abduction?

Well, she was alone now and would have to deal with whatever came.

As a rule, killers and extraterrestrials didn't announce themselves at the front door. Still, this was no time to start taking chances. She grabbed her father's single-malt by the neck and padded into the living room. The change from bright kitchen to gloom skewed her vision as blood shunted to her legs. Shadows clung to the beamed ceiling and brick fireplace. If the rocking chair in the corner moved, she'd pee her pants. That old gooseneck rocker starred in more than a few of her childhood nightmares—ever since her sister had mentioned that Great-Grandma Carson had died in it.

"Hello?" she called, her voice calm—but, darn, an octave too high. "Who's there?"

Silence.

The door didn't have a peephole. This was the Eastern Sierras, a place where shopkeepers left signs taped to their unlocked front doors saying, "Went to the bank, back in five minutes."

Think! Think! What's the game plan?

Retreat—not a choice. But more whisky was definitely a viable option. She opened the bottle, and the gulp seared her throat. At least the burn helped dissipate the cold fear knotting her stomach. She pressed her lips together while screwing the cap back on. *Here goes nothing.* Brandishing the bottle like a club, she flung open the door.

A light breeze blew across her face, cool despite the fact it was early July. Five Diamonds Farm sat at four thousand feet in elevation. She glanced around the porch. Empty. Unable to stand the suspense, she stepped forward, her bare toes grazing warm ceramic. A baking dish sat on the mat. Annie knit her brow and crouched—a neighborly casserole delivery? At this hour? Fat chance, but one could hope. She removed the lid, and an invisible fist squeezed her sternum.

If hope was a thing with feathers, all she had was chicken potpie.

Literally.

A toothpick anchored a Post-it note to the crust.

> *Caught your hen in my tomatoes.*
> *Chicken #2 will be nuggets.*
> *Welcome home.*

About the Authors

JENNIFER RYAN is the *New York Times* and *USA Today* best-selling author of The Hunted, McBride, and Montana Men series. She writes suspenseful contemporary romances with outrageous plot twists, deeply emotional love stories, high stakes, and higher drama. Her stories are filled with love, family, friendship, and the happily-ever-after we all hope to find. Jennifer lives in the San Francisco Bay Area with her husband and three children. When she finally leaves those fictional worlds, you'll find her in the garden, playing in the dirt and daydreaming about people who live only in her head, until she puts them on paper.

New York Times and *USA Today* best-selling author **MAISEY YATES** lives in rural Oregon with her three children and her husband, whose chiseled jaw and arresting features continue to make her swoon. She feels the epic trek she takes several times a day from her office to her coffeemaker is a true example of her pioneer spirit. Maisey divides her writing time between dark, passionate category romances set just about everywhere on earth and light sexy contemporary romances set practically in her backyard. She believes that she clearly has the best job in the world.

After studying at the University of Montana-Missoula, **LIA RILEY** scoured the world armed only with a backpack, overconfidence, and a terrible sense of direction. She counts shooting vodka with a Ukrainian mechanic in Antarctica, sipping yerba mate with gauchos in Chile, and swilling fourex with station hands in Outback Australia among her accomplishments.